Twilight Curtain

Also by Stella Shepherd

Black Justice (1988)
Murderous Remedy (1989)
Thinner Than Blood (1991)
A Lethal Fixation (1993)
Nurse Dawes is Dead (1994)
Something in the Cellar (1995)
Embers of Death (1996)

TWILIGHT CURTAIN

Stella Shepherd

Constable . London

First published in Great Britain 1998
by Constable & Company Limited
3 The Lanchesters, 162 Fulham Palace Road
London W6 9ER

ISBN 0 09 478910 X
Set in Palatino by Pure Tech India Ltd., Pondicherry
Printed and bound in Great Britain by MPG Books Ltd.,
Bodmin, Cornwall
A CIP catalogue record for this book is available from the
British Library

1

The shuffling stopped when the lights were dimmed. The murmuring, too, died abruptly, and for a few seconds the silence was almost absolute. Everyone's eyes were focused on the wooden stage where a middle-aged, very ordinary-looking woman was standing in semi-silhouette. As they watched she breathed deeply, as if steadying herself for the effort to come, her own gaze diffuse.

Rowena felt a faint chill across her shoulders, and cursed herself for succumbing so quickly to the atmosphere. Hidden in her left hand was a discreet note pad, but she was unlikely to be able to use it in *this* poor light. Likewise, she suspected the tape recorder would pick up very little from her station half-way down the hall. She had underestimated the surging popularity of a spiritualist's visit to this suburban community centre, and arriving fifteen minutes early had not been good enough to secure a seat near the front.

Alongside, a plump woman in a thick dark wool coat was crowding her, all elbows and a slight underwashed sourness. Beyond her, two other late-middle-aged females were poised, one giving a furtive little cough. Rowena instinctively classified these three as widows. She had already noted the preponderance of women in the room, an observation which conformed with her own expectations. Some would be there simply out of curiosity, but many others would be hoping, in various states of trepidation, to receive a personal message.

Up on the platform the medium, Dorothy Lambrook, stirred and wheeled slowly away from Rowena to face the right-hand side of the hall. She waved her arm in a sweeping gesture towards the front three rows. 'I have a gentleman here,' she said strongly. 'He's tall and wears a distinctive red scarf. Someone in this area knows him.' She waited. 'He's very practical, always mending things. He mentions the name Kate or Catherine...Can anyone take this one?'

Rowena glimpsed a tentatively raised hand. Mrs Lambrook nodded to the owner of the hand. 'Ah, good. Are you Catherine?'

'No. But my mother is Catherine, and she died recently. I think the man is my uncle George. He often wore an orange scarf.'

'That's right; his name is George. He says you've had a lot to handle over these last few months, but remember to take care of yourself. There's something about a domestic appliance...'

'I've had a new gas fire fitted.'

'That must be it. Yes... he wants you to get it checked. There might be a leak.'

'I shall. Thank you.'

'Everything will be fine, he's confident. They both send their love. Wait – George is saying something about Christmas. Do you remember that time there was too much turkey?'

'I'm not sure... oh, yes! One year it wouldn't fit into the oven. Mother had to cut the legs off.'

'They're laughing about it. Your uncle has quite a cheeky laugh...'

As the medium continued to speak, Rowena scratched a few blind shorthand hieroglyphics on her note pad. Cynical even before the proceedings had begun, she was fighting now to suppress a wave of real anger. 'That's right; his name is George.' 'Something about a domestic appliance.' How dared this woman batten on the gullible, get people to provide the information themselves then frighten them with vague warnings of faulty gas fires? And as for that turkey – she couldn't miss. If there'd been no story about its failure to fit into the oven (a common enough occurrence) she would simply have said, 'You were eating it up for days, weren't you?', an experience of every meat-eating family in the realm.

With a mental huff of disgust Rowena turned her attention back to Dorothy Lambrook, who had moved on to converse with an expensively dressed young man. An observation about a sports car triggered a laugh of recognition. Young man, fast car – hardly a surprise. She might even have seen him parking it... Now she was speaking of a woman with musical talent who had a message for someone in the back row. The letter D...

Rowena craned her head round to see an anxious-looking blonde girl raise her hand. 'It could be my sister Dinah,' she supplied quietly.

'And Dinah plays the piano.'

'Yes. Piano and guitar.'

'Dinah loves you. She hopes you have a very happy birthday. It's soon, isn't it?'

'Next week.'

'She says, have crackers like you always do. Does that make sense?'

The girl beamed. 'Yes. We always saved some of the Christmas crackers to have with dinner on our birthdays.'

'There's a dog, isn't there? She says he's getting too fat. Perhaps you should cut down on the Bonio. She's giving me a name. Rory? No... it's Rusty. Is that your dog?'

'Yes! That's his name.'

Rowena had turned back to face the platform, but there was no mistaking the note of excitement, of awed enthusiasm in the young woman's voice. She felt a strange rippling thrill herself, an involuntary acknowledgement that this latest dialogue was genuinely impressive and those who believed the hall was indeed full of shadowy beings trying to communicate with their loved ones had been given no reason to change their minds.

Keeping her eyes on Mrs Lambrook, Rowena scribbled a few more notes then sat back in her chair to watch the rest of the proceedings unencumbered. The medium gently quizzed an elderly lady and gave her messages of comfort, then moved on to a trilby-hatted gentleman with similar reassurances. Each recipient looked happier and more relaxed after the exchange; a secret smile played around the old man's lips, the sole outward manifestation of an inner glow which Rowena could sense. Perhaps this wasn't exploitation, she reasoned, but just another form of therapy...

Suddenly she realized that the medium was looking straight at her. She lowered her own gaze, unwilling to stare, and wondered with a leap of mixed hope and fear if Dorothy Lambrook was about to mention the name of Oliver. 'I have a man,' she heard. 'His name is Charlie. He had trouble with his chest.'

The plump woman in the next seat shot her hand into the air, brushing the side of Rowena's face with the scratchy coat sleeve. 'That's my husband,' she gasped.

'He's with an older man called Robert, or something similar.'

'My father, Richard.'

Mrs Lambrook gave a slow, considering nod. 'They want you to get some help in the garden when spring comes. And Charlie says not to worry about the clothes. Give them to people in need...' The conversation continued for some minutes, with Rowena's neighbour eagerly enlarging on the various scraps of information offered by the medium. Rowena continued to avert her eyes out of politeness, but she could hear the heavy, excited breathing of her companion. Sometimes a line of comments would appear to lead nowhere, but with such wholehearted co-operation the dialogue was always salvaged. It was notable, therefore, when one of the medium's gambits was met with complete blankness.

'A young girl has joined us,' she said. 'I'm afraid she's quite distressed. Her name is Ellen, or Ellie. Do you know Ellie?'

'I – I'm sorry. I can't just think...'

'She's a pretty girl, wearing a blue summer dress. She wants you to tell her mother that she's sorry she caused everyone so much worry, and she never meant to do it again... Do you know of any young girl who was in some kind of trouble before she passed over? I feel it wasn't so long ago.'

Rowena's neighbour frowned in concentration. 'I'm sorry,' she repeated after a pause. 'I can't think of anyone in this situation... There's been nobody called Ellie in our family.'

Unperturbed, Mrs Lambrook gave her a reassuring smile. 'Perhaps this message is for someone sitting near you. Can anybody else take this one?' Her eyes flicked across the row of seats, meeting Rowena's for a split second before moving on. Rowena felt a cold wave of nausea. *She* knew an Ellie, her own cousin, who had shared years of holidays and confidences with Rowena before suddenly rejecting everything their families stood for. Ellie had run off with New Age travellers, not once but twice, and to the best of Rowena's knowledge she was at this moment alive, filthy, and existing hand-to-mouth somewhere in the south-west of England.

'Nobody?' Mrs Lambrook was asking. 'Ah, well, perhaps it will come to you later. Ellie knows she should have stayed in touch. She's sorry for the hurt she's caused and she sends love to all the family. I think we should all join together and send our love to Ellie.'

As the people around her bowed their heads in silent respect, Rowena was racked by uncertainty. This message *couldn't* be meant for her; she didn't believe in such communications and besides, Ellie was alive – *wasn't she*?

There was a jumpy, nagging feeling in Rowena's stomach. *Almost* she wanted to raise her hand, to catch Mrs Lambrook's eye, admit that she might just be the person they were looking for. But the moment passed... the medium turned to a new area of the hall and Ellie, if it were she, was out of reach.

*

'Morning, Ro. How was the spook show?' Keith Aspinall half turned from his desk and twinkled at her through his small, round spectacles as she rushed to her own corner of the long office at the *North London News*.

Rowena thrust her shoulder bag under the desk, uncovered the word processor and switched it on before glancing towards him across the divide. 'It was – interesting,' she replied. 'I'm still trying to decide on an angle for the article.'

'"*Interesting*,"' scoffed Ed Tranter, one of the sports correspondents. 'What sort of word is that for a journalist to use? Tells you freak-all. Come on, what's the story? The audience must have had something for their money. Were there any *manifestations* – ectoplasm, or astrals, or whatever these things are?'

'No, it was all rather matter-of-fact. The medium didn't even go into a trance. She just – concentrated. She could see, or hear, things that the rest of us couldn't.'

'Allegedly.'

'Well, yes. But I must admit I was impressed. She seemed to know some quite specific details that she couldn't have picked up just by scrutinizing the individuals involved.'

'Lucky guesswork.' Ed folded his arms and parked his huge frame against the side of Rowena's desk, which shuddered in protest. Already he was chewing his favourite gum.

'Or a plant,' suggested Keith.

Of course, she thought with a strange little sag of disappointment. She had been so caught up with the atmosphere of the place, with the genuine-seeming reactions of the people around her, that the obvious possibility of a stooge's presence had never even crossed her mind. Throughout the audience faces had been enrapt, and wherever possible she had studied the recipients of the messages... they had glowed with an almost unearthly exaltation.

She didn't want to discuss these things with the boorish Ed. Fobbing him off with platitudes she prepared to focus on her work. This material was going to be difficult. She had not lied about her inability to find a perspective; it was surely axiomatic that writing a cogent article was well nigh impossible if one's own attitudes to the subject in question still awaited definition.

Rowena felt angry with herself, though she didn't know why. Was it because she, with all her supposed intelligence, had fallen for the wiles of an ordinary-looking middle-aged woman with a pleasant voice and sympathetic manner? For a short period the previous night she had actually found herself looking for reasons to believe... Or was it because she suspected that the topic of spiritualism was too weighty to present as a superficial, easy-to-read-over-coffee, 'women's interest' item in a none-too-important London weekly? Whether her piece was going to resonate with uncompromising scepticism or soften into a grudging acknowledgement that things might indeed occur which were beyond the ability of the vast majority of people to discern, this milieu would still be inadequate...

With a sigh, Rowena began to tap the keys. In the light of a looming deadline, further soul-seeking was futile. She had no alternative material to use.

At lunch time Keith returned whistling from an assignment and padded to Rowena's desk. 'Still at it?' he asked, peering at the monitor.

Deftly she clicked on 'File', and the straggling lines of prose were obscured. '*Be* cheerful,' she said, 'but preferably not here.'

'Ah. Things are going badly.'

'Your perspicacity is stunning...sorry, Keith. This piece is a mush. I'm trying to take a neutral line, and it's just – dead.'

'Passed over, you mean.'

She giggled. 'Yes. Damn it, I think I'll get a sandwich.'

He paused. 'Why don't you come to the Crown with me? It's a while since you've been down there; they've started doing a good cottage pie...'

'I – thanks for the offer, but I don't fancy eating lunch with the crowd. I've still got a few loose ends to tidy up here.' Not so long ago she would have accepted without demur, or even initiated the suggestion. Anyone not involved with interviews or desperately hammering out overdue copy would filter into the Crown around one o'clock for food and a pint. Among those present would be Keith, Ed – and Sebastian, her ex-beau, who had abruptly abandoned both Rowena and the *North London News* for a plum job as home affairs correspondent at the *Signal*. All he had left behind was his black and white rabbit, Flash.

'I didn't mean with Ed. I just met him on the stairs, and he's off to the Wellington. There'll only be me, and I promise to be quiet if you're struggling with syntax or axing auxiliary verbs.'

He lifted his eyebrows in a mild questioning gesture and Rowena nodded her acceptance. Keith was unthreatening with his granny glasses and his ubiquitous patterned jumpers. She had known him for three years, and held him in the same mental bracket as a pair of comfortable slippers. 'Perhaps I'll try the cottage pie,' she smiled.

Outside the building, snatches of raw March wind eddied along Great Wenlock Street, plucking rubbish from the gutter and whirling it a few inches in the air. She had worked for six of her twenty-six years in this urban environment, and usually enjoyed the feeling of energy it gave her, of people charged with purpose packed within an entirely man-made complex. Today, however, it seemed ugly, the winter drabness never-ending. Perhaps an Easter holiday would be a good idea.

Together they turned into the Crown, a Victorian pub with plenty of frosted glass, red velvet, mahogany dados and furniture. It was already three-quarters full, the air both smoky and moist with an underlying redolence of school dinners.

'Quick! The corner seat!' Keith tapped her arm and leapt towards it, just securing his claim before a florid-faced businessman lumbered across from the bar. Once Rowena had joined him on the bench, he stood up again. 'I'll go and order. What are you having?'

'Cottage pie, please. And, er, cider. Dry.'

She tried to pay him but he forestalled her with a wave of his hand. 'My treat,' he said, and turned to thread his way through the throng.

He was gone a long time. Rowena guarded his place with her bag, her mind roaming back to the abortive article. She knew perfectly well what was wrong with it. It was a piece of straight reporting – albeit with the names judiciously changed – completely devoid of an authorial voice. Usually she was prodigal with her opinions, didactic, even; their editor, Kevin Bastable, encouraged the style. On this occasion, however, she had shied away from such exposure, merely ending the piece with a question that readers might choose to answer for themselves.

Keith returned with their drinks. 'Cheers,' he said, grazing her glass with his own before eagerly downing a third of his pint of beer. 'I needed that,' he went on, sagging against the back of the bench. 'I've just spent all morning with a lady in Hendon whose terrier keeps savaging people.' They discussed his assignment, and soon their number was called for the food. It was a rich, tasty pie, made in the traditional way with lamb, and served with peas and parsnips.

'I got the impression you were somewhat ambivalent about last night,' said Keith as they ate. 'Tell me to mind my own business if you like, but I wondered if you wanted to talk? You weren't for talking much to Ed, but that's quite understandable.'

'He'd have laughed,' she said slowly.

'I won't.'

Rowena took a mouthful of parsnip and considered as she chewed. Keith was just a friend, one of the gang from the office. She knew very little about him beyond the fact that he shared a flat in Haringey with two salesmen. He was aware that her parents were currently living in Oman because of her father's international banking job, and that Sebastian was no longer on the scene. Perhaps he felt sorry for her. Perhaps he was just curious? Whatever the reason, she couldn't deny that the urge to confide in *someone* was strong.

'The event was held in a community centre,' she began. 'It had been advertised simply as a demonstration of clairvoyance, and you had to buy a ticket to get in. I think it's fair to say that my initial frame of mind was sceptical. I could see a lot of elderly women there, many of whom must have been widows. I was expecting to angle the article along the lines of "con merchant exploits the vulnerable".'

She took a sip of cider. 'The medium was a very ordinary-looking woman in her fifties. Her manner was matter-of-fact: no histrionics, no trances. I noticed early on that she got members of the audience to provide a lot of the information themselves, with her just prompting. That seemed to bolster my theory. But then...' Rowena leaned forward earnestly. 'She became very specific with one girl. She spoke of a family tradition with Christmas crackers, and she named a dog precisely. I couldn't work out how she'd done that. The girl sounded genuine... Anyway, the medium passed on some more messages to people, mainly general things, then turned to my part of the hall.'

'Did she pick on you?' asked Keith.

'No. I must admit I was rather anxious about that. I was afraid she would, then perversely disappointed because she didn't. She came up with the name Charlie, and the woman sitting next to me claimed him as her husband. They chatted for a while, and then...' She looked down at the glass, unable to continue.

'Then?'

'This will sound very unlikely. She said that a young girl in distress had joined us, called Ellie. She asserted that the girl was apologizing for not staying in touch with her family and for hurting them in some way. The woman who had been answering the questions forcefully denied knowing anyone called Ellie, so the medium said the message might be for someone else sitting close by.'

'Sounds like a convenient cop-out.'

'Yes, but – I know an Ellie. She's my cousin. My family was based in Amersham while I was growing up, and hers over in Gloucestershire, but we used to be very close. We spent a lot of holidays at each other's houses. She's three years younger than I am, but that didn't seem to make a difference, except possibly to encourage her to copy my clothes when she was thirteen or so. Her brother Jonathan never had much to do with us – he had his own friends – but Ellie and I seemed to like the same things and hold similar opinions…' She paused, pushing a dark memory into its proper place. 'Both of us have fathers who are away a lot. Ellie's is the Conservative MP for Wynchwold, while mine as you know has held various banking posts abroad. Mother used to stay at home while I was young, but now she's out there with him in Oman.

'At first, Ellie was interested when I took up a career in journalism, but later on she decided that wouldn't be her choice. She did a secretarial course and held down a job for about six months, then suddenly dropped out. She joined a group of New Age travellers stumbling around the West Country in rickety old vehicles. Apart from an initial note, there was no contact at all with her parents for weeks. Her father abandoned an important conference and went looking for her; when he found her sitting on a bench in South Molton one day, she didn't want to know him. It was the best part of a year before she finally came home of her own volition, a year during which my aunt June was ill with worry. Ellie was contrite. She got a job in a solicitor's office for a while, but still felt restless and decided to join a temping agency. She didn't like being tied down, you see. I think she felt that a more permanent job meant her whole life was suddenly mapped out for her, preordained, like a strait-jacket.

'She did a few conventional stints for the agency, then a position cropped up that was different. A famous medium called Caireen Malone wanted someone on a temporary basis to transcribe her memoirs. Well – Ellie called her famous. I have to admit I'd never heard of her. Ellie had developed quite an affinity for horoscopes, runes and the like while she was with the travellers, so she jumped at this opportunity. Mrs Malone would dictate sections of her autobiography to Ellie, who would record the material in shorthand there and then. They preferred that to tape: it felt more personal. Ellie would then type it up later, correcting any solecisms as far as she was able. Not her strong point, I'm afraid.

'Unfortunately, most of this took place in Cornwall – '

'I've heard of Caireen Malone,' interjected Keith. 'I thought she was London-based.'

'She is. She has a house in Maida Vale, but also a property on the south Cornish coast and another in Paris. Ellie started off all right, and her employer was satisfied. But then she met a hippie type called Patrick working on a nearby farm, someone she'd known before. He suddenly upped and left, stealing from the farmer in the process, and the next day Ellie, too, vanished. She hasn't been in contact since.'

Rowena became aware of Keith's frown of concentration. 'When was this?' he asked.

'Last summer. Investigations were made at the time, but the police didn't take it very seriously, especially with Ellie's history. Her parents made some private enquiries, then gave up after Christmas when she didn't so much as send them a card.' There had been no messages for her, either. She had felt piqued, but unsurprised this time, and gradually put Ellie out of her mind, accepting that they had separate lives, and separate aspirations.

'And you're worried about what the medium said.'

'Yes. I can't help it. It's been flickering around in my mind ever since. Yet that's not logical, because I still don't believe in spiritualism. At least, I don't think so...'

Keith drained his glass. 'As far as I can see, this woman has simply triggered in you a natural feeling of disquiet on behalf of someone who has been out of touch for a long time. Perhaps you should contact some of Ellie's old friends, find out if they've heard anything. It might be just family she's avoiding at present, because she's ashamed.'

'I suppose that would be sensible. Thank you, Keith. But *why* did the medium pick on that name, and deliver a message that I could identify with Ellie's circumstances?'

'There were probably about twenty people under her eye in your part of the hall. *Somebody* would have known someone called Ellie. And the message as you described it sounded flexible enough to me. Remember, you said that the medium cast the gambits but the audience provided the interpretations. You mustn't worry, Ro. I'm sure your cousin's all right.'

She nodded, only partially convinced, and they finished their meal without further discourse. Leaving the now jam-packed pub, they strode along the chilly drabness of Great Wenlock Street, swerving past groups of pinch-faced office workers coming the other way, turning their thoughts to the prospects of the afternoon.

'Kevin's going to bounce my article,' said Rowena with certainty. 'I can just hear him now. "Where are the *guts*, girl?"'

'That's a good imitation.'

They stepped aside once more to allow a cluster of girls to monopolize the pavement, and fetched up against the window ledge of a furniture shop. Inside, every item was a forbidding dark oak. 'Keith,' she said suddenly, 'do *you* believe?'

'In what? Guts?'

'No – life after death in some form or other.' Her eyes sought his; it was important that he took the question seriously.

He shrugged. 'I can't honestly say I've given it much thought. I'd need a lot of convincing.'

'You see, I have trouble viewing the medium I saw as a cold-hearted fraud. I thought so at first, but afterwards – no. She seemed so sincere, so low-key. But what alternative does that leave? If she isn't a clever con-woman, a plant here, a manipulation there, then – spirits must exist.'

'Not necessarily.' He edged round into the shop doorway to shelter from both elements and passers-by, and Rowena followed. 'What about telepathy?'

'Telepathy?'

'People in the audience are focusing on lost loved ones. The medium could be picking up on these vibes, sometimes enough to give out startlingly accurate information.'

'But isn't that a form of fraud?'

'It doesn't have to be. She may not be aware of the mechanism herself. She may believe that they are spiritual perceptions . . . Tell me, Ro, were you thinking of Ellie at all last night before she was named?'

'No. I was concentrating on what was going on.'

'When was the last time she'd crossed your mind?'

Rowena pondered. Through the dusty angled window she could see a long oak chest; it reminded her uncomfortably of a coffin. 'A few days before, when I saw the advertisement for the Demonstration of Clairvoyance. I thought, what a pity I can't ask Ellie for some background information in view of her last job. But it was only a fleeting notion, soon forgotten.'

'Maybe not... You'd bracketed Ellie in your mind with a medium, and shortly afterwards you watched a different medium performing. What's the betting you were *subliminally* thinking of Ellie, and the medium picked up on this?'

'I – I certainly wasn't aware of it.'

'Bet you that's what happened. But don't take my word for it – check up with Ellie's friends.'

2

At seven forty that evening Rowena emerged from Finchley underground station with weary relief. The tube had been delayed due to an IRA bomb scare and the day had seemed very long. She left the High Street and made her way as rapidly as possible to the tree-lined suburban road of semi-detached dwellings where she rented a ground-floor flat. Her four-year-old Clio stood in the gravelled space where the front garden had been; she gave it a cursory glance, checking for signs of vandalism in the light from a nearby streetlamp, then hurried to unlock the front door. Letters scraped across the mat: the usual circulars, nothing to fuel the soul.

Keeping her jacket on, she traversed the short hallway to the kitchen and half filled the kettle with water. Outside in the darkness, across the straggling strip of lawn which constituted the rear garden, Harry would be waiting impatiently for his supper. He would have to wait a few minutes longer.

Fortifying herself with freshly brewed tea, Rowena stirred the rest of the water into a handful of Rabbit Mix to create a 'hot mash'. In this weather, she reasoned, Harry too would appreciate some inner warmth. She seized a torch, unlocked the back door and padded across the grass towards the hutch. In the jolting torch-beam she caught the gleam of an eye and a flash of white muzzle.

'Here you are,' she soothed. 'Don't guzzle it all at once.' She stroked the silky ears as he lowered his head with single-minded gluttony, but was soon forced by the chill to retreat to the kitchen. 'Goodnight, Harry,' she called as she closed the door. Sebastian, as ever, came briefly to mind and she gave a wry smile. Without doubt she was a soft touch. Flash had been *his* rabbit, legacy of a previous fractured relationship, so named because of the prominent facial white zigzag on his otherwise ebony fur. Her one small act of rebellion had been to rechristen the creature Flash Harry as soon as he left, subsequently transmuted to Harry. It was a fitting reminder of Sebastian.

Shivering again, she darted into the sitting-room to turn on the small gas fire, then returned to the kitchen to ransack the cupboards for a quick and easy meal. Macaroni. That would do. She made a cheese sauce, cooked the pasta and stirred the two together; pouring this into a flat dish she sprinkled the top with grated cheese and crushed cornflakes, added a herb-coated half tomato and browned the dish under the grill.

To a background of Ella Fitzgerald, Rowena ate her meal in the sitting-room from a tray on her lap. Afterwards she sipped orange juice, reading the evening paper in a desultory manner, but soon the pages slipped to the floor and she was not of a mind to retrieve them. Ellie was back in her thoughts, crowding out mundanities such as the fate of the local cinema and the spate of car crime in the suburbs. She demanded attention.

Rowena rose abruptly, and crossed the hall to her bedroom. It was a long, generously sized chamber, running front-to-back with a window at each end. She had been proud of her painting and decorating efforts three years ago, transforming the room from a nightmare of puce floral splotches to matt walls of palest yellow, with cream paintwork and curtains. Her previous London residence, a cramped, musty bedsit near a railway line, had been beyond any kind of decorative redemption.

She opened one of the room's two wardrobes and reached down a pile of photograph albums from its top shelf. Spreading them carefully across the bed, she opened one with a blue cover and began to leaf through it. Here were pictures from her late teens: her father had given her an expensive automatic camera on her eighteenth birthday and she had spent a prodigal summer with Ellie's family in their Cotswold home photographing anything that breathed, and plenty of things that didn't. She flicked past the picture-postcard shots – golden cottages, a water wheel, an old smithy – and slowed down when the human beings began to appear. She saw Aunt June, taken unawares basting a turkey in her lovely pine kitchen, then Uncle Alan standing in his orchard, deep in conversation with the gardener. Here was one of Jonathan, slightly blurred as he turned his head away. And here... the fifteen-year-old Ellie, laughing gleefully as the rubbery lips of her pony Peppy tickled her outstretched palm.

Rowena bit her own lip. Ellie had been so unspoilt, still childlike that year. Her pleasures had been simple and spontaneous, her character warm and generous before the shutters came down and 'causes' began to dictate her every action. 'My materialistic years,' Ellie herself had described her adolescence later. 'My years of conforming.' Their philosophies had rapidly diverged with Rowena, by this stage a cub reporter struggling to manage on a meagre salary, resenting Ellie's open admiration for pressure groups and travellers whose welfare-imbursed freedoms were bought on the back of other people's toil. They had argued with some rancour... not long afterwards Ellie had become a traveller herself.

Rowena knew she had instinctively sought out this album because of the innocence it represented, a time when the poisonous clouds of discord had not even begun to gather. She turned another page and studied the pictures closely. Here was the whole family standing by a duck pond during a visit to Sudeley Castle, once the home of Henry the Eighth's sixth wife, Catherine Parr. This was one of the rare occasions when Jonathan had deigned to join them, presumably in response to a three-line-whip from his father. Two years older than Ellie, Jonathan had always preferred his own pursuits to the company of girls.

June was smiling charmingly as usual, her slightly overweight figure nonetheless graceful in a pale green linen dress. Ellie, the next in line, had her mother's smile and golden hair, but was slender as a dryad, almost ethereal in pure white. Jonathan towered above her, squinting in the sun, his brown hair tending to mocha like his father's. Alan, the veteran of many a photo-shoot, had perfected an easy, engaging expression, and this shot was no exception, but Rowena understood the term face value: both the Drinkwater men had a cold, hostile streak in their characters, and she had always been a little afraid of them.

She continued to flick through the album, her gaze meandering across the pages, then suddenly stopped. *This* was the picture she had really hoped to find – Ellie and herself in close-up, arms round each other's shoulders, laughing into the camera as June pressed the shutter. They had been picking strawberries, she remembered, huge quantities so that June could make jam for the WI.

Rowena peered at the faces. People had occasionally commented that Ellie and she looked alike, although she had never credited this herself. Her own blonde hair shaded to fawn as opposed to Ellie's golden bronze; her eyes were hazel while her cousin's were blue. Ellie had a sweet, heart-shaped face while Rowena knew hers was squarer and stronger. But perhaps there *were* subtle similarities: the arch of the eyebrows, the short, straight noses...just enough to mark them as distant members of the same family to someone with keen powers of observation.

Shouldn't I *know* if Ellie is alive or dead? she wondered. Shouldn't I feel some instinct inside? Closing the album, Rowena acknowledged that it was too late: the invisible threads of empathy had parted long ago. Whatever bond had linked them at the time of these photographs existed no longer.

Sighing, she rose from the bed and slowly paced the long room, rubbing her upper arms through the sleeves of her jumper. It was cold in here; she should have taken the album to the sitting-room where the gas fire still burned cheerfully. What was it Keith had suggested? 'Talk to Ellie's friends.' Easier said than done. Rowena no longer knew who Ellie's friends were, any more than Ellie was familiar with her own London crowd. But she had to do *something*.

Returning to the sitting-room she sat in the deep armchair by the telephone and lifted the receiver. She would try June. If Ellie had been in contact over the last three or four weeks the news might not yet have filtered through via Oman.

It was nine thirty on a weekday. Alan would be in his Westminster flat and June would have finished her supper long ago. Without giving herself time to find reasons not to ring, Rowena tapped out the Wynchwold code.

A male voice answered. 'Drinkwater.'

'Alan?' she asked tentatively.

'No, it's Jonathan. Who's speaking?'

'Rowena.'

'Oh.'

He didn't sound particularly delighted, she reflected, even though it was over two years since they had last been in direct contact. She decided not to waste time on platitudes. 'May I have a word with June, please?'

'She's out. Some play in Oxford. She's gone with a woman friend.'

Damn.

'...Can I give her a message?' he added as an afterthought.

'Er, no; it's all right. I'll try another time. There's something you could tell me, though. Has Ellie been in touch recently?'

'Why?'

Jonathan's naturally cool voice invested the monosyllable with several extra degrees of chill, and Rowena felt anger stir. June would never have asked such a question. It was typical that Jonathan, however, with his dry accountant's brain, should require a reason. For a bizarre moment she was tempted to tell him the truth, if only to puncture his equanimity, but immediately recoiled. Not for anything would she upset her aunt with half-formed theories of the paranormal.

'I found a bracelet of Ellie's last week,' she improvised. 'I wondered if she wanted it back.'

'I doubt she's interested in jewellery sitting round whichever camp-fire in whichever muddy field has taken her fancy. Except perhaps as something to sell.'

There was bitterness in his sneering tone, and Rowena felt constrained to probe further. 'You've had no news at all?'

'None. Which is just how she likes it. Not for Ellie the responsibilities of staying in touch with one's parents. Save that for mature adults.'

'I'm sorry, Jonathan. Will you tell June I rang and give her my love?'

There was a short silence. 'All right. I won't mention this bracelet, though, if it's all the same to you. Mention of Ellie distresses her. Dad and I have got the message, though, and frankly I don't give a monkey's now whether or not Ellie chooses to return. She's had it as far as I'm concerned.'

Rowena wondered fleetingly whether it was a sense of family duty keeping the twenty-five-year-old Jonathan at home, or sheer convenience as she had previously imagined. He had a girlfriend in Banbury, Sally something-or-other. 'How is Sally?' she asked.

'Okay.'

'I heard you both went skiing in January. La Tania, wasn't it?'

'Yes.'

'Was there much snow?'

'Enough.'

Rowena found her hand tightening around the telephone receiver, and decided to give up. There was just one more thing she needed to know. 'Aunt June...' she began. 'She hasn't been ill again?' 'Ill' was the euphemism used within the family for June's quasi nervous breakdown the first time Ellie disappeared.

'No,' he said shortly. 'And we want it to stay that way.'

There was nothing more to be said. Rowena murmured polite valedictions and replaced the receiver. Beside her, the gas fire glowed invitingly. She had turned down the lights in the room, and the only other source of illumination was a faint sheen from the streetlamp outside, just visible beneath the curtains.

She hunched in the chair, ambivalent and troubled. Though Jonathan had merely confirmed what she had expected all along, that Ellie for whatever reason had not yet contacted her family, she felt a new sense of foreboding deep in her gut.

A fugitive white streak flickered across the wall opposite as the quartz halogen headlights from a turning car briefly probed the gap behind the curtains. For a moment Rowena was reminded of a spirit: she saw Ellie, slender and white-clad as in the Sudeley picture, beckoning her with pale fingers.

'No,' murmured Rowena, turning decisively to face the interior of the room. Across the Indian hearth rug, behind two threadbare armchairs disguised by vivid throws, stood her grandmother's long oak sideboard. Suddenly she was back with Keith in the doorway of the furniture shop, asking him if he believed, seeing a coffin in the place of an innocent oak trunk.

She found herself shuddering, two feet from the gas fire. It was *her* threshold of credulity she had to grapple with, not Keith's. He had not been present when the medium had demonstrated her powers so convincingly. What *do* I believe? wondered Rowena. If I think she's a fake, why can't I get her words out of my brain? And if I believe she's genuine...

Then Ellie is dead.

3

Rowena had little time to brood over the next three weeks. The blustery equinoctial weather ushered in a wave of staff sickness in the form of an unidentified flu virus, and those stalwarts who battled to keep the *North London News* supplied with copy also had to contend with Kevin Bastable's peevishness. Racked with bronchitis, he nevertheless staggered to his desk every day, but his natural irritability was augmented fivefold. Nothing seemed to please him, and the remnants of the newsroom staff were soon in an advanced state of paranoia. In their rare free moments they converged in huddles of discontent.

Rowena saw little of Keith throughout this time. He came and went almost unannounced, his face pinched and vole-like under the hood of a dark olive parka. It seemed amazing now that she had confided in him so freely – slightly embarrassing, even. Beyond the usual camaraderie of colleagues in more leisured times she scarcely knew him, and the brevity of his current greetings seemed to indicate that this was how he would like it to stay.

It was a surprise, therefore, to find him falling into step with her one evening as she left the office after another stint of unofficial overtime.

'How are things with you?' he asked, ignoring the lift and following her to the stairs.

'Oh, same as for everyone else – a bit short in the fun department. You seem to be busy.'

'Yes. I'm covering for Peter *and* Clive.'

She made a sympathetic grimace as they tapped down the stairs, two flights to the ground floor. The short corridor to the foyer was deserted. Beside her, Keith glanced to right and left as if to make sure.

'Did you manage to track down your cousin?' he enquired with an attempt at a casual tone which did not quite ring true.

She slowed down. 'No, unfortunately. I tried her family, then mine, and one school friend. I couldn't probe too deeply – it seemed to catch people on the raw – but the basic answer was the same: Ellie hasn't been in touch.'

'I'm sorry. I was hoping you might have had some definitive news.'

His manner seemed discomfited, somehow oblique. Rowena sensed that he was debating whether or not to say more. 'Thanks for asking.'

He nodded jerkily, still ill at ease. 'What will you do now?' he asked after a pause.

'I don't know. The trail seems pretty cold. I suppose I could try the National Missing Persons Helpline, or the Salvation Army: Aunt June did that the first time she went missing; I'm not sure about the second. I know they tried a private detective for a while last September, but he wasn't any good. I expect Ellie and Patrick were keeping a low profile because he'd robbed the farmer...' She bit her lip. Ellie had always been so honest – and fastidious. Sometimes it was hard to believe that she'd changed so completely. Perhaps the influence was more than Patrick. Perhaps it was drugs.

Keith's eyes were searching her face. 'I wasn't sure whether to mention this,' he began, 'but that woman Caireen Malone – she's in London at present. I saw an advert last night for one of her demonstrations.' Reaching into the inside pocket of his parka he drew out a torn square of newspaper and handed it to her.

'Wimbledon Theatre...' she read. 'The twenty-eighth. When's that – oh, this Saturday. I wonder if they've got any tickets left...' Her mind was racing. Ellie had worked closely with this woman for three months, enthusing about her to Rowena in a sudden, all-too-brief wellspring of letters and cards. 'Caireen is wonderful' was one of the phrases she had used. Perhaps they had exchanged confidences; perhaps Caireen was the unwitting custodian of a clue as to Ellie's whereabouts. She would, of course, have been interviewed by the police, but in the context of a listless, perfunctory enquiry imaginative questioning was unlikely...

Rowena scoured the advert again, as if attempting to imbibe some impression of Caireen Malone's character from the smudged print. She might be hostile to any mention of Ellie – from her perspective this was simply a feckless girl who had left her employer in the lurch. Perhaps Ellie had even stolen from *her*, and she had generously kept quiet. Anything was possible...

'Do you want me to come with you, Ro?'

She blinked, dislodged from her chain of thought. 'What?'

'In case – you know.'

Keith had had more time to think about this; suddenly she realized what he was implying. 'In case Ellie tries to make contact?'

'Well – in case one of the messages sounds a bit like Ellie, which might be upsetting.'

There. He *did* feel sorry for her. He also believed she was over-credulous. 'I don't think that's likely,' she said briskly. 'I was visualizing Mrs Malone more in the context of an ordinary witness than as a medium. I was wondering how I might get to talk to her privately in a theatre packed with hundreds of people. I can't really play the "journalist" card south of the river.'

'You might catch her afterwards, if you lurk by the stage door,' he suggested.

Wryly she noticed that he was looking relieved. 'I don't know... Maybe they'll announce some contact details for people who want to arrange private sittings.'

'She should be in the phone book.'

'There must be scores of Malones.'

'I meant the Yellow Pages, under psychic, or spiritualist, or whatever. How else would clients reach her?'

'You're probably right. But I still want to see her anonymously first, in public – get an idea of her personality before I blunder in with questions.'

'Good idea. If you need moral support, I'm still willing to come.'

'Keith... thanks, but...' She laid a mollifying hand on his arm. 'I think I'll concentrate best on my own. I'm grateful to you, though, for pointing out this ad.'

He accepted her decision with easy grace, underlying her suspicion that he had only offered out of a sense of duty.

'Let me buy you a coffee down the road,' she said. 'It's cold out there.'

Wimbledon Theatre was a tall Victorian edifice which usually played host to repertory companies, choirs and occasional orchestras. There was also ballet, according to the leaflets in the foyer where Rowena surged forward with the crush of people queuing to enter the stalls, clutching her ticket and wondering if she would see anything at all from seat 19S.

The auditorium itself proved to be cooler. Rowena sank into the worn velvet seat and absorbed her surroundings: the dusty chandeliers, the elaborate, faded gilding, the overall feel of shabby splendour which reminded her of Brighton. Tonight there could be no written programmes as such, but with the ticket she had been given a delicate mauve flyer on which was printed a black and white portrait of Caireen Malone and a few scant lines of biography. Caireen had inherited psychic gifts from her mother, had been a medium for thirty years and had assisted clients from every continent.

The picture was scarcely more informative. It was a three-quarter view of a woman of indeterminate age, forties perhaps, with short, softly curling hair, good cheekbones and a slight gathering fullness beneath the chin. She wore ear-rings in the design of a Celtic cross, and stared out from the paper with a blurred, long-distance focus which may have owed more to poor reproductive technology than to distant spiritual contemplation.

Rowena smiled grimly to herself. Having spent two hours the night before doing assiduous homework with the newspaper archives, she was in a good position to assess both the photograph and the text. Caireen Malone, she knew, was fifty-four and hadn't looked like this for years. She had two sons by two different husbands and Brett, the elder son, worked as her business manager. She had been extraordinarily successful as a medium, helping many famous people including minor royalty, though Rowena had detected a faint underlying flavour in recent articles suggesting that her career had now passed its zenith...

There was an anticipatory rustle as the lights in the auditorium began to dim. On stage, the heavy curtains swung aside to reveal bare planks and two four-foot stands of gilded wrought iron, each surmounted by a pale candlestick. As the throat-clearing died away to silence, a tall, dark-haired young man strode purposefully out from the wings and stopped in the centre of the stage, facing the audience.

'Ladies and gentlemen,' he said, 'good evening. We are delighted that so many of you have come here to join us tonight. We want you to enjoy a feeling of fellowship over these next two hours, the knowledge that even though Caireen cannot offer messages to all of you, the glimpses of hope and optimism are for everyone to share.'

He smiled, a flash of bright teeth. 'My mother has just come back from a tour of France. Luckily she can manage the language, because the spirits made no concessions! If, however, somebody here has an uncle from the Czech Republic who is desperate to make contact, then you'll have to help us out!' He paused while the onlookers responded with a collective chuckle. Rowena felt some of the prevailing tension dissipate, and mentally congratulated him on his approach.

'Enough from me,' he went on. 'Let me introduce my mother, the stunning and gifted Caireen Malone.' He raised a hand towards the wings, bowed briefly in acknowledgement to the audience itself and made a smart exit at the other side of the stage. For a few seconds the platform was bare; Rowena, like the others, held her breath and imperceptibly leaned forward before a small figure glided into view from the right-hand side.

'Thank you, Brett.' Her voice was light, with a faint indefinable lilt, yet the sound projected perfectly to 'S' row with no visible microphonic assistance. Rowena scrutinized her with interest; under a cap of short, curling Titian-red hair, Caireen Malone's face was beautifully made-up: from this distance she looked about thirty. She wore a shimmering violet gown, cut low on the bodice but with loose elbow-length sleeves and a flowing A-line skirt which effectively masked any tell-tale thickening of upper arm or hip. A glitter of crystal at her throat and ear-lobes – diamonds? paste? – completed the ensemble.

'I have been meditating off-stage,' she said, 'and I feel the room is full of spirits tonight, so I shall start without further ado. I want as many people as possible to receive their messages, and I shall do my very best to convey them accurately.' She gave a little nod, then stood stock still and closed her eyes.

The auditorium lights dimmed further to a state of low-key illumination. A young man entered from stage left bearing a lighted taper, but this was not Brett: he was shorter and slighter, with hair which was a paler version of Caireen Malone's rich auburn-red. This must be Daniel, thought Rowena, Brett's half-brother. He padded to each of the candlesticks in turn and left two slow-burning lights in his wake. When he had disappeared from sight his mother slowly raised her head.

For the next two hours Caireen Malone was as good as her word. She worked tirelessly to provide a channel of communication between whatever she could see or hear and the audience in front of her, and her messages were well received. Barring occasional non-sequiturs, the information seemed to be of high quality, and Rowena was impressed. She found Caireen's manner more distant, more polished than that of Dorothy Lambrook, but it was only to be expected; this woman was a professional medium with a world-wide reputation, performing here in front of over a thousand people.

Just before the scheduled end of the evening, a young man near the front was picked out by the medium. 'I have a message here from Wilfred,' she said strongly. 'He says he's your father.'

The young man was at first too stunned to reply, then he gasped out, 'My father's name *is* Wilfred.'

'And he is now in the spirit world – yes?'

'Yes . . .'

She smiled, perhaps in response to the doubt in his tone. 'He says he passed over five months ago. He tells me you live in a terraced house with a green door, and some kind of plant in the window – aspidistra, I think. Is that correct?'

'Yes!'

'He's standing right behind you. He wants you to know that he feels better than he has done for years – no pain, no shortness of breath. He asks you to look after Muriel, and –' here she chuckled – 'give Furball a cuddle for him. Does that mean something to you?'

'Oh yes. Definitely. Thank you... thank you so much.'

Rowena was particularly affected by this encounter. The man didn't sound at all like a stooge, yet how else...? She shook her head, and resolved to try to get close to him as he left the theatre.

She became aware that everyone around her was applauding fiercely, and up on the stage Caireen Malone now stood limply in a spotlight. Rowena could sense her exhaustion, the shattering weariness that follows the squandering of nervous energy.

When his mother had left the stage, Brett returned. 'Thank you for your warm appreciation,' he said. 'We know from past experience that some of our audience wait a long time outside in the cold for Caireen's autograph, or the opportunity to book a private sitting. The management have kindly allowed us the use of the green-room backstage for the next forty-five minutes for this purpose.' He indicated a door to the side of the stage. 'If interested parties would like to wait *here*, I can tell you that Caireen is in London for the next three weeks and will try to accommodate as many people as she can who wish for a private sitting. Thank you.'

Rowena stood up with the rest of her row, hopelessly torn. This would be a perfect way to meet Caireen Malone – book a sitting tonight, then admit later in private that she had really come to discuss Ellie. But she also wanted to follow the young man, son of 'Wilfred'... With great difficulty she kept him in sight as he forged his way up the central aisle, apparently in the company of a bespectacled young woman. They passed her and struggled through into the foyer, where they paused by the side of the tall glass doors.

'Let me put on my coat,' said the girl. 'It's freezing outside.'

The man slipped it over her arms and shoulders while Rowena stood nearby, pretending to fumble in her shoulder bag.

'Thanks,' said the girl, then her face changed. 'How did she *do* that, David? How did she *know*?'

'I don't know. I didn't believe it was possible, but now... It really felt like Dad.'

'Will you tell your mother?'

'I need to think about that...' They joined the queue pouring out through the doorway and were swallowed up by the frosty night. Shelving her perplexity, Rowena fought against the flow to regain the auditorium and take her place at the back of that other queue, the substantial body of people eager for further contact with Caireen Malone.

The crocodile moved fairly quickly, and Rowena suspected that Brett's brisk efficiency was to be credited. As she shuffled through the door into a spartan backstage corridor, she tried to recall some more of the fruits of her archive search. Brett was the son of Caireen's first husband, an American businessman called Lonsdale Saunders. That marriage had lasted five years before ending with his death from a heart attack. Caireen then married Daniel Malone, an Irish musician, who had encouraged her to develop her psychic gifts. Sadly he too had died young, leaving her with sons of fifteen and six to bring up...

Everyone around Rowena was chatting animatedly, albeit in low voices. The verdict on Caireen Malone's powers was uniformly favourable. 'I've seen six mediums,' she heard one person say, 'and she's the best of the lot. Really convincing.'

Gradually, her own turn in the green-room came nearer. She wondered why one of the front-of-house reception rooms hadn't been chosen, since theatre backstage areas were without exception grim, filthy places, but reflected that it was easier for Caireen Malone this way. Ahead, the queue stopped, winding round in a dog-leg through the green-room doorway. A woman came out wearing a beatific expression, clutching her piece of violet paper. A genuine fan – Ellie's words, 'Caireen is wonderful', came back to mind. Rowena tried to quash an illogical surge of apprehension. She had been more relieved than she dared admit to herself that Ellie had not 'come through' this evening, but who knew what Caireen Malone might yet detect?

Once inside the room she saw that it was bare like the corridor, with just a trestle table, two chairs and a lamp. Caireen sat behind the table, smiling graciously at the female supplicant opposite while Brett tapped at the keys of a lap-top computer. The woman got up to leave, and as Caireen welcomed the next person in the queue, Brett's dark blue eyes made a quick assessing sweep towards the doorway. His would-be glance halted as it reached Rowena. For two or three seconds he stared at her, the expression on his sharp-hewn, handsome face a compound of thoughtfulness and hostility, before he turned his attention to the next potential client.

Rowena's trepidation flooded back with renewed force. Suddenly she was confused, just when she needed to take plain, decisive action. Had he recognized her as a relative of Ellie's? Did that make any difference? She had never intended to hide the fact. But why had he looked so...baleful?

Within two minutes she would be sitting in that chair herself, committed. She wasn't ready. Some instinct of danger was rising in her chest, telling her to go away and think things through. As the remnants of the queue moved forward again, Rowena checked behind her. A few latecomers had joined even after she had – she would go to the back and gain a few precious minutes of breathing space.

Murmuring an apology to a woman pressing hard against her shoulder, Rowena broke out of the line and almost ran through the doorway. Head down, she started up the corridor, but was brought up short by something soft. She heard a yelp of alarm and a rattling sound; drops of hot liquid splattered her left hand before the crash of shattering crockery echoed from the walls.

'Oh, I *am* sorry,' she began. A man with light, coppery hair was kneeling at her feet, picking up the broken pieces of a white china cup and saucer. He looked up at her; she saw a sweet, poetic face, as fair as a girl's. The guileless blue eyes were friendly, and the shapely mouth was curved into a shy smile. *Daniel Malone*, thought Rowena with dismay. It would be.

'Don't worry,' he said. 'I can easily get another.' His voice was soft with the merest hint of a lilt, just like his mother's.

Rowena bent to collect the remaining scattered fragments and followed him up the corridor to a narrow kitchenette, where they dropped the pieces into a waste bin.

'I'm sorry,' she repeated as he switched on the electric kettle. 'I didn't look where I was going. I thought I was about to miss my train, but I've remembered now that there's another one...You're Daniel Malone, aren't you?'

He looked gauchely pleased that she should recognize him. 'Yes...Did you get to see Mother?'

'I'm afraid I didn't. I wasn't sure if I was doing the right thing anyway. You see –' she took a deep breath – 'I'm a journalist and I was wondering if she would agree to an interview.'

'Oh. She usually does.'

Rowena affected an embarrassed shrug. 'We're not exactly a national daily. It's the *North London News*, to be precise. The circulation isn't huge.'

'North London?' He looked puzzled.

'She's a resident of Maida Vale, and her clients come from all points of the compass.'

'Oh yes; of course.'

He nodded as he spooned leaf tea into a pot and poured on boiling water. Rowena felt the tension in her abdomen begin to relax. Some instinct had sent her down this previously rejected road; she could hide behind a professional façade until she was more sure of these people.

'This tea is for Mother,' Daniel was saying. 'She gets so exhausted. She gives everything to her audience, because for many it's their only opportunity to make contact... I've been trying to take notes. I bet you'd laugh at them, being a journalist. I can't do proper shorthand – I was never taught.'

'What are the notes for?' asked Rowena casually.

'Mother's autobiography. Sometimes something startling happens, then she tells me afterwards we should include it. I daren't miss anything, really, just in case... I wish she had a proper secretary. Mrs Burkitt has just left, and Mother doesn't want anyone else until we go to Cornwall. Brett and I are filling in at present.'

'Cornwall!' sighed Rowena with feeling. 'I envy you. There are times when I feel as if I never want to see London again.'

He laughed, but a gleam of interest had kindled in his eye, enlivening his delicate face. 'I wish you could come with us. We need someone who's used to words and phrases, to help with Mother's book. She's discovered she needs a writer, someone who can make the incidents come alive. She's been enquiring as to who might be free... We had a typist once, but she was only employed to take down Mother's dictation. She looked a bit like you...'

Rowena gave a polite half-smile.

'She wasn't a writer, though, and that's what we need just now. I say, you don't suppose your boss will grant you leave of absence for three or four months? A kind of sabbatical? It would be *so* nice if you could come.'

'I – I don't think...' Rowena was dumbfounded. His boyish enthusiasm sounded genuine, in contrast to the suspicious glower of his brother. She had never even entertained the idea of attempting to work for them. Yet the attractions were undeniable. She was desperately in need of a change of scene; she felt both jaded and frustrated at the *North London News*. Perhaps here was the trigger for handing in her cards.

Daniel poured the rich dark tea, then pulled at her wrist like an eager child. 'Come and meet Mother,' he said. 'She'll persuade you even if I can't.'

Caireen Malone was just signing her last autograph as Daniel laid the cup at her elbow.

'Sorry it's late, Mother,' he said as the supplicant, another middle-aged lady, bustled out beaming. 'I was talking.' He gestured towards Rowena. 'Mother, this is Rowena. She could be the answer to our problem. She's a writer!'

The veil of weariness seemed to slough away from Caireen's face as she turned her full attention to the newcomer, but she remained seated. 'I'm pleased to meet you. This is my son Brett... What kind of writing do you do? Novels?'

'I'm a journalist.'

Caireen's well-painted eyebrows rose a fraction. 'That was quick. We've only just begun to put out feelers in that quarter. I have to say, though, that we are really looking for someone with experience of biography.'

Brett glanced stonily towards Rowena then leaned down to his mother. 'I've heard that Tristram Veluce is available.'

She shuddered. 'Ghastly little man! He's so sly and gossipy about everyone else, he wouldn't be above doing an oh-so-subtle hatchet job on me, if that isn't too much of a paradox. All I want is someone who will translate my story into sympathetic prose.' She scrutinized Rowena thoughtfully. 'Did you bring a curriculum vitae and samples of your work?'

Daniel glowed, but Rowena felt obliged to put a stop to this spurious momentum. 'Perhaps I should explain,' she said. 'I came here tonight as a representative of the *North London News*, hoping that you might grant an interview while you're in London. But Daniel explained to me that you need a collaborator for your autobiography, and – I must admit, I'm interested.'

'It could take six months,' said Brett coolly. 'Are you ready to give up your job?'

She paused. 'Yes. I was already looking around for something else...'

'It won't be six months,' stated Caireen. 'We've got all the information. It's purely a matter of converting a series of incidents into a smooth, readable text. I'd say three or four months. How much has Daniel told you? Whoever takes this job would be resident with us in Cornwall. I should work mornings only on the script, but the writer would, of course, have more to do. Does this accord with your expectations?'

'I didn't know the details, but it sounds very reasonable.'

'You haven't asked about pay.' For a moment Caireen's eyes were sharp, like Brett's, then she gave a warm chuckle. 'We're so used to negotiating business deals that it's refreshing to meet someone who's reticent about the pounds and pence. We'll discuss figures when we've seen some of your work. These days I don't pay per hour – that encourages laziness. I'll pay an agreed sum for the job as a whole. Have you any questions for Rowena, Brett?'

He stifled a yawn. 'I presume you've written features, not just accounts of Joe Bloggs arraigned at the Magistrates' Court?'

'Of course.'

'And what did you say your surname was?'

'I didn't. It's Kemp.'

'Ah. Well: fax us copies of your six best articles before Wednesday, plus a full CV. Here's the number. We'll get back to you when we've considered. Okay?'

Rowena nodded, matching him for *sang-froid*. They would say this to anyone, she reminded herself. Despite Daniel's enthusiasm, the chance of an internationally renowned medium engaging a twenty-six-year-old nobody to write her precious biography was almost nil. But if it *did* come off, what an opportunity! She herself would be able to retrace Ellie's footsteps from the very place she was last seen, talk to local people, gain a picture of her health and state of mind. Rowena felt the hunger even as she bade Caireen Malone a dispassionate goodnight. She wanted this job, badly. And it would never do to let them know.

'You want to leave us?' Keith was dismayed.

'Shh. Don't tell everyone else. There's nothing definite yet. But I really do need a change…even if this doesn't work out, I might well look for something else.'

'It's the winter blues. Seasonal affective disorder, or whatever. You'll be all right when the sunshine reappears.'

'It's not as simple as that.'

He seemed to shrink. 'This is my fault. I wish I'd never shown you that item on Caireen Malone. Ro, you don't have to throw in your job and *work* with her. You could still see her just the once here in London, as you intended, and ask whatever you need about your cousin...'

'That's not the same. I feel... I honestly feel this was meant to be.'

'Ellie leading you there? Ro – for goodness' sake!'

He tried hard to keep the note of shocked derision out of his voice, but Rowena could still detect it. 'You don't understand,' she said stiffly.

He shrugged, defeated. 'Evidently not.'

*

'So, you want to leave us?' echoed Kevin Bastable ten days later.

Rowena stood in the untidy office, once more feigning insouciance, but her heart was hammering a furious tattoo against her rib-cage. Kevin Bastable terrified everybody, even Ed Tranter.

'A bit of flu in the office, a bit of extra work, and you pull the whining martyr. I thought you were professional, girl. I thought we were *nurturing* your *skills,* so that you would rise above mere competence to excellence. And what thanks do we get?'

From Rowena's perspective, they had enjoyed cut-price labour from her over several years, and it was time for a change. To her astonishment, Brett Saunders had telephoned her five days after their meeting in the Wimbledon Theatre. They were considering her for the position, he had said, but needed some more evidence of her capabilities. He had faxed her a bundle of diary papers relating to an episode of clairvoyance when Caireen was twelve years old, and asked her to write it up in eight hundred words in the first person. She had worked all night, honing her adjectives, weeding out sentimentality whilst retaining sincerity. The result had impressed them to such a degree that she had been invited to Maida Vale...

Kevin's question must have been rhetorical, because he continued without pause. 'I assume you've been secretly fixing yourself up with something else, just like that bloody Sebastian.'

'I was head-hunted,' she said quietly. It was true in a way. 'Sebastian is nothing to do with it.'

Bastable flushed darkly. 'It's as well no one's asked me for references,' he snarled. 'I shan't have to find words to describe your puerile copy.'

Perversely, she found his aura of pique heartening. If I'm so useless, she thought, then why are you angry? He was acting as if he had discovered her true value too late. Ignoring his outburst she continued calmly, 'I'm owed a lot of annual leave. I'm hoping we can agree to waive eight days of my notice.' Caireen Malone wanted her in Cornwall in exactly two and a half weeks. If Kevin proved difficult now, the job might be jeopardized.

'So they want you in a hurry,' he sneered. 'I'm not sure...' He thumped his heavy forearms down on the desk, pressed his stubby fingers together and splayed them, staring at her all the while. 'Tell me about this job you're going to.'

'Is that relevant?'

'It might be.'

Sighing, she outlined her brief without names or places.

'Who's the ego-tripper?'

'It doesn't matter.'

Within the pouchy lids his eyes gleamed cunningly. 'You know I'll find out,' he said.

That was true. Her friends were bound to discuss Caireen's commission, and Kevin had at least one mole in the office. 'It's Caireen Malone, the medium,' she answered.

He rocked back and forth, mentally computing possibilities. 'I've got a deal for you,' he said at length. 'Do your book, then come back here. There'll be an extra 4K per annum.'

She gulped. This was unprecedented. 'I shall need to think about it,' she said.

'You've got thirty seconds.' He watched her face then nodded, satisfied, before she even spoke. 'Good,' he went on. 'In the interim, we'll be expecting regular articles.'

'I thought my copy was puerile.'

'There have been a few naff efforts recently, but your work is usually passable.'

He leered at her, and Rowena sensed that he had known her situation all along and was now playing some kind of game. 'I shall be in Cornwall. That won't interest North London readers.'

'*Au contraire,* Miss Kemp. People living in the great metropolis, hearing the rumble of traffic every day, breathing the polluted air, *long* for tales of the unspoilt countryside. That's why they listen to *The Archers*. Our great mistake is that we're too parochial. We need an "out and about" page to show that we're aware of events outside our patch.'

'Nature notes?' she murmured helplessly.

'Nah. Start with Caireen Malone and her Cornish mansion. Describe the rooms, the garden, the domestic set-up.'

'Like that awful glossy, *Coo-ee*?'

'If necessary. Then move on to her so-called psychic powers.'

' "So-called"?'

'She's a fraud, of course. They all are, but the public gulp it up like thirsty lap dogs. Then we use that as a link to the Cornish paranormal.'

'I'm sorry...?'

Bastable let out his breath in a snort. 'And I thought you were intelligent. It's a weird land beyond the Tamar. Think of all the inbreeding in those villages, the Celtic mythology...Seek out the Beast of Bodmin, the Panther of Pendeen. Our readers'll love it.'

'I suppose I could manage that.' Privately, she doubted any such thing was to be found. She had yet to travel further west than Devon herself, but she knew that Cornwall had long enjoyed the benefits of A-roads and telephones; isolated pockets of 'weirdness' were likely to be few and far between.

Rowena was just about to ask him to clarify his definition of 'regular' when Kevin leaned forward and lowered his voice confidentially. 'It's all cover, of course. What I really want from you is some good, old-fashioned investigative journalism. Let me tell you how to go about it...'

'How did you get on with Kevin?' asked Keith artlessly an hour later.

'As if you didn't know. Stop trying to play the innocent. *Someone* primed him with my intentions, and I'd lay fifty to one it was you.'

'Ro...We like you here. We didn't want you to go. Yes, it was me. But I only hinted, I didn't tell him anything specific. I suggested a compromise might be possible, then left him to work it out for himself.'

'Keith, you could have got me sacked!'

'You were already determined to leave. And I know that Kevin values your work. He's said so. He looks upon you as his protégée, rightly so, and if you weren't so paranoid recently you'd have spotted that yourself.'

He stood there, defiant in a sage green jumper covered with lambs, and Rowena was speechless. '*Never* do that again!' she spluttered at last.

'I won't...so what *is* going to happen? Are you coming back afterwards?'

She told him the arrangement that had been hammered out with Kevin, even the rise, though she avoided specifying the amount.

'Get that in writing,' warned Keith. 'Not to mention whatever figure Caireen Malone is offering you. Make sure you get royalties as well as a flat fee. Will you be named as one of the book's authors?'

'I thought about it. I could have asked for "Caireen Malone with Rowena Kemp" on the jacket, but that might have suggested an endorsement of the contents. As it is, I've no idea how accurate the material is. No one has been round interviewing friends, relatives, clients; the book will simply be her own recollections of events.'

'A self-hagiography.'

'Exactly. So I'd rather just be the ghost in the background. There's the question of belief, too...my own opinion of spiritualism won't matter.' Momentarily she frowned, hovering on the edge of a confidence, but drew back. A noisy office was not the place. 'It's going to be a challenging spring,' she went on. 'Not one job, but two, and a flat and a rabbit to sort out. The time-scale isn't long enough for subletting, so I'll probably just get my mail rerouted and pop back to London for odd weekends.'

'So much for taking a holiday,' said Keith with a wry grimace. 'What *are* you going to do with your rabbit?'

'I haven't a clue. It's a pity the family upstairs are so odd. They'd probably eat him, given half a chance.'

'He could stay at my place if you're desperate. I'm sure the other chaps wouldn't mind. There's a wide hall where people keep bicycles and the like...I reckon there'd be room for a hutch.'

'Thank you, Keith. I might yet take you up on that.'

'Call it expiation. Am I forgiven?'

'For interfering? You meant well.'

He pulled another face. 'Those must be three of the most crushing words in the English language.'

Rowena thrust her fork into another plump piece of *pasta penne* and marvelled at the change in the weather. Now that April was well established, her garden was actually looking attractive, with clusters of daffodils alongside the hedge and a hearty display from the forsythia in the corner. She had dragged the kitchen table out on to the narrow back patio for Saturday lunch in the thin sunshine; from her seat she could see Harry jinking across the lawn, springing twistily into the air, unaware that his freedom was about to be curtailed.

Across the table, Keith took an appreciative swig of Chianti. 'Thanks for doing pasta,' he said. 'I love it.'

'You're welcome. I'm grateful to you for taking Harry off my hands and offering to check the flat. While I *hope* to be back once a fortnight, that might prove difficult.'

'It's a long way,' he mused. 'Must be over three hundred miles. You'll only have Saturdays clear if you travel up late on Fridays... Don't worry. See how it goes. If I come across any mail that's slipped the net, I'll forward it. I expect you'll be busy finding your feet for the first few weeks anyway. How soon does Kevin expect his first article?'

'Too soon. In his parlance, "a blank page is no bloody good". I explained the situation to Caireen, and assured her it wouldn't affect my work for her. She understands that was the price for my release. I have a strong impression that they needed someone in a hurry, so that Mistral can get the book out in time for Christmas sales this year, and an American version can be available to coincide with her west coast tour there next spring. Brett isn't best pleased, I can tell.'

She watched as Flash Harry lolloped to the table and began to nuzzle Keith's ankle. 'Kevin gave me an extra brief,' she went on. 'The "secret agenda", he called it. In his eyes, all mediums are frauds. He wants me to find hard evidence against Caireen so that he can print an exposé. She's still a big name among the *cognoscenti* – it would be quite a scoop.'

'Will you do it?'

'Talk about biting the hand that feeds! Certainly not. I'll send him reports on extra-large foxes wandering the Cornish moorland, or covens on the Lizard, or whatever, but as for the rest, I shall prevaricate... Don't let Harry ruin your sock.'

Keith bent down and gently disengaged the rabbit, who had begun to nibble in earnest. He guided him back towards the lawn, and slowly chewed his own last mouthful of the side salad. 'Ro...' he said at length, 'have you told Caireen who you are?'

The clear bird-song suddenly receded and the splashes of garden yellow shrank to bright pinpoints. Rowena sat very still. 'No,' she said. 'I was going to, at first. That night, at the Wimbledon

Theatre... that was the whole point. But when I met her family, I changed my mind. I felt it might not be wise.' She raised her eyes to his, and saw concern. 'You know why, don't you?'

He nodded.

'Ellie stayed with those people in Cornwall,' she went on. 'When you brush aside all the speculation and preconceived ideas, one fact remains: their home is the last place she is known to have been alive.'

4

By nine o'clock the next morning Rowena had loaded up the Clio and negotiated her way westwards out of London to the M25. This orbital motorway, dubbed by many 'the world's largest car-park', was mercifully free from heavy traffic early on a Sunday.

Initially she had planned to take the M4 as far as Bristol, then swing down the peninsula on the M5, but the dawning of another crisp, bright day had encouraged a change of mind. The M3/A303 route through lower Wiltshire and Somerset was much more scenic, and Rowena was keen to imbibe the atmosphere of the changing landscapes. She felt an increasing sense of freedom as London slipped ever further behind, and later a burst of vindication when the megalithic circle of Stonehenge came suddenly into view as she powered down one of Wiltshire's hills. It seemed to represent a gateway to the West Country, the transition to an older land of mystery and legend.

She stopped in a lay-by for coffee and sandwiches, then resumed her journey, impatient now to see Uplands, Graw Head, at first hand, but knowing it lay at least three hours ahead. People had warned her not to underestimate the length of England's south-west peninsula; there was Dartmoor to skirt, followed by Bodmin Moor, and her final rocky destination was on the far side of Helston.

Annoyingly, the traffic had now begun to bunch and slow. She had passed Yeovil, but not yet reached Exeter, and the road at this point was single carriageway in each direction. Rowena willed herself not to become irritated; slipping a cassette of Brahms music into the dashboard slot, she gently tapped the wheel in time with the rhythm. Five minutes passed, then the line of vehicles slowly began to move again, but it was a false cue – almost immediately they ground to another halt.

Rowena took a swig of bottled water, unwrapped and began to chew a mint, and rotated each ankle in turn to ward off calf stiffness. Idly she scanned the local scenery: flattish fields here, a cottage, a few tall trees... In the distance she could see some kind of encampment – gypsies, perhaps, or New Age travellers; it was too random and unkempt to be a commercial site. With a twisting ache of poignancy she thought of Ellie, attracted to the romance of open skies, clean air and a specious sense of autonomy. How soon had the romance turned to squalor after a rainstorm – to cold and filth and insecurity? Had she really chosen this life twice over, or had something happened to force her hand – a drugs habit, blackmail? Rowena had never expected to find herself praying that even that might be the reason for Ellie's silence...

With a burst of choking blue-grey exhaust, the 'eco-friendly' diesel car ahead of her lurched forwards, and the slow winding pilgrimage was resumed. When she eventually reached Exeter, she called in at a service station to freshen up and refuel the Clio for the last stretch of her journey. Setting off again, she passed the edge of Dartmoor and made good time to Plymouth. Here the broad river Tamar marked the boundary between Devon and Cornwall; Rowena suddenly found herself queuing to cross the tall suspension bridge spanning the water. There was little opportunity to admire the parallel railway bridge, or peer out at the toy-like boats over a hundred feet below: within minutes she was climbing through Saltash on the Cornish side and heading for Liskeard.

The high afternoon sun glared straight in through the windscreen as she drove on westwards. Each pinpoint of dirt, each sadly splattered insect, seemed to magnify the reflection, and Rowena squinted as she tried to concentrate on the road ahead. Mentally she ticked off the names of the key route towns she passed... Bodmin... Redruth... Brett Saunders had recommended that she stay on the fast A30 for the last stretch and double back eastwards from Penzance. Graw Head was a coastal promontory on the southern, 'instep' part of Cornwall's 'foot' as it kicked out into the Atlantic. The headland was situated roughly between Penzance and Helston, on the steepest, most isolated part of that coastline.

Daniel had sketched for her a rudimentary map showing the route between Anwith, the nearest village, and Uplands. *Narrow lanes,* he had emphasized with much underlining. As she purred along the final section of main road, Rowena began to prepare herself for the challenge of meeting his family again and living among them. The low sun was now behind her – blessed relief! – and she could search without handicap for the village sign.

Anwith was modest: a few granite houses, a pub, a small post office with white-washed walls. A square grey building might have been the church. She swung off the road on to a narrow track bordered by high hedgerows; bumping and jolting, she followed its curves as it wound down into a shallow saucer-shaped valley. She saw a field of cabbages, a scatter of outbuildings, a farmhouse.

Reaching a fork in the lane, she found that one road led past three terraced cottages to the farmhouse; a young woman with blowzy dark hair was just entering the middle cottage door. Rowena quickly consulted Daniel's map and turned the opposite way. After five minutes of steady climbing, the Clio suddenly crested the rise. Rowena gasped: spread out before her was a patchwork of green, ochre and blue as fields gave way to furzy scrubland, then sea, then sky. She could see the headland, an exposed-looking promontory with a single dwelling perched near the tip, crudely man-made among so much natural beauty.

Soon she reached the entrance gateway, a wide portal flanked by weathered stone pillars, each surmounted by a ten-inch stone sphere. There were no actual gates. A large notice on the boundary wall shouted 'PRIVATE PROPERTY' in scarlet letters; beneath, the words 'NT path' had been added in green, with an arrow pointing to the right.

Rowena slowed the Clio right down as she drove towards the house. Kevin was going to be very disappointed, she thought – here was no *Coo-ee*-style garden, just grass slopes, bare patches of granite and a few stunted, windswept bushes. Apart from the house itself, a 1930s construction, only a roughly paved car-parking area obliquely in front of the building evinced any kind of human effort. There was a Mercedes already *in situ*, and a Volkswagen Golf; she parked next to the smaller car.

As she climbed out of the Clio, shrugging the strap of her bag over her shoulder, Rowena could smell the clean, salty air. Even on this leeward side of the house eddies of wind plucked at her hair, and she could hear the sea's restless seething far below, out of sight over the edge of the promontory. Fighting an urge to stand there breathing deeply, she marched straight-backed to the front door, which opened before she rang the bell.

'Rowena! Come in. Did you have a good journey?'

It was Caireen herself. She ushered Rowena into a spacious entrance hall beautifully decorated in antique pink. 'I'll show you to your room. You'll want to freshen up before we tour the house. Mrs Trelowan has stayed on to meet you; she'll make us some tea.'

Brett Saunders silently materialized from one of the hall's many doorways and nodded to Rowena. 'I'll bring your case,' he said, holding out his hand for her car keys.

Rowena followed Caireen up a wide, curved staircase, her feet sinking into thick carpet. The landing was galleried; opposite the banisters a large south-facing picture window showed a stunning view of open sea.

Caireen smiled at Rowena's obvious delight. 'Most people find this house unprepossessing from the outside,' she said. 'I did myself. But once I had entered, I just had to buy it. I've been coming here for nine years now.' She slid the plush pink curtain further aside and pointed out far left through the glass. 'You see that land mass on the horizon? That's the Lizard peninsula. Round to the right, out of sight from here, is the Penwith peninsula, and the water between them is Mount's Bay.'

'St Michael's Mount?' Rowena knew about the famous causeway-linked island near Penzance, and would have digressed to visit it in other circumstances.

'That's right. There was a priory on the outcrop for several centuries before the present castle. You've been there? No? Then we must arrange a visit. Now... this is your room.' Caireen led the way into a modest bedchamber decorated in primrose and pale blue, with fresh floral-patterned curtains, cushions and bedspread. There was a white-painted wardrobe, chest-of-drawers and dressing-table, but no desk that Rowena could see. 'I've allocated a small study for you downstairs,' continued her employer.

Brett came in as Rowena was craning towards the window and deposited her suitcase by the bed. 'Your bathroom's next door,' he told her. 'Come down when you're ready and we'll show you the rest.'

When they had gone, she studied the view. Her window looked out along the irregular axis of the cliff edge; it rose, fell and meandered before climbing again to form the next headland's grassy horizon. Along the raw seaward side rocks spilled sideways at the base in a tumble of solid slabs, and she could see the lazy creaming swell of the surf as it surged and ebbed in this dark playground.

It felt odd to hear no murmuring sound through the double glazing.

Aware of the need to be prompt, Rowena detached herself from the window and made a quick survey of her surroundings. The bathroom was not *en suite* – its door linked only with the main passageway – but it was for her use alone. The porcelain units were an inoffensive pale turquoise. Just like the ground floor, there were several other doors opening from the corridor, the whole house being, in the parlance of estate agents, 'deceptively spacious'. (Deceptively poky didn't appear quite so often in their literature.)

Downstairs again, Rowena was drawn to the sound of voices coming from a room with its door ajar. Softly she knocked, then pushed the door open wider at Caireen's bidding. The room beyond was long and golden, flooded with westerly light which poured in through three broad windows, each stretching from floor to ceiling. Stepping inside, she realized that the central 'window' was in fact a sliding patio door, though it was closed at present. A coal fire flickered in the grate beneath an imposing marble mantel the colour of ivory. Brett and his mother sat in comfortable cream brocade armchairs on opposite sides of the grate; he had been reading the Sunday papers, and a supplement lay sprawled across his lap.

'Sit down, Rowena.' Caireen indicated a third chair, adjacent to a low tiled table. 'You're just in time for some tea.'

Rowena too could hear the rattling of crockery, and a moment later a tall, grey-haired woman of sixty or so entered the room and placed a laden tray on the table.

'Thank you for staying on, Mrs Trelowan. This is Rowena Kemp, who has come to help me with the book.'

They nodded acknowledgement to each other. 'I've put the salad in the dining-room, as usual,' said the woman to Caireen.

'Thank you. We'll manage now. You go home, Mrs Trelowan.'

When the door had closed Caireen explained, 'Mrs Trelowan is our cook-housekeeper. Her home is one of those farm cottages on this side of Anwith – you saw them? I can never persuade her to live in while we are in residence, so you'll see her riding to and fro on her bicycle. Usually she cooks breakfast and dinner, and leaves us a cold lunch, but on Sundays we have a traditional roast lunch, so her hours are reversed. She stayed on today to see you – I think these crumpets must be in your honour. She knows you had a long journey.'

Brett, after an almost inaudible huff which might have been annoyance, was pouring the tea. There were four cups.

'Where *is* Danny?' Caireen asked him.

'He went for one of his walks. That was hours ago. You know how he forgets.' His dark eyes slid towards Rowena with a sardonic glint. 'He was looking forward to showing you around. You're his protégée.'

'Ah, but you were in charge of the *serious* vetting,' she answered lightly, accepting a cup from him.

'Time will tell, as far as you're concerned. We're hoping you'll take the job more seriously than the last girl.'

As Rowena hesitated, feeling it might be premature to press for more details, a shadow fell across the window. Even as she glanced towards it, the silhouette had gone, but she sensed that it had been a human shape, peering in – Daniel.

Caireen was offering her a crumpet. Rowena accepted one, and bit gratefully into its soft, buttery texture – she was hungry now. She found herself nurturing the ignoble hope that the 'salad in the dining-room' was for early and communal consumption.

Behind them in the house, a door banged. Daniel hurried into the drawing-room, his skin rosily flushed, the pale coppery curls dishevelled. 'Sorry I'm late, Mother,' he gasped. 'I went along the cliff to the ruined mines and lost track of the time.' He turned to Rowena. 'I meant to be here when you arrived. I'm so glad you've come. Have they shown you everything?'

'No, Danny,' answered Caireen. 'We waited. Have your tea while it's hot, then we'll all go round together.'

He took a few gulps, but remained standing, shifting his weight impatiently from foot to foot. 'I'm ready,' he announced. 'Let's go outside first.' He seized Rowena's sleeve and pulled her towards the french door. As cool air rushed into the room she noted the wry, resigned expression on Brett's face. He remained seated as they stepped out on to the side terrace.

'This is the patio. If it isn't too breezy in the evenings we sometimes sit out here…' Enthusiastically Daniel led the way in a circumnavigation of the house. As Rowena had already observed, the gardens were sparse, and the building's southern façade rose only a handful of yards from the cliff edge, but the headland was granite and the house looked solidly built – neither was likely to collapse into the sea as far as she could determine.

Once inside again, she was shown the well-equipped kitchen, the pantry, the utility passage. A brief visit to the dining-room revealed a substantial chicken salad laid out on the long table – good! They continued anticlockwise past the drawing-room, where Brett was still relaxing, to a series of closed doors.

'This is Brett's study. He's got *the view*, lucky thing!'

'Brett has business interests of his own,' added Caireen. 'Although he's standing in as secretary just now, he'll be going up to London periodically, and Danny will help us.' She opened the next door herself. This was a large, well-equipped study in beige and pale yellow. The window here also had 'the view': the tussocky, curling edge of the cliff, the sea below, now a deepening blue as the evening advanced, the distant, lilac-streaked sky.

For a moment, Caireen paused, her gaze distant. 'Looking at the sea,' she murmured, 'I always feel that we are in the benign hands of something greater than ourselves. Call it Nature, call it God...' She shrugged, and turned briskly to the next room which contained only armchairs and a small table. 'My clients wait in here if they're early, or if I'm meditating to focus my mind on the forthcoming session. I like them to focus, too, so there are no books or papers to distract them.'

The view on this eastern side was obscured by an outbuilding and part of a wall. Just a glimpse of the next headland could be seen in one corner. They moved to the adjacent room; here the outside world was blotted out completely by long, deep purple curtains. The whole room had an intimate, womb-like feel, and Rowena found it wholly superfluous to be told that this was where the actual consultations took place.

Daniel had been quiet for five minutes; now he eagerly took charge again. 'That's just a washroom,' he said with a dismissive gesture towards the door nearest the main entrance, 'but *this* is the study you'll be using.'

Rowena had already worked out the orientation of the window and was prepared for the view to be uninspiring. In fact, there were two windows. The light from one was partially obscured by the same side wall she had seen from the clients' waiting-room, while the other faced north across the car-parking area. The internal decorations were predominantly dark greens and browns. Ah well, she thought; distractions aren't likely to be a problem.

There was a telephone on the desk as well as a computer. 'When we have a secretary she works from this room,' said Caireen, 'but we're seriously thinking of waiting to engage another until the book's finished. I've scaled down my commitments accordingly, and Brett will handle the rest from his own study.'

'Everything's very nice,' said Rowena. 'I think you have a wonderful house here.'

Daniel beamed, and his mother nodded graciously. They returned to Brett, then to Rowena's gratification all four proceeded to share the chicken salad.

'I'm sure you'd like to unpack and have an early night,' said Caireen after the meal. 'There's plenty of hot water if you want a bath. We'll talk about your duties in the morning.'

Rowena acquiesced thankfully and headed for the stairs. After a twenty-minute soak in 'Woodland Lily' essence she padded to the door to see if it was safe to emerge into the corridor.

Daniel was just passing, a thin paper under his arm. He turned as she began to retreat. 'Goodnight, Rowena.'

'Goodnight, Daniel.'

He disappeared into a distant room and Rowena scuttled into her own.

She was thoughtful as she towelled her hair. Daniel's paper had been festooned with highly coloured illustrations; among them she had recognized the figures of Tintin and Snowy.

Her brow creased into a tiny frown. On current evidence, it seemed that Daniel's choice of bedtime reading encompassed the cartoon section of the *Sunday Times*.

Rowena slept well, and was down at the dining-room by seven forty the next morning. The table was laid for breakfast; Caireen stood by the sideboard, helping herself from a small selection of fruit and cereals.

'Mrs Trelowan will cook anything you want – bacon, eggs, kippers,' said Caireen. 'She brings in toast automatically as soon as we appear.'

Rowena chose a half grapefruit. 'This'll be fine, thanks.'

They sat together, and she learned that Brett was already 'out on business' and Daniel would come 'when he is ready'.

Caireen took a sip of tea. 'Our usual schedule,' she went on briskly, 'will be work together each morning in my study, from eight thirty until lunch time. In the afternoons you can transcribe the information into a readable form. I may have sittings, but if I'm available and you want to check anything, you can of course do so. Weekends will be free.' She smiled. 'I know you'll wish to spend some of them in London, but you are welcome to stay here for the others. Just inform Mrs Trelowan in reasonable time.'

Rowena nodded; she knew she would need some of these weekends to amass suitable material for Kevin. Her evenings would be occupied with writing up features for the *North London News*.

Caireen was still speaking. 'Today and tomorrow,' she said, 'I thought it would be more fruitful if you read through the papers your predecessor compiled last summer. I have some local engagements.'

After breakfast she handed over the file, a thick sheaf of typed notes. 'This was ten weeks' work,' she said. 'You'll find it's only half the story. I'm afraid the girl was too flighty for the job. At the time, I was annoyed, but now I think perhaps it was for the best, because a collaborative writer was what I really needed.'

When Caireen had left, Rowena settled down on the swivel chair for some steady reading. The study's dark, earthy colours looked less of a hibernaculum this morning, she felt – sunlight streamed over the eastern garden wall and in through her side window, a few dust motes pirouetting in the beam.

Musingly she stroked the typescript. Ellie had handled this. Here were *her* spelling mistakes (she had always accused computer spell-checkers of curtailing her freedom), *her* page layouts... Rowena paused, her head cocked towards the ceiling. Ellie, where are you now? she wondered. Are you watching me? Do you know I'm here?

By eleven o'clock her limbs were stiff. The text, a verbatim account of Caireen's recollections, was necessarily both rambling and disjointed, but already a fascinating story was gleaming through.

Caireen, she now knew, had been born in County Kerry in 1944. Her father had worked as a draper, and her mother Mary had assisted in his shop. Mary was known locally for her psychic powers. As a schoolgirl, she used to hold objects supplied by classmates, describe the character of each owner and predict their future circumstances. Details of husbands-to-be were greatly in demand. Sometimes she whispered contemporary secrets to the stunned owners of the watches and pens – health problems, ambitions, 'crushes' – and always she was right. Her accuracy was just as sound if the objects were submitted by proxy.

Mary married during the Second World War. Her elder sister Frances was already the wife of an Ulster Protestant and was living in County Tyrone.

One night, Mary woke up with a jolt to find her brother-in-law Kieran watching her from across the bedroom. He was dressed in his army uniform and his left temple was obliterated by a ghastly wound. 'Tell Frances I'm sorry,' he said, then disappeared. Nine days later his death during active service was confirmed; he had been shot in the head on the same date Mary saw him at her home in Kerry.

Two months later, while Frances was visiting Kerry, Kieran appeared to Mary again. This time, he instructed her to hold a seance. Mary was confused; she had never done such a thing before. While she had accepted her powers of psychometry, this was new ground, and even seemed slightly ungodly. Frances begged her to try, however, so one evening the two sisters sat down at the parlour table with Mary's husband, held hands and waited for something to happen.

'It was the concentration of three minds that did it,' Mary was to tell her daughter later – 'it' being the reappearance of Kieran, floating close to Frances's shoulder and visible only to Mary. Mary passed on his messages, obscure advice about legal documents which meant nothing to her but plenty to Frances. The letters of the alphabet her own husband had prepared in case of failure remained unused, along with the glass, on the sideboard.

Neighbours soon got to hear of the remarkable seance, and humbly asked if she would hold further sessions for them. Good-hearted Mary was unable to refuse; though still reticent about her abilities, she was willing to try, and over the following years became an ever-stronger conduit between the deceased of County Kerry and their loved ones. She never charged a penny for her time and effort, and made do her whole life with very modest means...

Rowena laid down the typescript and wondered whether someone would let her make a hot drink. Outside in the hall, a tantalizing aroma of percolating coffee enticed her to the dining-room, where a glass jug stood on a heating element with cups and saucers alongside. Presumably we help ourselves, she thought. Through the hatchway to the kitchen she could hear Mrs Trelowan on the domestic telephone, ordering a delivery of vegetables. Overhead came the faint rumble of a vacuum cleaner.

She returned to the study without meeting anyone, and settled once more to the task.

In 1949, she read, Frances died in Northern Ireland of breast cancer. The child Caireen, wandering around her Kerry home in a dressing-gown that same evening, emerged from the kitchen saying, 'Auntie wants to talk to you, Mam.' It was the first intimation that she had inherited Mary's psychic awareness.

As a schoolgirl, Caireen attempted some psychometric predictions, encouraged by friends who knew her mother's reputation, but felt no confidence in this area. ('I had to make up a lot of the stories,' she had admitted to Ellie, who had dutifully made note of this.) Despite her small clutch of CSEs, Caireen found job prospects locally to be poor, so she left for Dublin at the age of seventeen. She took work as a waitress in a large hotel, and wondered what on earth she was going to do with the rest of her life.

A decision of sorts arrived unexpectedly in the shape of a New York businessman called Lonsdale Saunders. A youngest son and something of a maverick, he took a shine to her when she served him his *canard à l'orange* and stayed on to date her. On her eighteenth birthday they were married. His family were horrified, and so were hers.

The Saunders moved to England, and two years later Brett was born. Lonsdale failed to carve the business niche he had craved in the capital, and died suddenly of a heart attack when Brett was three. Left with only debts, Caireen returned to waitressing, and bar work in clubs. Brett was looked after by friends or, more often, concealed about her places of employment. He learned to be a quiet, obedient child.

It was while Caireen was pouring drinks in the Flamingo, a jazz club, that she met the love of her life. Daniel Malone had a wistful face, tousled copper hair and half-inch eyelashes. He played jazz fiddle with a group from Dublin who were touring London. After two foot-tapping numbers the other band members fell back and left him alone, a small slender figure, at the front of the low stage.

Caireen abandoned the bottles and stood enrapt as a sweet, haunting melody filled the smoky den. Its cadences were unmistakably Irish, and unlocked a piercing nostalgia for her mother country. At the end, there was silence, then – a crescendo of applause.

Later she was to learn that the piece had been his own composition. *That* was the sort of music he really wanted to play, but his membership of the jazz group paid the rent.

They married and moved back to Ireland, together with Brett, settling in Cork. Daniel joined another group and supplemented his meagre income with music teaching, but life remained a financial struggle, especially when baby Danny was born. Hardship notwithstanding, Daniel the elder was bursting with pride. 'The little feller!' he would cry, bouncing the baby in the air. (Did Brett watch solemnly from across the room, wondered Rowena, or was he 'bounced in the air' as well?)

An old school friend of Caireen's came to visit, and told Daniel about the psychometric sessions at school. 'She said I'd marry a bricklayer called Liam, and I did!' the woman told him excitedly. 'She promised me four fine sons, and I've got five! Sure, an' it's a wonderful gift!'

'You should develop this gift,' said Daniel seriously to Caireen when the friend had gone. He had known about Mary's talents, but Caireen had concealed her own patchy abilities.

'I'm not as good as my mother,' she demurred, but he insisted.

'You only need to unblock the psychic channels,' he said. 'You've been chosen to do good for other people. It's both a gift and a responsibility. It mustn't be wasted.'

So Caireen began to cycle miles to attend a Spiritualist church. She watched mediums at work, spoke with them, and was eventually put in touch with a development circle. Soon her powers had sharpened and she felt able to hold sessions herself.

'We mustn't profit from this,' said Daniel earnestly when her first private clients began to arrive. Obediently she asked for no fee, but the clients determinedly paid in kind: chickens, eggs, bottles of whiskey – even a bag of peat! Her reputation grew and grew . . .

Rowena laid aside the manuscript and stretched. She was tempted to read more, but already it was one thirty and her stomach demanded food. She returned to the dining-room, but once again the room was deserted and there was no sign of anything to eat.

Blast, she thought, and decided to raid the kitchen. The nearest shop was clearly miles away, and by the time she reached the pub it would be closed.

As she approached the kitchen, its door obligingly opened.

'Oh!' Mrs Trelowan, one hand buttoning her coat, was equally surprised. 'I didn't know you were here, Miss Kemp. I thought you'd gone out with Mrs Malone and Mr Daniel.'

'No. I've been in the study, keeping quiet. I just wondered if I could have a piece of toast, or something.'

'Of course. Let me get it – no, I insist. I would have left some lunch out if I'd realized. Would you like soup?'

'Only if you'll have some as well.'

Within ten minutes they were sitting at opposite sides of the large scrubbed pine kitchen table, enjoying carrot soup with hunks of fresh white bread and talking freely of their lives and experiences. Rowena's initial impression of Mrs Trelowan as being a taciturn individual was proving to be totally unfounded.

'You live near the farm, I gather,' she prompted after describing her own life in Amersham, in London and as a journalist.

'Yes. I have a cottage on Mr Polzeath's land. My husband used to work on the farm, but he died of a stroke five years ago. Mr Polzeath has been very kind to me. He lets me stay for very little rent.'

'I'm sorry about your husband. Things must have been hard. Do you have any children?'

The housekeeper shook her head. 'We weren't blessed.'

'Mm.' Rowena hastily took another spoonful of soup. 'I saw a dark-haired girl at the cottages as I drove past yesterday. Rather gypsy-like. Is she your neighbour?'

'Unfortunately.' Mrs Trelowan's mouth contracted into a grim line. 'If it's Ginette you mean. Her "common-law" husband worked as a labourer for Mr Polzeath, but he left her two years ago and went up country. He couldn't stand her playing around, you see. She was always down at the Young Farmers' Association, and staying out late... Anyway, he went, and she's lived off the Social ever since.'

'There must be seasonal work down here,' mused Rowena. 'All these hotels and restaurants... perhaps Mrs Malone could offer her something at Uplands?'

'She did do. A cleaning job, last year. Ginette made no effort at all, and was sacked within a fortnight.'

'Oh, dear. Mrs Malone doesn't seem to be very lucky with her staff. She said the girl who was transcribing her autobiography left suddenly.'

'That was Ellie. I liked her; we got on well.'

'Why did she go?'

Mrs Trelowan stared into the middle distance. 'I wish I knew. I was surprised... not so much at her going, but the fact that she didn't tell me. I thought we were friends. I suppose... I suppose she was ashamed.'

'Do you think she was dismissed as well?'

'No. It seems she got into bad company.'

Rowena decided to push for more information another time. 'Ah,' she said lightly. 'I must make sure I don't disappoint Mrs Malone.' She checked her watch. 'I'd better get back to work. Thanks for the lunch, Mrs Trelowan. I hope I haven't held you up too much.'

'It's been a pleasure talking. No – leave those dishes. You've plenty to do.'

Back in the study, Rowena settled once more to Caireen's life story: the burgeoning local fame, the tragic discovery that Daniel senior had developed a malignant lymphoma, a cancer of the lymph glands. He was ill for four years before he died leaving Caireen a near-penniless widow of thirty-five.

Dimly Rowena registered the sound of Caireen's car returning, but she remained engrossed in the recollections of a life which made her own seem hopelessly privileged. At length, she laid down the script and flicked back through the pages. Which had been the seminal moment when Caireen first displayed unusual powers? Her vision of the aunt who had just died in Ulster... Clearly, though, Caireen herself had not appreciated the significance at that stage. She was only five.

'I knelt by the range, stroking the cat,' she had dictated. 'Suddenly he went stiff, and his fur stood on end. I looked up, but it was only Auntie Frances. She was wearing a nightdress, like me, and her hair was down. It wasn't very tidy. I remember thinking I hadn't heard her knock...'

A quiet tapping sounded at Rowena's door.

'Sorry to disturb you.' Daniel peered around the doorway in answer to her summons. 'I wondered if you'd like a walk with me while there's still some sunshine.'

'I...' She glanced at her watch – four o'clock. 'I haven't really done a full day's work yet. Perhaps some other time?'

'Mother said I could ask you. Please come.'

'In that case, I'd be delighted.'

Warned that they would be crossing the cliff-tops, Rowena donned trousers and stout shoes, and soon they were striding eastwards above the seething water and dark tumbles of rock.

'I love it here,' said Daniel. 'I can't wait to leave London and come to Cornwall. The Celts lived here, you know. It's a different...' He made a flapping gesture of frustration.

'... atmosphere,' supplied Rowena. 'I agree. It feels more spiritual, doesn't it?'

He nodded, happy with her understanding, and they continued without further conversation until Uplands was out of sight. There was only one more person on the path, a young man with a rucksack who tramped nearer and nearer, finally passing them with a murmured greeting.

'The Cornwall coast path goes all the way around the peninsula,' explained Daniel. 'In summer we get lots of hikers. They stay in the youth hostels. Mother gets cross when they cut across our headland, because it's supposed to be private.'

Rowena remembered the notice by the gatepost. 'Is she bothered by admirers? Celebrity spotters?'

'Sometimes. One man had a camera with an enormous lens. Brett knows how to sort them out, though.'

She could well imagine.

Eventually they reached two ruined tin mine engine houses set in the shoulder of the hill. They had already passed one, restored by the National Trust as a monument, but these had a wilder, more isolated setting.

Daniel flopped down in the grass, his back against the decaying granite wall, and patted the ground beside him. 'The main tinners' coast was west of here,' he told her as she sat alongside. 'Between Cape Cornwall and Pendeen. They dug out under the Atlantic... But of course there were inland mines as well, like Ding Dong. You come across the shells of the engine houses up on the moors, rising out of the heather and bracken...'

Rowena tilted her face up to the thin sunshine. 'Do you usually come here alone?' she asked him.

There was a silence, and she flicked her eyes open in time to catch his fleeting expression of bewildered pain. 'I used to bring Ellie,' he said slowly. 'You know – the girl you reminded me of when we first met. She loved it up on these cliffs. She'd wear blue skirts and dresses that billowed in the wind. We'd have picnics and share secrets...'

'Secrets, Daniel?'

He reached out for her hand and gripped it hard. 'Call me Danny. Ellie always did. Special people are allowed to.'

'Thank you... Danny. I hope we'll be able to share secrets, too.'

He looked at her unblinkingly, a twenty-five-year-old man with the appraising stare of a child, then gave a shy smile. His features were perfect, if slightly feminine; weak sunshine kindled flecks of gold in his pale blue eyes. Unaccountably, Rowena felt a faint swill of disquiet.

'Will you tell me one now?' he whispered.

'Yes.' She swallowed, recovering quickly. 'Sometimes I don't like being a journalist, poking and prying into people's private affairs. I'd rather be a novelist, except it's very difficult to make a living that way. I did write a novel once, about a London family at the time of the Great Plague, but I couldn't find a publisher who was interested. I hope you won't tell your mother – she'd probably sack me! What about you, Danny? What are your secret vices?'

'You mustn't tell Mother, either. Promise? Well...I've got some psychic awareness, too. She doesn't like that; she says for me it's more of a curse than a blessing. She thinks I've given up trying to develop my powers, but she's wrong. I've been learning about auras. A lady called Lavinia in Glastonbury teaches me, but I can't go there very often. It's a long way from here. Somerset.'

'Do you see colours surrounding people?' asked Rowena.

'Just hazily, when I'm not really looking. If I look too hard, they go away.'

'Aren't colours supposed to have different meanings?' she hazarded vaguely.

'Oh, yes. Not just in the auras. We're affected by the colours all around us. You can change the way you feel by "colour breathing". You absorb the electromagnetic vibrations of the colour. For instance, if you can't sleep, concentrate on something dark blue. If you need to wake up, try orange. And for brain-power, look at yellow. That's the colour of the intellect.'

'That could be useful. Thanks, Danny.' She remembered Ellie's mentioning auras in one of her letters, along with Tarot cards and runes. 'Did you tell Ellie about this, as well?'

'Yes. She was really interested. She went to Glastonbury with me once.' Abruptly his face darkened. 'We were friends. She had no right to go off and see *him*. Not behind my back.' He scrambled to his feet and kicked at the unyielding granite pile. '*No right!*'

Stunned, Rowena gaped at him. As she rose to her own feet a hearty laugh sounded from the pathway.

'I don't think you'll manage to push it into the sea *that* way, Danny,' smiled a plumpish woman of sixty in a bright print dress. 'You might damage your foot, though!'

Daniel flushed. 'Miss Granger,' he mumbled.

'I was just taking a walk in this lovely air,' she told them. 'I can't resist, now that spring has actually arrived.' She turned to Rowena. 'I'm Madeleine Granger. I live in a valley just beyond Porthleven.' She pointed east over the headland. 'My brother and I are old friends of Caireen's.'

'He's a colonel,' said Daniel.

'Retired.' Madeleine Granger looked expectantly at Daniel; eventually he grasped the cause of her hesitation.

'Oh. This is Rowena Kemp. She's staying with us and writing Mother's biography. She works for a newspaper in London as well.'

'Sounds like a busy life. I feel quite ashamed of my freedoms. You must come and visit us with Caireen. Come for dinner. I'll give her a ring and fix an evening.'

'I'd like that. Thank you.'

They parted after a few more minutes' polite discourse, and Rowena felt reluctant to raise the subject of Ellie again with Daniel so soon. She was frustrated by the interruption. Presumably he had been referring to the hippie Patrick Sullivan, but she would have preferred to have clarified this. As it was, they took the path back to Uplands indian-file, which limited further conversation to occasional sea-bird observations.

Daniel seemed to have made a full recovery from his fit of rage by the time they arrived back at the property. 'You'll come again, won't you?' he urged Rowena. 'I've got much more to tell you about colours.'

'Of course,' she said, slightly distracted by a dark figure behind one of the windows.

He beamed as they entered the house, and almost skipped away to wash before dinner.

Rowena was sure the watcher had been Brett. He stared at her with a kind of sardonic amusement throughout much of the evening, and she found it difficult to maintain a balanced response. Ignoring him would, she knew, constitute as much of a statement as an aggressive challenge.

After the meal, Caireen took leave to return to her study, and Rowena thankfully followed her lead. In her own office she jotted down key points from the undisciplined stack of memoirs and began to work out suitable chapter divisions. At ten thirty, tired out by her ramble in the fresh sea air, she prepared for bed.

'Miss Kemp.'

She managed to avoid a gasp of surprise as Brett materialized in the hall behind her. 'Yes?'

'There's something I think perhaps you should know. Can you spare a minute for a private word?'

'Er, yes. My study?'

'A good choice.'

He sank loosely into the easy chair as she closed the door behind them. 'You seemed to have an enjoyable time with Danny this afternoon,' he said. 'Mother was glad – she likes him to be happy, and if someone's with him he tends not to wander so far.' His eyes regarded her with a kind of lazy shrewdness. 'I expect you noticed something – shall we say *unusual* – about Danny?'

'Well...'

'Of course you did. You're an intelligent woman. If you're embarrassed, I'll put it into words for you: Danny has a childlike quality which is quite appealing on first acquaintance, but later seems – unnatural, unbecoming in someone his age. Yes? It's clear you know what I'm talking about. There is a reason. You see, Danny is thirteen.'

'What?'

'Danny is thirteen and will always be thirteen. He had a viral encephalitis at that age, and everything just stopped. His mental development completely arrested at that point, although luckily most of his personality survived intact. Mother has always suffered from perfectly needless guilt on his behalf, and overcompensates by spoiling him.'

Perched on the high office chair, Rowena found that her first reaction was deep sadness for Danny, for the opportunities he would not now experience. Hopefully his sunny disposition would protect him against most of life's slings and arrows, but on the other hand...today she had witnessed an ugly outburst, triggered by a mere recollection. Brain diseases often did leave their victims emotionally labile, unable to cope with frustration of any kind. And what of poor Caireen – yet another tragedy.

This initial gut response was swiftly followed by surprise at Brett's frankness. A few seconds' further consideration, however, provided perspective. He had known she would quickly divine that all was not well with Daniel; there was nothing to be gained by withholding a sensible explanation.

'I'm sorry,' she said to Brett.

He rose to his feet with a long-limbed gracefulness. 'I just thought you ought to know.'

5

Rowena could find no mention of Danny's illness when she completed her reading of the typescript the next day. Presumably Caireen was protecting her son.

What she did find, however, was the close linkage of Brett with the commercialization of Caireen's talents. He was only fifteen when Daniel Malone died, but already it was clear that he possessed a hefty share of the genes for business acumen which were scattered throughout the Saunders family. He left school at the first opportunity and became his mother's manager...

Caireen must have had enough of poverty at that point. For years she had been giving away something for free that people wanted. If, as these papers suggested, the idea of building that something into a paying career had come from Brett, then she probably hadn't needed much persuasion.

Rowena's days began to settle into a pattern. At first she found the slight upstairs/downstairs dichotomy confusing. Like the governess in a Victorian household, she didn't quite fit into either niche. Over time, however, a tacit compromise was reached. If specifically invited to dine with the family, she would, but otherwise she was free to eat with Mrs Trelowan or make her own arrangements. That was a relief, because she needed flexibility in the evenings in order to fulfil her obligations to Kevin.

Caireen had graciously consented to a formal interview, which Rowena faxed to him in lieu of glossy details about the house. She needed examples of 'Cornish weirdness' quickly, however. Searching through newspaper archives would take too long; she decided to employ a short cut.

An old friend of Ed Tranter's called Mick Vean was now a journalist with *West Country News* in Truro, and Ed had offered to contact him on Rowena's behalf. Swallowing her preference for total independence, she accepted Ed's mediation, and late one evening found herself meeting Mick Vean in a Helston pub. Perhaps inevitably for a friend of Ed's he was a tall, flabby chain-smoker with overfamiliar hands. 'Sure, I can get you some stuff on the Beast of Bodmin,' he said agreeably, pressing his ham-like thigh hard against her own as they sat together on a bench. She tried to slide away, but was trapped by the wall on the other side.

'Thanks, Mick.'

'You'll have dinner with me later this week, won't you?'

Now his hand was snaking around her back, probing the ribs on the far side. She was suddenly reminded of the old schoolgirl couplet, 'Roman hands, Russian fingers', and gave an involuntary snort of laughter. Seamlessly she turned it into a cough, and endured a series of earth-shaking back-slaps before she was allowed to speak. 'Sorry about that. Yes – dinner would be nice, but you must let me pay since you're doing me a favour.'

'We'll see.'

'No deal otherwise.'

'Phoo...' He tried unsuccessfully to pout. 'Okay – business only. At least until you appreciate what a good deal I *can* give you.'

She gave a stiff smile, and managed to fend him off until closing time. When they met in an Italian restaurant two evenings later, she was surprised to find that he had been as good as his word: the packet of cuttings he handed over represented a comprehensive catalogue of feral creatures glimpsed on various horizons, unexpected encounters, savaged sheep. There was no copyright on facts; she could create a review article from this lot with minimal effort, or use it as a springboard for her own local interviews.

She thanked him again, and watched in wry amusement as he wolfed down his pasta, fists clenched around the cutlery, pausing only to slurp wine at intervals with a noise like a faulty cistern. His manner was such a contrast to Keith's careful fastidiousness with pasta.

She waited until Mick was glutted (though still miraculously able to manage a double helping of cassata) before introducing the subject of Ellie. 'Funnily enough, there seems to be a bit of a "Cornish mystery" where I'm working just at present,' she said, idly folding her napkin into small triangles.

'What, with the psychic woman?'

'No. The girl who was typing up her memoirs last year suddenly disappeared. At least, that's what I've been told. A young blonde girl called Ellen Drinkwater. I wondered if there was a story in that. Does it ring any bells with you?'

'I can't say it does... but I don't report crime. I can find out if you like. Have you any more gen?'

'Well... it's all hearsay, really. She was said to be friendly with a New Age type called Patrick Sullivan. He was doing temporary work on a nearby farm, owned by an Adrian Polzeath, before he suddenly absconded with some of Mr Polzeath's valuables. The girl Ellen vanished the following day.'

His look of interest ebbed. 'Seems straightforward enough. I thought you were angling for suspicious death. If the guy had disappeared the day after Ellen or even the same day, you might have been on to something. As it is, it sounds as if they've met up by prearrangement and scarpered together.'

'People at the house seem to think it was out of character for her. Would you check for me anyway? Thanks. There must be something I can do for you. Professionally, that is. I know – Caireen is approving a news release soon, to do with some forthcoming guest appearances at Cornish Spiritualist churches. I'll make sure your paper gets it first, plus enough background material for a full article.'

'You're on.'

Rowena drove back from Helston in the darkness, her mind assembling the scant facts she had given Mick in endless permutations. He was right, of course, about the timing of Ellie's disappearance. If it had coincided with Patrick's, or occurred earlier, people might indeed have considered Patrick as a possible murder suspect. Certainly they would have viewed the whole situation more seriously.

Why not flee together, though? Why would Patrick run all the risks of waiting for a day in the very area where police would be searching for him? Perhaps Ellie was caught by surprise. Did Patrick throw gentle handfuls of gravel at her window one night, explain when she came down how an opportunity had suddenly arisen that day and he had robbed his employer? Rowena could imagine the urgent whispers in the lee of Uplands, the cloud-wreathed moon, the slow susurration of the waves far below... 'Ellie, you've got a choice. Leave now with me or you'll never see me again.' She wasn't prepared; she needed more time. 'All right. I'll wait out at the old mine until midnight tomorrow, but then I go.' Perhaps he exhorted her not to arrive empty-handed: they would need more items to pawn or sell in order to get by. Caireen was a rich woman; she wouldn't miss a few baubles...

All pure conjecture, Rowena chided herself. And doubtless unnecessarily complicated. Maybe Ellie had known Patrick's intentions all along, and leaving separately was a naïve part of their plan, allowing Ellie to mislead the police, perhaps...

Rowena turned off the main road, passed through Anwith and cautiously negotiated the rutted lane past the farm. Lights burned in the farm building itself and in two of the cottages. *These* people know the facts, she thought to herself. Mrs Trelowan, Adrian Polzeath, the girl Ginette. They know – at least, a lot more than I do. Is it actually *true* that Ellie left the day after Patrick? Was she seen? Or did someone simply *say* so? Their relationship... is that a fact, or merely an assumption?

I'm wallowing in hearsay, she thought angrily, and I can't openly interrogate people without giving the game away. Only the police can do that...

She revved the Clio and entered the Uplands estate, passing the welcoming 'PRIVATE PROPERTY' sign. Parking next to Caireen's Golf (the Mercedes, she had discovered, belonged to Brett), Rowena reluctantly concluded that the police might well be her only hope of unbiased information. She needed to know if they spoke to Ellie after Patrick was reported missing. For if they didn't...

Perhaps the same hand had killed two people.

'You need to know if Patrick is alive. It's as simple as that.'

Rowena was glad that she could approach Keith for a neutral, dispassionate opinion. Apart from a brief call on her mobile phone to let him know she had arrived safely, and a faxed handwritten note to clarify her whereabouts for the second weekend, she had been too busy for telephone calls. Now she stood in Anwith's public phone box, one of the few remaining old-fashioned red ones, and felt cheered to hear his voice.

'The police weren't able to find him,' she said. 'So how can I?'

'How hard did they look? I bet they gave up after day one. You could hire a private detective.'

Alan Drinkwater had done that – but not for long. Rowena recalled the bitter resignation in Jonathan's voice. No. That second disappearance, coupled with theft, had put Ellie beyond the pale.

'They cost an arm and a leg, don't they?'

'You're earning two salaries,' he said mercilessly.

'True. Well, that's an idea, for sure. How are the gang? I met Ed's friend the other night.'

'Ed says he forgot to warn you that Mick is something of a ladies' man.'

'Does that describe Ed's estimate of his shimmering magnetism, or Mick's own? I'd believe the latter. Don't worry. I can handle bundles of quivering flesh. He was actually quite helpful. Tell Ed thanks.'

'Kevin liked your piece on feral beasties. For some reason he's linked it up with reports of wild boar on the loose in Kent and Sussex.'

'So relevant to the North London reader.'

'Come on, you know why he's doing it. He's deliberately encouraging the residents of the metropolis to feel that everyone outside the capital is vaguely eccentric, their lifestyles bizarre. It gives them no end of a superiority complex.'

'Pff! London has always patronized the rest of the country. Nothing new there... How's Harry, by the way?'

'Er... Harry?'

She felt a jolt of alarm. 'Yes. My rabbit.'

'*Ah*. He's very popular in the flat. Slightly overfed, perhaps... but his name's Gordon.'

'Gordon?'

'Definitely. You see, I told the chaps he was Flash before, when you and Sebastian had him, and without prompting they dubbed him Gordon. It suits his temperament. He's adventurous. He likes it.'

'Flash Gordon... We shall have words about this when I come up to London.'

'Will that be soon?' He sounded rather plaintive.

'Maybe in a couple of weeks' time. Caireen is doing a demonstration this weekend and I'm supposed to be on the lookout for moments of special poignancy or accuracy.'

'Stay as an onlooker, Ro. Remember to keep it third party.'

'I shall. Damn, I think my money's about to run out. Thanks for keeping an eye on everything for me, Keith. I'll keep you posted with events this end.'

'Ro. Remember, don't let her get inside your head –'

Abruptly the connection was lost and she replaced the receiver. Keith warned her endlessly about Caireen's probable powers of telepathy and use of practical psychology. He seemed afraid that she would succumb to the temptation of becoming a client herself. Nothing was further from her mind. Here, among these people, she wanted nobody to make the connection between Ellie and herself.

Brett had been her main source of anxiety on that score, but since her arrival at Uplands, neither word nor deed on his part had suggested that he knew. She still caught him watching her on occasions, his face thoughtful, but she was no longer afraid of him. In fact, she felt confident enough to grill him about Caireen.

'This book is your mother's autobiography,' she said to him the next morning when they met by chance in the hall. 'She doesn't want me chasing up long-lost relatives for their recollections – they might even conflict with her own. But you don't suppose she'd object if I ask for extra perspectives from you and Daniel?'

'Probably not. What do you want to know?'

'Your role interests me. You've made her into a rich woman. Materialistic things are now a way of life with her, but that wasn't always so. Was it difficult to persuade her to abandon the concept of vocation?'

'What a dumb question. You're suggesting the two things are mutually exclusive, a decent living versus a "vocation". Why should they be? Just listen to nurses squeal for their pay rises.'

She smiled. 'Voluntary work is a luxury for the rich?'

'That's one interpretation.' He paused as the door to Caireen's consulting-room opened and two elderly sisters shuffled out, thanking Caireen profusely. 'They just paid forty pounds. Do they look unhappy? Caireen exhausts herself providing a service.'

Smoothly he detached himself from her, nodded at the sisters and escorted them to the front door.

Caireen emerged from her own doorway, dressed in a deep purple gown. She wore heavy crystal ear-rings and a matching necklace; Rowena could see the stagey curtains in the room behind her.

'Coffee,' she murmured at Rowena, and disappeared into the dining-room as Brett returned.

'Do you think the clients expect evening clothes and a mysterious dark room, or do you think simplicity would be more effective?' she asked him, thinking of the uncomplicated sincerity radiated by Dorothy Lambrook.

'God, you're a lot more impertinent than the last girl!' he exclaimed. 'This is Caireen's way of doing things and purple, for your information, is a very spiritual colour. Just ask Danny.'

'Ask me what?' Daniel peered from the kitchen door, and Rowena had a fleeting impression that he had been listening.

'Colours. They're your forte, aren't they, Danny?'

'Shh. I'm not supposed to... you know that.'

Brett was clearly teasing him. 'I'm secure from all these "vocation" anxieties,' he said. 'I haven't a psychic bone in my body. But Danny here thinks he has. Maybe he's right – or maybe someone's conning him into believing he has special aptitudes.'

Daniel flushed, confused, and ran off down the hall. Rowena felt a shadowy stirring of recognition of Brett's attitude, a muddied picture from her own past. Nevertheless, she turned on him angrily. 'That wasn't very kind.'

'It's for his own good. If he tries to follow that path he'll be exploited by unscrupulous people.'

Like you exploit his mother? she wondered. Not quite; Caireen was far too strong a character to be manipulated by her eldest son.

'Will you look out for Danny when he's older?' she asked.

Brett shrugged. 'That won't be necessary. He and Caireen are welded together.'

But Caireen wouldn't live for ever... 'How would you summarize your role in this family?'

'Is that the intrusive journalist speaking?'

'I'm interested.'

He considered. The reply, when it came, was not quite what she had expected.

'I see myself as my mother's protector,' he said.

'I'm glad you're staying this weekend,' said Caireen on the Saturday as they prepared to leave for St Christopher's church. 'Madeleine Granger has invited us for lunch tomorrow, and she particularly asked for you. The colonel has had a cold, or they would have contacted us sooner.'

They climbed into the Mercedes, where Brett was already seated at the wheel; Daniel was staying behind to watch television. Rowena kept a respectful silence during the journey, knowing that Caireen was meditating.

The Spiritualist church was small and plain. Rowena melted into the congregation at the back while Caireen was welcomed by the officials. Two jolly hymns followed, then Caireen was introduced publicly, and invited to take the dais.

Her hour of clairvoyance began. She was toning down her performance, it seemed to Rowena, in order to harmonize with her surroundings. Nevertheless, her presence was commanding – all the more so, Rowena felt, because of the contrast with her soft voice and shortish stature. Certainly those around her were enrapt, a look almost of hero-worship in their eyes.

Five members of the congregation were given messages in turn; all identified the lost loved ones Caireen described, nodding fervently 'yes, yes,' and 'thank you, thank you.' Rowena experienced the now-familiar tingle between her shoulder blades. *Something* was happening in that room, a kind of mass sharpening of the senses, but whether telepathy was at work or the dead really *had* come to communicate, she could not be sure...

Suddenly Caireen was looking in her direction, her violet-blue eyes resembling deep sockets in the dimly lit room. 'Rowena, my dear... there's somebody here who insists on speaking to you.'

Rowena was numb. Her heart began to beat in slow, sickening thuds and a high-pitched ringing sounded in her ears. No! cried her brain. Not me! Not Ellie – please.

She heard Caireen's light voice as if from a vast distance. 'It's a little boy. His name is something like Oliver. I'm sure it's you he wants. Do you know an Oliver?'

People turned towards her. Wordlessly, she nodded, strangled with resurgent grief and a deep sense of shock.

'He says everything is all right. He's happy and has friends to play with. He just wanted you to know...' Rowena's eyes filled with tears as the soft Irish voice continued in this vein, talking about the little brother of whom she had been so jealous, who had been knocked off his bike and killed before she could make up for all her petty cruelties. Oliver... he had not been in her thoughts at all this time, yet he had seized upon the channel offered by Caireen to come and reassure her.

'Thank you,' she murmured, just like all the others. Caireen gave her a warm, slow smile before turning to an elderly gentleman nearby.

Afterwards, in the car, Caireen was full of concern. 'I didn't mean to upset you, Rowena,' she said. 'I didn't mean to single you out at all. Not one of my own people. But he was insistent... a very bright, forceful little boy.'

'That's Oliver,' she answered. She felt peculiar, both elated and fragile.

'Forgive me. I didn't feel I had any choice.'

'Of course.'

Caireen took her hand in the dark and gave it a small squeeze, an unexpected gesture from one whose usual manner had so far been professionally distant.

'It's all right, honestly,' went on Rowena. 'Tell me about the Grangers. I understand they live somewhere between Uplands and the Lizard peninsula.'

'Yes – at Cober Pool. There's a part of the coast where the cliff-line is breached by what used to be a river estuary. Years of silting led to the formation of a sand-bar across the old estuary mouth; the sea pounds one side, while a freshwater lake nestles on the other; Charles and Madeleine live by the upper reaches of the lake, about a mile inland from the bar.'

'The National Trust owns a lot of the land,' commented Brett over his shoulder, 'but the gardens immediately around the house are private. You'll like the area; it's most attractive at this time of year.'

Rowena found that Brett had predicted accurately. The Grangers lived in a modified seventeenth-century house flanked by woodland, a short walk from the edge of the 'pool'. The lake itself was irregularly shaped, with creeks projecting from the long central axis, their shorelines sometimes wooded, sometimes marshy.

Colonel Granger proved to be a bluff, florid-faced man in his late sixties with a luxuriant pepper and salt moustache. It was clear to Rowena within a very few minutes that he harboured tender feelings towards Caireen. The solicitous little gestures, the wink when he thought no one was looking... in return, Caireen teased him like a brother.

Daniel was with them, but not Brett. He had stayed behind pleading 'pressure of paperwork'; she suspected he was merely feeling antisocial.

'And have you been to Cornwall before, Miss Kemp?' asked the colonel as they sat down to roast lamb.

'I'm afraid not. As a family we tended to go to Scotland or France. I've just discovered what I've been missing.'

'You must make sure Caireen allows you some time off,' said Madeleine. 'Our shops can't compare with London's, of course, but

Truro will give you a pleasant day out. Or you might like to visit the new Tate Gallery at St Ives...'

'I think the coast is Cornwall's strength,' answered Rowena. 'I shall definitely go to Land's End, and Caireen has kindly offered to show me St Michael's Mount.'

'Good.' Madeleine nodded her satisfaction, and the meal progressed amicably. Afterwards, they rose for a slow stroll along the lakeside.

'This is a fascinating stretch of water,' expounded the colonel. 'It's the largest freshwater lake in the county. Shallow and reedy up here, but nearly thirty feet deep near the sand-bar. There's a legend connecting it with King Arthur's Excalibur, as well as some grimmer ones about people disappearing and never being seen again.'

'The huntsman and his horse,' chipped in Madeleine.

'That's right. They fell in together and only the horse reappeared... But we don't find the water at all sinister. Perhaps a little unpleasant when algae get a grip in high summer, but otherwise most picturesque.'

'It's a haven for birds,' said Madeleine.

Daniel swung round to Rowena. 'Yes! I've seen coots, and swans and tufted duck... There's a hide over there.' He pointed across the water. 'Colonel, may I show Rowena the hide?'

'Of course, young man. We'll take our time, and you can catch us up.'

As their elders disappeared into a plantation of trees Rowena and Daniel doubled back past the house, across a small stone bridge and round to the northern shore of the lake. Soon they came upon a dilapidated wooden construction at the water's edge.

'Is that the hide?' asked Rowena, knowing that it wasn't.

'No, silly. That's the boathouse. It's very old, but...' He hesitated, then ploughed on. 'I'll tell you a secret. There's a rowing boat inside. Look...' He led her to a thin crack in the planking; beyond it she could just make out part of the thwart of a dinghy, and the gleam of a rowlock.

'We took it once,' he whispered. 'Brett and I. It was exciting...'

'Tell me.'

His face closed, like the sun going behind a cloud. 'No. That's my secret with him. We never had a secret before. He trusts me.'

'All right, Danny. Where's the hide?'

'Along here...' They returned to the main path, but soon branched off again. 'Behind these bushes,' he hissed, ducking into a small enclosure. 'You lean against these wooden supports and look out through these holes.'

The hide was angled towards the reedy shallows at the edge of Cober Marsh, though it was possible by craning to visualize part of the longer stretch of Cober Pool.

'What are those copper-headed birds?' asked Rowena.

'Wigeons. Male ones. Their backs are grey. That's how you can tell them from pochards.'

'Ah. Thanks.' Rowena knew nothing of either species. She could just about recognize the swan gliding past. 'I suppose we'd better catch up with the others. They must be half-way to the bar by now.'

Together they hurried round the north-west tip of the lake, then southwards through the tree plantation. At length they saw the bright splash of Madeleine's primrose jacket just ahead, and were soon within earshot.

'How *is* your girl shaping up?' the colonel was asking Caireen. 'Can she cut the mustard?'

'Yes. She has a vigorous style, and I'm very pleased with her work so far.'

'Good. Your story deserves the best. I really don't mind if you want to include Hester...No, Madeleine, it could inspire others in the same position, give them hope...'

Caireen held up a mollifying hand. 'That's kind, Charles, but it's quite all right. We have plenty of material.'

Rowena was keen to catch up and avoid further unintentional eavesdropping. She coughed, but no one heard, and a moment later Daniel had seized her arm. 'Look. Out there, through the trees. That's a teal. See the green stripe behind the eye?'

'Yes, Danny. Let's just catch up with the others, then you can show everyone.'

They approached once more, and to her profound discomfort they were talking about Ellie.

'What was it she stole from you? Silverware, wasn't it?' The colonel's voice was rough and indignant. 'You give these people a chance, and *that*'s how they repay you. She's the one who persuaded Adrian to take on that Sullivan layabout. It was all a well-planned con.'

'I'm worried about Adrian,' said Madeleine. 'He's been depressed for years, but that theft seemed to knock the stuffing out of him completely. The police are quite useless. I don't know why we bother to pay our community charge – we get nothing for it.'

Rowena began to speak loudly to Daniel about a nearby tree and the group turned round, a practised social smile on each face.

'Monterey pine, my dear,' supplied the colonel. 'We're very near the sand-bar. Are you game for a bit more of a stroll?'

'Definitely.'

The bar was wider than Rowena had expected, but she found it strange nevertheless to contrast the still, mysterious depths of the pool on one side with the restless waves of open sea on the other.

'Never try to swim from here,' Madeleine warned her. 'The currents are treacherous; people have died underestimating the force of the water.'

'Lethal undertow,' nodded the colonel.

'Oh – is Graw Cove just as dangerous?' Rowena had hoped to swim from the beach closest to Uplands. Now she looked to Caireen for reassurance.

'No, Graw is safe. But you must be careful further down the coast. There's a narrow inlet just beneath the ruined mines which can look temptingly secluded, but there's barely time to climb round there from the adjacent rocks before it's cut off by the tide. Any tourist who has tried it has ended up a sodden guest of the inshore lifeboat crew...'

Daniel whispered to her as they retraced their steps. 'I've been to that cleft. It's got adits from the mine – you know, passages – but they're all blocked with rubble.'

It sounded an unsavoury place; Rowena had no desire to investigate. They meandered back to the house for afternoon tea before Caireen began the polite prelude to leave-taking.

'Just a moment, young fellow,' said Colonel Granger to Daniel as they stood in the hall. 'I've got something you might like to borrow.' He hurried away and returned with a slender stack of copies of *The Magnet*, all in near-pristine condition despite their venerable age. 'You enjoyed those others, didn't you? Bunter, the Fat Owl of the Remove? Bob Cherry? Harry Wharton?'

'*"Yaroo! Leggo, you beasts!"*' responded Daniel with enthusiasm.

'Hah! They were my father's,' he explained to Rowena, 'but when a television series about Greyfriars was screened in the 'fifties I must admit I sneaked a look on more than one occasion.'

She smiled, recognizing that he was going out of his way to be kind to Daniel. Throughout the short journey to Uplands Daniel pointed out amusing illustrations, or read out some of the more colourful passages. Rowena scarcely concentrated: her mind was on

Adrian Polzeath, farmer, 'depressed for years', plunged even deeper into despair by the actions of Patrick Sullivan. He was certain to know some of the solid details she craved concerning the disappearance of that young man.

Somehow she had to persuade him to share those details with a perfect stranger.

6

'I got the impression yesterday that the colonel is rather fond of Mrs Malone.' Rowena finished a light lunch with Mrs Trelowan at the kitchen table and rose to carry her dishes to the sink.

'Yes, indeed. He's been trying to court her for the best part of seven years, but he never seems to get any closer. His wife Hester died after a long illness, and a friend persuaded him to consult Mrs Malone. She gave him a lot of comfort.'

'Has he any children?'

'Two sons, but they have lives of their own. One lives in Malta, the other in Brussels.'

'Ah. Perhaps Mrs Malone feels the time isn't right yet for commitment – she's a busy professional woman.'

'I'm sure that must be the case. She keeps the relationship going up to a point. While Miss Granger is always invited here along with the colonel, Mrs Malone has on occasions dined with him alone in Penzance or St Ives.'

Dinners *à deux*, reflected Rowena. Caireen could definitely have the colonel if she wanted him. He accepted Daniel's role in her life. Where would they live, though? Cober House was larger than Uplands, with more architectural merit, but its setting was far less spectacular. And what would Madeleine's position become? Mere housekeeper for the colourful couple? She was pleasant and friendly, yet some of her comments by the pool the previous day had seemed to indicate that she held some reservations where Caireen was concerned. Was this pure self-interest, or something more?

'Does Miss Granger get on with Mrs Malone?' she asked guilelessly.

'I... Well enough, I think.'

'She didn't appear too keen to have Hester included in the book.'

Mrs Trelowan hesitated. 'I don't want to speak out of turn,' she said, 'but Miss Granger never did like her brother meddling, as she called it, with spiritualism. She thought psychic people would take advantage of him. It was the talk of Helston. But I think she can see that it's done him good, whatever she feels about it herself.'

Rowena made tea for them both, and prepared to carry her own cup through to the study. 'I'm making good progress with the book,' she said, 'but my editor in London still wants me to send him articles on aspects of coastal and rural life. Do you think Mr Polzeath at the farm would be willing to talk to me about his work?'

'I doubt it. He used to have a wonderful dairy herd, the pride of the peninsula, but then the European Union slashed the milk quotas and wrecked his livelihood. He turned to beef instead, but two years ago was forced to cull four-fifths of his herd because of the BSE scare. He grows vegetables now, but it's a struggle to make a living.'

'If he's upset about EU rulings, I could tie that in with the viewpoint of Newlyn fishermen...'

'He won't talk to you. He won't talk to anyone unless he has to. His wife and children left him years ago and he hasn't been the same since. They couldn't stand the hardship and anxiety.' She blinked and lowered her eyes. 'I've offered several times to leave the cottage, so he can get more rent from someone else, but he won't hear of it. He's a fine man. Loyal. But life has treated him badly...'

Kicked him in the teeth good and proper, mused Rowena. No family, his livelihood destroyed by political regulations beyond his control, his goods stolen by a casual worker he had employed at Ellie's behest...

Adrian Polzeath must have known Ellie quite well. She had to meet him, and soon.

An opportunity presented itself the following Saturday. Mrs Trelowan had professed a liking for lupins, but found them too tall for the narrow strip of earth in front of her cottage. Rowena, poking around at a local village fête for unusual games or customs, found a row of potted dwarf lupins on one of the stalls, and bought them. She drove carefully along the rutted lane to the farm cottages with the pots clinking in the Clio's boot; parking alongside the end dwelling, she climbed out and knocked on the door.

All was quiet inside. Rowena could glimpse the tiny sitting-room through the window – open fireplace, gleaming brass, neat floral sofa. She tapped again then stood back, craning thoughtfully at the upper windows.

The door of the middle cottage creaked open and a girl in her mid-twenties emerged, hands on hips. She had tangled dark hair, overgenerous lips and a voluptuous figure. One of her blouse buttons was missing – perhaps unable to take the strain.

'Mrs Trelowan's out,' she announced with something like haughty pleasure.

'Pity,' said Rowena. 'I've brought her some plants. I don't suppose you know when she'll be back?'

'No idea.'

More sneering satisfaction, which Rowena ignored. 'I'm Rowena Kemp,' she said, nodding at the girl. 'I'm working for a few months at Uplands.'

'Thought you must be. We've heard of you hereabouts.' Her harsh Cornish voice evinced little interest in Rowena and her concerns. Doubtless she still held a grudge against the entire household for that short-lived cleaning job. A question suddenly arrowed across Rowena's brain. *When was Ginette sacked?*

'You must be Ginette,' she smiled. 'Mrs Trelowan said you were her neighbour. I'm pleased to meet you.'

With a pitying look the young woman flounced back across her doorstep, and Rowena accepted defeat. It wasn't Ginette's information she wanted just now, but when the day came she knew instinctively that loosening that pink tongue would entail thrusting cash into one of those grasping little palms.

As she unloaded the plant pots and assembled them by Mrs Trelowan's doorstep, Rowena cast covert glances along the lane towards the farm itself. The gate was open – probably a permanent state in view of its pronounced sag. There were no animals now to pen... Beyond an untidy yard she could see the granite farmhouse and part of a barn. The house's exterior paintwork needed renewal; even from this distance it was obvious. No gay tubs of pansies or geraniums stood outside to brighten the pervading air of drab utilitarianism.

Aware of Ginette's sharp brown eyes focused through the window on the small of her back, Rowena walked boldly into the farmyard. The door of the house had a wrought-iron knocker with peeling black paint. As she reached out towards it, a tall man emerged from beyond the barn.

'Can I help you?' he asked in unenthusiastic tones.

He was in his early forties. His face was weathered, as befitted an outdoor worker, but there was a greyness beneath, an exhaustion of the soul. Deep lines were etched across his forehead and past the corners of his mouth, and his dark brown hair was mottled with silver.

Beneath the green plaid shirt and mud-encrusted trousers his limbs were unnaturally thin, though she could sense their strength. This, then, was Adrian Polzeath. The stigmata of depression she had expected: what no one had mentioned, however, was the fact that he had once been a handsome man. Good bones were harder to wither than ephemeral flesh...

She made her own voice bright and sociable. 'Hello. I'm sorry to bother you. I brought some lupins for Mrs Trelowan, and she's not at home. I wondered if you could spare a scrap of paper so I can write her a note?' Her bulging note pad was safely tucked away in the Clio's glove compartment.

He frowned at her suspiciously for a moment, then seemed to accept the story. 'I suppose so. Wait there a minute...'

She followed him as if he hadn't really meant the instruction. 'I'm Rowena Kemp. I'm doing some work for Mrs Malone at Uplands. Are you Mr Polzeath, by any chance?'

'Yes.'

'Mrs Trelowan speaks very highly of you.'

He raised his eyebrows in a deprecating gesture and entered the farmhouse. This time she did wait, and saw his shape on the other side of the window flicking through a stack of documents in a desultory way.

'I can let you have this,' he said at length, reappearing with a used brown envelope. 'Sorry it's not much.'

'That'll be fine. I'm grateful. This is a wonderful site for a farm. Do you –'

'You'll excuse me,' he cut across her. 'I'm rather busy.'

'Of course. Thanks again.'

Well, at least we've met, she thought as she scribbled a few lines on the envelope. She could create an opportunity to build on the introduction later... Today was Saturday. How would a depressed loner spend his Saturday evenings? He would either lurk at home with the television or sink a few morose pints in the Tinner's Reach... She would visit the pub herself tonight.

Half-way through an afternoon of intense concentration, Rowena heard a soft knock on the study door.

Daniel responded to her murmured 'Come in'. 'I've brought you some lemonade,' he said, balancing a small tray with two glasses. 'The sunshine is so beautiful. Will you walk out to the mines with me?'

'Oh... Danny, I'm sorry. I'm really tied up at present. I have to get this piece finished and sent to my editor, then work on another chapter for your mother. I'd love to come another time.'

'But I want you *now*!' His lip began to pucker dangerously. 'It's no fun on my own. I want to show you things.'

'And I'd like to see them. Can't you save them for me?'

'It's not the same. The weather changes...'

'Soon, Danny, I promise. But I've got to finish this. What about Brett? Is he around?'

'He's in London. All right – I'm going.' His eyes glinted redly. 'You're just like her – you pretend to be interested, and then it's all too much trouble.'

'That's not true...' She sighed deeply as he ignored her and flung himself out of the room, leaving both glasses of lemonade behind. Minutes later his figure could be seen striding erratically but determinedly up the driveway from the house. He didn't turn right on to the cliff path, but kept on going towards Anwith.

Rowena thrust aside her faint niggle of guilt. It was Keith who deserved such feelings on her behalf, if anyone. She had intended to return to London herself this weekend and they had made tentative plans for a meal out to share news, but she had withdrawn on the Thursday, finding herself overwhelmed with work. Must ring him tomorrow, she muttered.

Daniel was back by supper time, with an air both flustered and smug – rebellion fulfilled. Caireen's violet eyes appraised him sharply, but she forbore to question him in front of Rowena. 'Do have lunch with us tomorrow', she said pleasantly to Rowena. 'Mrs Trelowan cooks a superb loin of pork.'

'Thank you. I shall look forward to that.' She left as soon as it was polite to do so, glad that they accepted her autonomy: it made for a much more relaxed household.

In the bedroom she changed from the smart 'secretarial' appearance which Caireen favoured to a more casual ensemble. There was still a nip in the air each evening: Rowena chose chestnut slacks and a hip-length cream jumper. She brushed her corn-coloured hair until it swirled and shone; with amber ear-rings and a slick of coral lip-gloss she was ready for the fray.

The Tinner's Reach was already packed when she parked the Clio in Anwith and pushed open the creaking oak door. There was just one lounge bar, narrow and low-ceilinged; across the smoke haze she could see ruddy rural faces, farmers among others enjoying rare leisure time.

Adrian Polzeath leaned moodily against the bar, staring into his pint glass. She squeezed through the clutch of drinkers milling between them and fetched up adjacent to him. 'Dry cider, please,' she said brightly to the barman, before turning to Adrian in apparent surprise. 'Hello, Mr Polzeath. I didn't expect to see a familiar face. I thought I'd see where the local people spend their Saturday evenings.'

'Down Barn,' murmured a voice behind her.

'Barn?' she echoed.

'It's a night-club.' The speaker was a sturdy young man in his late teens, standing with a group of his friends. 'We'll take you, if you like.'

'Er, thanks, but no. I'm not in the mood for dancing.' She turned confidingly to Adrian. 'I thought this might be a place to pick up local stories – find out from people's conversation the real issues of interest.'

'And why would you want to do that?'

She was sure that he knew. 'Sorry,' she smiled. 'Mrs Trelowan's such a talker, I assumed she'd have told you. I'm a journalist for a London newspaper, and I'm writing a few articles on West Country life for my editor in parallel with working for Mrs Malone. I've covered odd things like the Panther of Pendeen, but he's also interested in ordinary rural life, the effects of distant politics – that kind of thing.'

'The egg scare, the beef scare,' nodded the barman sagely. 'You could help her with that.'

'No thanks,' said Polzeath curtly. 'I'm no one's provincial specimen.'

Rowena sipped her cider. 'It's more of an opportunity to air justifiable discontent,' she said. 'People all over the country have their lives ruled by directives from the capital, or beyond. London needs to know first-hand what effects these rulings are having on individuals.'

Polzeath eyed her, his expression bored. 'Funny, I thought that's why we had democratically elected representatives at Westminster – to put across local views.'

'Yes, and how often do they get a chance to speak or put down a bill?'

He didn't answer. The barman leaned over. 'And how much good have our MPs done *you* these last few years?' he clucked.

As Polzeath drank, refusing to be drawn, two old men sitting at a corner table laid out a chess board and began to set out the pieces. One removed a pawn of each colour and concealed them behind his back; he then offered clenched hands to his opponent, who tapped one set of knuckles. The hand was opened to reveal a black pawn; the pawns were replaced and the game began. A few people drifted over to watch, but the rest continued to chat at high volume.

'I can't play chess if there's background noise,' said Rowena to the air between Polzeath and the barman.

'I can't fathom the moves,' said the barman. 'I like draughts. Adrian, here, though – he plays chess.'

'I don't.'

'Oh, yes 'e do.'

Rowena recognized the broad Cornish voice of Ginette and turned around slowly, just in time to see the girl detach herself from the group of young men who had mentioned the night-club. She hadn't known that Ginette was in the pub; perhaps she had just returned from the washroom.

Polzeath's tenant was pink-cheeked and already slightly unsteady on her feet. She wore a gold micro-skirt, showing clumpy legs, and a skin-tight, low-cut black top. Her eyes were narrowed balefully in his direction. 'E were happy enough to play chess with Little Miss Ellie,' she went on mockingly.

Adrian's face was white and taut.

'Chess and goodness knows what else.'

'That's a damned lie.'

'Couldn't get it up, could 'e? Dear, dear.'

Thankfully the sturdy young man chose to intervene. 'Come on, Ginnie,' he shouted. 'We're going down Barn.' He grasped her arm and pulled her away from the bar, but not before she had made an unpleasant gesture in Adrian's direction.

'I haven't played for a while,' mused Rowena before the silence became even more uncomfortable. 'I'd love to have a game with somebody. I don't suppose you'd be willing, Mr Polzeath?'

'No.'

'Oh, go on, Adrian,' cajoled the barman. 'It'll do you good. Too much introspection rots the brain.'

'And chess is a gregarious, outgoing pastime? Besides... Miss – *Kemp* has already stated that she can't concentrate in a noisy environment. Perhaps you'll offer her a game of draughts, Bill.'

'Not me, I'm afraid. I have customers to serve.' As if on cue a large man stepped up to the bar with a multiple order, and Bill's attention moved elsewhere.

Rowena stood awkwardly with Adrian Polzeath. If she missed this opportunity, there might never be another, and Ginette's words had been troubling... Maybe it wasn't only the hospitality of this tall farmer which had been betrayed. 'It's lonely up at the house,' she began. 'Of course, I'm only an employee, so although they're very kind, I don't quite fit in. It would be really nice if someone here *would* play chess once in a while.'

She saw him consider, drawn by her careful tone of hesitant sincerity... almost she hated herself for her journalist's fine-honed facility for acting.

'Well...' He glanced around the room, as if to propose someone else, then met her gaze briefly before studying her feet. 'I haven't played recently, but I suppose, if you're sure you want to, we could have a game...'

He enjoyed chess, she could tell. This wasn't just altruism. He was tempted, against some kind of better judgement.

'I'd look forward to that. I'd invite you to Uplands, but I don't have a sitting-room of my own there. Shall we try this pub one lunch time, when it's quiet?'

In the far corner a whoop of sound mushroomed around the two old men. 'No. I don't like being watched and heckled.'

Rowena kept her face pleasant and neutral as he made up his mind. Once again she studied his features as he stared at the floor. Strength was hidden there behind the grey mask of trouble, strength which had attracted Ellie. She knew that Ellie had been unable to play chess as recently as three years ago. Perhaps Adrian had been teaching her...

'Tomorrow,' he said. 'Better make it an evening. Can you come to the farmhouse?'

'Yes.' She felt a sudden furtive need to look around, even though Ginette had long gone. Everything seemed normal. She turned back to Adrian with a warm smile. 'Yes,' she repeated.

'You're playing chess tonight with a farmer?' echoed Keith when she told him the next morning.

'Yes. He knew both Ellie and Patrick. I have to gain his trust before I can ask the right sort of questions.'

'I didn't know you could play chess. Two rooks on an open board and I'm lethal. We've missed out there.'

'How's your weekend going?' She had already apologized for not travelling to London.

'Bit quiet. I went to Kew Gardens yesterday. Today I'm catching up on some reading. Gordon would send his regards if he could remember who you are.'

She let that pass. 'Any comments from Kevin?'

'Yes. He wants more bizarre items, general weirdness.'

'I can't just *manufacture* weirdness, Keith, though I'll carry on doing my best to unearth any that exists. Anything else?'

'He wants to know if you've got "the dirt", as he calls it, on the Malone woman yet.'

Her skin went cold. 'I told you I wasn't going to bite the hand that feeds,' she said slowly. 'I also believe Caireen is genuine.'

She thought she had succeeded in sounding casual, but immediately she felt the pulse of his alarm over the telephone wires. 'Ro – you haven't had a private sitting with her?'

'No. Certainly not.'

'Why do you say she's genuine?'

'I've heard satisfied clients talking. I've seen more of her public demonstrations. She's *stunningly* accurate, Keith.' And my little brother chose her. He must have been waiting all these years for a channel.

'People like Caireen Malone get inside your head, Ro. It's – pervasive. Please be careful.'

'*You*'ve been to a psychic!' she suddenly burst out.

'Yes.' He sounded muffled. 'Just a public demo, like you. They *get* to you – I know now. What they're offering is so – desirable, we're all desperate to believe. Every one of us.'

Rowena could feel her heart thumping, beating a deep tattoo against her chest wall. 'Caireen is very modest about her skills,' she told him. 'She dresses up and to a degree performs, but she feels that's expected. Her own heroine is Eileen Garrett, a powerful trance medium who was also Irish. Eileen died in 1970, but throughout her life she was keen to understand her curious abilities and allowed all kinds of scientific researchers to investigate her. She's regarded as one of the most honest mediums ever to practise.'

'Do I take it, then, that Caireen's all ready to submit to objective examination?'

'Don't be flippant, Keith. She doesn't need to.'

'Exactly.'

They were straying on to dangerous ground. Rowena bit back a retort; Keith was an enormous help and she didn't want to alienate him. 'Ellie hasn't come through,' she said lightly. 'I must say I'm relieved. I'm keeping my enquiries strictly this side of the twilight curtain.'

'Good. Did you engage a PI?'

'What – oh. Private investigator. Not yet. He'd only ask for a photograph or at least a description of Sullivan, and I don't have either yet. I don't want to overplay my hand with these local people, or I'll be rumbled.'

'Fair enough. So I'll be seeing you next Saturday, then?'

'Definitely.'

Mrs Trelowan's roast loin of pork proved to be as delicious as Caireen had promised. There were only two of the family at lunch, as Brett was still in London, and Rowena found herself glancing covertly at Daniel, trying to assess his mood.

He *seemed* to have recovered from his pique the previous day. He joined in the general small-talk, ate heartily, even smiled. Towards Caireen he was particularly attentive, passing her cruet, gravy, apple sauce, all without being asked. Eventually the reason became clear. 'Mother...' he began. 'I wondered if perhaps I could go to Glastonbury this week. I thought maybe Wednesday. It's been nearly a year since last time...'

He looked so appealing that Rowena couldn't imagine Caireen turning him down.

'How will you get there?' asked Caireen.

'On trains and taxis, like before. I've got a timetable.'

Caireen frowned thoughtfully. 'I have sitters on Wednesday, otherwise I'd take you in the car. Thursday is busy, too. How about the week after?'

'I'd rather go soon.'

'Perhaps I can help?' Rowena decided to intervene. She needed to be back in Danny's good books. 'I'd be happy to drive

Daniel, if you can spare me. I've never visited Glastonbury before.'

Caireen's face cleared. 'That would be very kind of you. Danny – you can show Rowena the view from the Tor. And of course the Abbey, and the Chalice Well.'

He nodded enthusiastically, playing the game. Rowena wondered how much Caireen knew, or suspected, about his true plans. She seemed relieved that he had a chaperone, someone with whom he was now obliged to spend a large part of his day – although her reasons could stem from simple protectiveness...

Later, when Daniel had gone and the two women lingered over their coffee, Caireen smiled at Rowena. 'I'm glad Danny will be with you,' she said. 'He's loved Glastonbury ever since the first time we took him. He can potter for hours in a crystal shop; left to himself, he'd probably miss the train back, and it *is* a long way. I hope you have a pleasant day – you know the town's reputation, do you?'

Somehow Rowena didn't think she was referring to its status as venue for the country's noisiest pop festival. 'Spiritual centre of England,' she said vaguely.

'That's right. England's first Christian church was founded there, reputedly by Joseph of Arimathea. Just a little wattle and daub construction – he can't have imagined what a magnificent Abbey would be standing on the site centuries later. St Dunstan was the most famous abbot... There are legends of King Arthur at Glastonbury, too, and the chalice from Christ's Last Supper is said to be buried near a well at the foot of the Tor.'

'The Holy Grail,' murmured Rowena.

'Yes. Much of Somerset was under water in the Dark Ages, and Celtic mythology has identified Glastonbury's hills as Avalon – the Island of the Blessed Souls. So you can understand why people are drawn to the place... I should mention that New Age travellers in particular cluster around the town. You'll see some odd-looking people.'

New Age travellers... Rowena felt a stir of excitement. Perhaps, just perhaps, her path might cross that of Patrick Sullivan.

7

A fine mist wreathed Graw Head as Rowena and Daniel climbed into the Clio at 6 a.m. the following Wednesday, but within an hour it had dissipated. The climbing sun strengthened rapidly as they sped up the peninsula, and Daniel's mood of happy anticipation began to affect his chauffeuse.

Rowena had hoped to milk details of Sullivan's appearance from Adrian Polzeath the previous Sunday evening, but she had been obliged to tread carefully. Polzeath had been polite, but distant. He had shown her into his stone-flagged kitchen and offered her a seat at the scrubbed pine table before providing tea in a chipped mug. Even if Rowena had not been aware of his domestic situation, the substantial room bore witness to it, from the sintered food splatters defacing the kitchen range to the crumbling, cobweb-draped dried flowers hanging high in the corner. He didn't even seem to have a cat or dog, which to her had always represented an integral part of life on a farm.

They had played two games of chess, of which Polzeath had won the first easily, and the second against a prolonged rearguard action. Rowena was happy that he had not patronized her by letting her win. His victories had allowed her to smile ruefully at the end, and demand an early rematch to secure her revenge. He had agreed, unable to suppress the brief spark of pleasure in his eyes. She left convinced that he had enjoyed the evening, though of course no such admission had passed his lips.

Next time, she decided, as the Clio forged beyond Bodmin's bleak moorland to cross the Devon border, she would take a bottle of wine to the farm and ensure that Polzeath drank most of it. The small-talk on Sunday had been stiff, safe, conventional: chess openings, cabbages, Cornish weather. Next time, spartan kitchen notwithstanding, she would create an *ambiance* of snug intimacy where gossip could flourish...

In the passenger seat beside her, Daniel was shooting her suspicious looks. 'You haven't been listening to a word I've been saying!' he accused.

'I have,' she replied calmly. 'You told me that the summit of the hill they call Glastonbury Tor is over five hundred feet above sea level, and it's on two major ley lines, one of which includes Stonehenge. You said that many people believe the terraces cut along the hillside represent a prehistoric maze, or labyrinth, which would mean that it was a centre for pagan worship long before its links with Christianity. You also mentioned that there may be a cave deep inside the Tor, although excavations have so far failed to reveal it...how am I doing? Finally you described how the topography of the Somerset countryside around and to the south of the Tor has been found to resemble a perfect circle of zodiac symbols. So there! Of course I was listening!' She ruffled his hair, and he chuckled merrily.

By nine o'clock they were approaching Glastonbury, and Rowena could see the awe-inspiring landmark for herself. The town proved to be small; she found a quiet back-street car-park and paid a day's tariff.

'Right,' she said brightly. 'Lead on, MacDuff.'

Daniel guided her to the narrow High Street and pointed across the road to a medieval building with mullioned windows. 'That's the Tribunal,' he said. 'It was a courthouse once, but now it's the Tourist Information Centre. Do you want to go inside?'

'Maybe later. Show me how we get into the Abbey.' She had glimpsed sections of the honey-coloured ruins whilst circumnavigating the town.

The pavements already seethed with people as they walked down the street, and Rowena felt that Caireen's warning about 'odd-looking' people was not ill-founded. Many young women simply wore long skirts, brightly coloured shawls, indigo lipstick and rows of jangling beads, but others were tattooed, with asymmetrically shaven heads and grubby male companions sporting matted pigtails. There was almost an air of carnival, but not quite: in the distance a New Age beggar with aggressive boots had staked out his patch and was practising psychological warfare on passers-by.

'Look!' said Daniel, drawing her attention to a shop window full of crystals. Among shimmering chunks of rose quartz and citrine knelt plaster Hindu maidens, their exposed bellies filled with either amethyst clusters or ammonites – curved fossils. Presumably these symbolized fertility, though Rowena found the open bellies less inspiring than slightly sinister. Daniel innocently enthused before taking her hand and leading her onwards, past a candle shop to another selling mystic books.

Outside stood a bearded New Age man, and Rowena decided this was her opening. As they discussed the unusual titles, she discreetly drew Daniel's attention to the man. 'Danny,' she whispered, 'Mrs Trelowan told me that it was a hippie who masterminded the loss of your mother's silver last year. Glastonbury seems to be full of them... supposing he's here as well? If you can tell me what he looks like, I'll keep my eyes open.'

To her ear that sounded light and spontaneous, but Daniel didn't immediately reply. He stared at the display of mystical volumes, his face tense.

Rowena affected not to notice. 'She said he was called Patrick Sullivan. Is that right?'

'Yes.'

'Well, the police didn't help your mother very much. Perhaps we can do better. Was he tall, or short? Blond? Dark-haired?'

Daniel swallowed. 'He was my height – about five foot nine. Untidy fair hair down to his shoulders, and a *stupid* little beard, just on the chin. There was some sort of tattoo on his left forearm – flowers in a trellis, as far as I could see.'

'Where did you meet him, Danny?'

He frowned at her. 'Why does that matter?'

'Because if it was some public event, then there's just a chance that someone may have taken a photograph with him on it.'

'We were at Anwith village fête. He played the fiddle all afternoon.'

She hoped he was telling the truth. She herself had been frank, for once, and the possibility, though faint, of being able to present a photograph of Sullivan to a private detective was exciting. Mick Vean had been unable to come up with anything; indeed, there was every evidence that the story of the robbery had been suppressed. Perhaps Caireen hadn't wanted the wrong kind of publicity.

They meandered slowly to the Abbey entrance, Rowena covertly examining the left forearm of every passing blond male. As they approached the glass-walled Visitor Centre where tickets could be bought, Daniel seemed ever more reluctant to proceed. At the last moment he turned to her with a face of supplication. 'Rowena – did my mother instruct you to chaperone me today?'

'Well... she made the comment that she was glad I would be with you, which isn't quite the same thing.'

'You know why I come. Lavinia teaches me about auras. She says I have a real talent for reading them. She – she's expecting me at ten. I rang her last week. *Please* can I keep my appointment?'

'Does she live locally?'

'Yes. Out near the Tor.' He fidgeted. 'She said we could spend the whole day on study if I could get here. It's such an opportunity . . .'

Rowena considered. 'I'm quite happy being a tourist here on my own, but I think I should meet Lavinia and know where you are. I want your word that you won't wander off anywhere else.'

'I promise, I promise.'

Lavinia turned out to be a plump lady of forty, who seemed pleasant and sensible. She welcomed Daniel with an easy familiarity, and Rowena felt reassured that he would be in good hands. They arranged to meet again at five; Rowena walked back into the town.

She felt strangely flat. *Something* had drawn her to Glastonbury – she had felt an inner conviction of this throughout the journey. Daniel had simply been the means to an end. Yet now she was here, what exactly was the purpose? A day spent meandering around the ruined Abbey, the Museum of Rural Life? A day examining every New Age traveller she could find, in the scant hope that one of them would be Patrick Sullivan?

She drank a cup of coffee in a small restaurant, then prepared to cross the road to the Abbey entrance. Suddenly, on the other side, she glimpsed the backs of a young couple. The man was of middle height with unkempt fair hair; the girl, also fair, looked slender and fragile, and wore some kind of sky-blue shift . . .

'*Ellie*!'

Rowena realized she was shouting, desperately trying to project her message as an unusual surge of vehicles filled the road between them. For a moment, it seemed as if the girl had heard: she half turned her head, and Rowena glimpsed a short, straight nose and familiar jawline before a stout tourist wielding a camcorder elbowed past them and obscured the view.

They were disappearing, melting into the crowd. Rowena saw one tantalizing flash of hair before they rounded a corner into the High Street. Jinking across the road to a chorus of car-horns, she forced her way between two tall men with backpacks, darted around a group of window-shoppers admiring coloured boots, and finally gained the High Street herself.

It was narrow, steep and crowded at this point. Wildly she scanned both sides of the road, each individual shopper . . . there was no sign of the couple.

They *can't* have got far, she told herself. There hasn't been time. They're inside a shop, that's all. That candle shop, or the one selling crystals . . .

A fist seemed to be lodged under her diaphragm; she felt breathless and sick. She hovered on the threshold of each shop in turn, peering inside, praying no one would try to engage her in conversation. Nothing . . . A covered passageway loomed on the right, leading to more retail premises clustered around a gay courtyard. Rowena hesitated. Her quarry might be here, but if she paused to explore this area, they could elude her completely.

What to do . . . As she stood at the entrance, chewing her lip, the decision was made for her. The couple emerged from a tiny doorway, laughing and bantering. Hands linked, they came straight towards her.

The girl was not Ellie. Her face was broader, the eyes wider set. As the man went past, Rowena skimmed a searching gaze over both his arms. There were no tattoos.

They turned once more into the High Street, and she leaned against the nearest wall, more deflated than ever. Why did I do that? she asked herself wearily. Did I really think that girl was Ellie?

In recent weeks, whenever she had considered Patrick Sullivan, her imagination had sketched a shadowy, solitary figure. Even when Daniel had described him – an oblique spotlight glancing off scruffy fair hair and a mysterious tattoo – still the figure had stood alone. Sheer gut instinct had prevented Rowena from placing a slender blonde girl at his side. Yet today a maverick flare of optimism had overridden that deeper instinct and sent her thrusting though the crowds in pursuit of an innocent pair of hippies.

Rational? Irrational? She no longer knew. Her actions today brutally underlined the basic ambivalence of her current existence. She had come to the south-west to uncover facts, facts which so far offered no proof as to whether or not Ellie still lived . . . *Yet* – primitive instinct, or perhaps that telepathic bond she thought had long been severed, had over the same time-scale strengthened her conviction that Ellie was dead. She had almost believed that Ellie herself had occasioned this trip to Glastonbury . . .

Sighing, Rowena stood up straight, aware now that the wall she was leaning against was not in fact a wall, but a sheet of glass. She looked more closely: along one side of the passageway stretched a glass-fronted notice-board, festooned with posters and bulletins. Some advertised treatments such as holistic massage and spiritual healing, some offered group activities – Aikido, Meditation with Crystals, Fellowship at a Fasting Retreat – while others described forthcoming lectures on subjects such as the Michael Line.

Definitely no Fasting Retreat, she thought, then suddenly noticed a discreet pink card pinned in the bottom corner. 'Lost loved ones? Let me help you reconnect. Mary: psychometrist.' A telephone number appeared below.

Rowena's heart thumped forcefully as she stared at the card. It was uncanny... surely she had been led here? Almost immediately she heard Keith's voice in the back of her mind, reminding her that in Glastonbury, on a board replete with details of psychic practices, one notice was bound to catch her eye and assume disproportionate significance.

Mary, though... such a down-to earth name – but also auspicious: Mary had been the name of Caireen's gifted mother, now dead. This woman would be comfortable and middle-aged. Rowena copied down the telephone number, telling herself it was just for reference...

Ten minutes later she was on the line to Mary.

'Come and see me,' a pleasant contralto voice invited her. 'Five Rainbow Street – just behind the car-park. It's easy to find: my neighbour on the left has an outdoor aviary.'

Hands shaking, Rowena replaced the receiver. She was committed now – but wait. A psychometrist would need something of Ellie's to hold, to feel the vibrations, or whatever. All she had with her was Ellie's last letter, which was permanently housed in the side pocket of her shoulder bag – part talisman, part reminder of her quest. With a nostalgic smile, she unfolded the pale blue paper, two pages covered with Ellie's hurried, rather childlike scrawl, and scanned the content... 'We enjoyed the village fête. Caireen actually made some jam – at least, she said it was hers! I forgot to tell you, I met a friend in Penzance the other week, someone I knew at the Avebury camp. Small world, isn't it? He came to the fête. Danny won the boot-throwing competition, which was amazing against all those brawny Young Farmers. We're going to Glastonbury next week...'

The letter was chatty, insubstantial. Damn it, Ellie, Rowena wanted to hiss, who *else* was at the fête? And this friend in Penzance – was it Patrick Sullivan? What happened then?

Unfortunately, after a brief burst of correspondence, Ellie had lost the enthusiasm engendered by the novelty of her situation, or had become too busy to write. And five weeks later, she disappeared...

'Mary' had been right; her home was easy to find. It was a modest terraced house a short walk from the High Street, with a partial view of the Abbey ruins across the high car-park wall. Her tiny garden was paved; it held terracotta planters full of nasturtiums and pansies, a cat carved in blue lias stone, and another cat with black fur, very much alive. As Mary had mentioned, her neighbour on the left had an aviary full of yellow birds; Rowena could only assume that they and the cat had worked out some kind of peaceful New Age coexistence.

'Hello, I'm Mary. Do come in.'

A thin girl with long black hair answered Rowena's knock. She was unexpectedly young – twenty, perhaps – and wore a knubby black jumper and multicoloured leggings.

Faintly fazed, but determined to suspend judgement, Rowena followed her into the interior, which bore evidence of domestic cleaning interrupted. 'If I'm disturbing you, I can come back later,' she said.

'No, best to start now. I feel that your time is limited. Come through here...'

It was a diminutive sitting-room with three elderly armchairs, an antique table and an Indian rug, enlivened by green ceramic vases of spring flowers. Mary motioned her to a seat. 'Tell me about the problem,' she invited.

Rowena swallowed. In for a penny... 'My cousin is missing. She had a nomadic lifestyle for eighteen months before she took up a job in Cornwall, and seemed to settle down. She wrote to her parents, and to me, expressing enthusiasm for her new work. Then suddenly, early last September, she disappeared. We haven't heard from her since. Most people think she left with a New Age traveller whom she'd known before, but I'm not convinced. I'm very worried about her.'

Mary nodded gravely, her vivid green eyes seeming to take in all the details of Rowena's appearance at a glance. Her own face was thin and pale; her hands, which were lightly clasped in her lap, had long fingers and bony knuckles. 'Have you something belonging to your cousin?' she asked.

'Only this letter, I'm afraid. I wasn't expecting to see your card today.' She handed it over, the written pages hidden inside the resealed envelope. Mary took it in one hand, closed her eyes and smoothed her other palm across the paper, pressing firmly, before holding it still between the flat of both hands. Her forehead began to corrugate in a frown of concentration.

'What is your cousin's name?' she murmured after two minutes of silence.

Rowena hesitated as doubts began to emerge. This girl could be a complete charlatan, supplementing her Social Security with donations from the gullible. 'Just tell me if you can feel if she's alive,' she said.

Mary resumed her stroking of the envelope. 'Two names have come into my head,' she said. 'June, and Ellie... I believe your cousin was called Ellie.'

Rowena felt her eyes widen and stare. There was an icy tingle at the back of her neck. 'Yes – her name's Ellie. What have you found?'

Mary laid a finger across her lips, eyes still closed. 'Please...' she whispered.

For ten minutes she was absolutely still, then she sat back with a sigh and unleashed her green gaze. 'I'm sorry,' she said. 'This letter isn't quite enough. Nothing's clear... I need something she wore, or carried. Something with her imprint.'

'You said – she *was* called Ellie.'

Now it was Mary's turn to waver. 'It was just a figure of speech,' she said after a pause. 'I'm not quite sure at the moment. I feel close, but there isn't quite enough contact. Do you think you could bring me something else?'

Rowena's brain flashed through the options. Ellie's belongings would be at Wynchwold; anything she had left in Cornwall had presumably been handed back to Alan and June. Daniel wasn't expecting to see her until five... a return trip to the Cotswolds was *just* feasible. June was normally at home during the day... 'I don't suppose...' she began, then cleared her throat. 'I don't suppose, if Ellie *is* dead, you can communicate with her, or act as a channel for her to speak to us?'

'I'm sorry. You're not the first person to ask, but I've never had any talent as a spiritualist. I need something to hold, something to pass on the essence of its former owner. Then I tap into that essence, and sense impressions of where they might be, or what may have happened to them.'

'Have you ever – succeeded? I mean, found someone who was lost?'

'Oh, yes. Several times. Two young boys wandered off from their party during a school trip to Cheddar Gorge. The mother of one of them knows me: she was frantic, and asked me for help that same evening, even as the police were searching. She brought her son's pyjamas. As soon as I held them, I knew that the boys weren't lost in a rocky place at all. I felt they weren't even in the gorge; they seemed to be near water. At midnight they were found unharmed three miles away, across a busy main road – on the banks of a reservoir.'

'And if someone's – dead, can you still sense where they are?'

'Usually. Not always. It partly depends on what I'm holding...'

Rowena stood up in a rush of decision. 'I could bring you something else,' she said. 'It means a journey, so it would be later today, but would you be willing to try again?'

'Of course.'

Back in the Clio, Rowena swung out of Glastonbury and headed for the motorway, eschewing the slower scenic route. She hadn't telephoned June; it was hard to know what to say, and somehow it seemed appropriate to leave matters in the hands of fate.

Seventy minutes later the car crawled to the end of the exclusive cul-de-sac where Ellie's old home stood in leafy splendour. June's Metro was in the drive – good. Rowena parked behind it and climbed out apprehensively.

'Rowena!' June's voice was full of startled delight as she emerged from a shrub border with a pair of secateurs in her hand.

'June.' They embraced, and Rowena drew back to look at her aunt.

There was very little of her former plumpness left. Her once lustrous blue eyes were sunken, blurred and shadowy behind purple-grey lids; her cheeks had lost their rounded bloom, and seemed shapeless and drawn, with cruel new lines around the mouth. Only the bright gold hair remained, now merely a tribute to artful tinting.

Rowena smiled to hide her shock. 'I was in Glastonbury with a friend and he had things to do, so I thought I'd take a chance and see if you were in.'

'I'm so glad you did. I was just about to have some lunch. Have you got time?'

'Plenty.' Rowena followed June round the side of the house and in through the conservatory, where Alan liked to grow strange subtropical plants. Soon they were sitting down to salad and home-made quiche at the large pine kitchen table.

'It's funny,' said June, 'I was just thinking of you yesterday. Kitty wrote that you were doing some work in Cornwall, though she didn't specify. Are you still based there?'

'Temporarily, yes. It's a writing assignment, though the newspaper is keeping me on and I'm sending them sporadic articles.'

'This is a lovely time of year to be in the West Country. I used to have holidays there as a child. The cliff-tops become pink with sea-thrift, and the lanes are alive with campion and may-blossom. Ellie loved it, too. Her last letter was full of enthusiasm for the coast and its wildlife...'

Loved it, thought Rowena. June, just like Mary, had used the past tense. 'I wanted to ask you about Ellie,' she said carefully. 'I don't suppose...?'

June shook her head. 'No. Nothing.'

'I'm sorry. Is Uncle Alan still retaining a detective?'

'Not this time. That robbery hurt him, Ro. He feels – alienated from her. So does Jonathan. Even if she was coerced, they feel she's let the side down once too often, and what happens now is her choice. I wish I could believe that.'

Her normally animated voice was slowed with a kind of defeated exhaustion and Rowena suddenly sensed with certainty that *loved* had not been an inadvertent slip of the tongue. June knew, or felt that she knew, and no one in the family would talk about it: the subject had been decreed taboo.

As she struggled to find the right words to express fellowship, June herself unlocked the door.

'I can see it in your face, Ro. I'm right, aren't I? You think she's dead, too. For months I've fought against it, telling myself that no news is good news, and Ellie did this once before. But I know this time is different. *Ellie* was different last year, more mature, more balanced. She finally realized how her lack of communication had caused us all such anguish. She was enjoying her work. Even if something dark like drugs or blackmail forced her to leave, she would have found a way to send us a message, however indirect...'

She stared down at her wedding ring, which looked loose on the finger. 'Last time she disappeared, I was worried sick about who she was with, whether she was ill, or hungry, or afraid – but deep inside, some spark was telling me that she was at least alive. Now – I feel that spark has gone. There's a cold blank, an emptiness that I can't fill no matter how much I try. All I can conjure up is guilt, guilt that her own mother has given up on her and thinks she's dead, while her father and brother, who believe she's alive, won't even voice her name.'

Tears flooded her eyes and she turned away with a murmured apology. Rowena, torn between a preference for discretion and pity for her aunt's lonely battle, decided to confide more than she had planned. 'June,' she began, 'let me tell you what I'm doing in Cornwall...'

Ten minutes later she had provided a condensed account of her movements since March, her work for Caireen Malone. Only Dorothy Lambrook's message from a girl in distress was omitted; Rowena presented the story as one of unease about Ellie, curiosity about Caireen, coincidence that the Malones were looking for a writer. It was nearly all true. '...So I've been making careful enquiries,' she finished up.

June's lifeless eyes had kindled with a new vitality as she had listened to the unfolding report. 'Ro,' she said, 'I can't tell you how thankful I am that someone is taking Ellie's disappearance seriously. If you do find Patrick Sullivan, though, you will leave matters to the police? He could be a very dangerous young man.'

Rowena nodded. 'I looked for him in Glastonbury this morning. Silly, really – he could be anywhere. But I found something else – the address of a woman with psychometric skills.' She shot a brief, assessing glance across the table, but June's expression remained open and receptive. 'I felt we couldn't ignore any avenue, so I went to see her. All I had was a letter of Ellie's, which I kept sealed, but when she held it she told me Ellie's name. She couldn't glean any more from the paper because it hadn't been in enough contact with Ellie, but she's willing to try again if I can give her something more personal. Would you mind, June? I'd really like to give this a chance.'

'Ro – these last few weeks I've been telling myself I'd try *anything*. Indeed, I even thought about Mrs Malone, and wondered whether I dared approach her and ask for a formal session of spiritualism, despite all the unpleasantness about the robbery. Ellie had said she was kind...But I knew Alan would be hostile to the idea, and I didn't have the courage to pursue it alone. You must think me very feeble.'

'Never.'

'Bless you. Please do go to this lady. What would help her the most?'

'Something Ellie used to wear; something she was fond of.'

June frowned in concentration. 'She took her watch, of course, and her rings, but she only took a small selection of practical clothes. The rest were left at Mrs Malone's house, and handed over to Alan when he went there in response to Mr Saunders's telephone call. They're upstairs now.'

As they climbed the wide, blue-carpeted stairway to Ellie's room, Rowena reflected on the third-hand pieces of information she had received via her parents at the time. Hushed, disapproving voices had spoken of 'scandal... Ellie up to her tricks again... Alan has gone to sort it out... best if June isn't involved... she'll only get upset...' None of them had so much as considered that June might have *wanted* to be there.

So between them Alan Drinkwater, MP, and Caireen Malone, international medium, had hushed up the incident. Perhaps he had even offered her compensation for her lost silver...

It was a jolt to enter Ellie's room again. That bed under the window, where they had sat so often and shared schoolgirl secrets; that poster of the pop group A-Ha, which Ellie had kept *in situ* since her early teens: three clean-cut young Norwegian men... Rowena remembered asking Ellie which one she fancied, and the giggling reply, 'I'd have them all!'

June opened the wardrobe and drew out from a protective pillowcase a white nightshirt with a jolly row of ducks across the front. 'I – I didn't wash it,' she said. 'She must have worn it just before she left; it actually smells of Ellie.'

'I'll take good care of this,' vowed Rowena as the shirt was rewrapped and handed to her. She stared around the room, nostalgic and troubled.

June gave her a weak smile. 'Ellie had a little album of photographs,' she said. 'They were her favourites from childhood onwards. Pictures of you, me, her father and Jonathan, Peppy, the dogs... everyone who mattered to her. That was never returned, so she must have packed it when she left. I like to think it gave her comfort. Don't imagine she forgot us, Ro. She didn't.'

Downstairs, Rowena took a fond leave of her aunt, accepting a bag of strawberries and promising to inform her of any positive developments. As soon as she had left the cul-de-sac she slammed down the accelerator pedal and headed for Glastonbury.

Mary was still at home. They settled once more in the tiny sitting-room, and Rowena unwrapped the pillowcase.

'This is much better,' said Mary instantly as she was handed the nightshirt. 'I think we have a good chance now.'

Soon her eyes were closed and she was breathing slowly and deeply. 'Water...' she murmured. 'Still water – and waves. The sound of waves. Sometimes distant, sometimes closer...' She lapsed into silence again, then, 'Jacket...roll... restriction...green darkness...'

Rowena felt herself shudder.

'Water,' repeated Mary, then opened her eyes; for a moment before the pupils contracted the green darkness was reflected there.

'I'm so sorry,' she said. 'Ellie is dead. I think she's been dead for some time. She's lying in water, wrapped in something...the water is still, but I can also hear the sea. I don't quite understand that.'

All the strength had gone from Rowena's limbs. Like someone nursing a relative with a terminal illness, she had always known the outcome was likely to be one of loss, yet actually hearing the news had proved devastating. 'Can you tell where the place is?' she croaked through a throat suddenly dry.

'I'm sorry. I was trying to, but I couldn't visualize any landmarks.'

'It's all right. Thank you very much.' She stumbled to her feet, retrieved the nightshirt and tried to offer a fee.

'No,' said Mary.

'Please. I've taken up a lot of your time.'

'No. Not when it's bad news. I wish there'd been something hopeful to tell you...'

Outside, walking dazedly towards the Tor and Daniel, Rowena felt the cold blankness in her stomach that June experienced every day. Her mind, however, teemed with images of cliffs and surf and wheeling sea-birds. As if seen from an aerial camera, Graw Head flashed beneath, then the entire cliff-line to the east, Porthleven harbour, the beach beyond...In a dizzying downspiral of closer focus she saw the sand-bar enlarging, and finally the mysterious green depths of Cober Pool.

8

Daniel was in good spirits when Rowena arrived at Lavinia's home. There was much laughter as she was shown inside, and she discovered that a small circle of students was present.

'We hoped you might come sooner,' said Daniel. 'We wanted to read your aura – we've done our own.'

'I'm sure mine's very dull,' she said hurriedly.

They were all sitting on the floor around a central tea-tray. Before she could extricate Daniel and disappear, Lavinia had poured her a cup and indicated a space in the circle. 'A cup for the road,' she said.

Rowena couldn't refuse. She sat down carefully between a bearded man with bare feet and an intense-looking girl. The man smiled, then seemed to stare at a point above her left shoulder. 'You are opening the door,' he said in portentous tones. 'You are learning.'

'I think we're all learning,' she said; he nodded in sage approbation.

Desperately she tried to meet Daniel's eye but Lavinia intervened. 'Did you enjoy the Abbey?' she asked pleasantly.

'Oh – er, yes. It's magnificent.'

'You saw the thorn?'

Rowena thought rapidly. She had read about the famous Glastonbury thorn, said to have sprouted from the staff of Joseph of Arimathea on a place called Wearyall Hill, to flower on Christmas Day ever since.

'I didn't go as far as Wearyall Hill,' she murmured.

'No – it's in the Abbey grounds. At least, a cutting is. The original has long gone. What a pity you missed the tree. Such a lot of blossom. It's just outside the display centre.'

'Too busy studying the ruins,' grinned Rowena, aware that any moment now she could make a more serious gaffe. These people – they seemed to see right through her. Or was that just her own guilty imagination?

'Psychic powers helped with the excavation of those ruins,' announced Daniel from across the room.

'That's right,' agreed Lavinia. 'The architect in charge, one Frederick Bligh Bond, was shown the existence of the Edgar Chapel by means of automatic writing. The spirit monks of Glastonbury were guiding his hand.'

'When was this?' asked Rowena.

'Not so long ago – about seventy years. It was an important discovery because the chapel was behind the altar and it made the Great Church the longest in England.'

Rowena fielded well-meaning queries about the Chalice Well before managing to make a graceful exit with Daniel. 'We'd better go back,' she said.

He shook his head. 'The Tor. I always go up the Tor. You haven't been, have you? No... then please let's go.'

She sighed. 'Or spoil the ship for a hap'oth of tar? I think the spoiling is all in your direction.'

'Mother would agree with you,' he acknowledged solemnly. He led the way through a field of sheep and a gateway to a path which followed the spine of the whale-backed hill. By the time they reached the small bare chapel at the summit, Rowena was out of breath.

'I didn't think it would be so windy,' she complained, pulling the lapels of her thin jacket together at the neck. 'I should have guessed. It's the height.'

'But look at the view,' enthused Daniel. 'Surely that's worthwhile?'

Green countryside stretched in all directions, from the flat Somerset Levels to the rolling hills of Wiltshire. Daniel pointed out landmarks, then turned to her with a sly smirk. 'Roger liked you,' he said.

'The bearded man with no shoes?'

'Yes. He was analysing your aura.'

'That's a relief. I thought he had a problem with his eyes.'

'He says I've got talent, Rowena, and he's nearly as good as Lavinia so his opinion counts. Thank you for letting me join them today. You won't tell Mother, will you?'

'Of course not.'

Rowena cowered in the lee of the chapel as Daniel strode exultantly along the edge where earth seemed to meet sky. 'You know about the last Abbot of Glastonbury, don't you?' he asked on his return.

'What about him?'

'He was hung here when Henry the Eighth was destroying all the monasteries: Henry's agents were supposed to have found a book in his possession which criticized the King's divorce from Catherine of Aragon... I bet it was planted, so they could make an example of him. They hung him right here on the Tor, then chopped his head off and sent quarters of his body for public display in local towns.'

Rowena watched Danny's face as he spoke. It was full of the ghoulish glee of a child. What went on in that brain of his? she wondered. How much of the adult world did he really understand? Sometimes he seemed almost normal, and other times...

'How horrible!' she stated, aware that he expected a response. 'That's typical Henry.'

She continued to ponder the enigma of Danny as he returned to the edge and milled his arms in a mock fall. Recent memories of another high place had returned... Danny by the cliff-top mine, kicking the stones in fury and frustration – fury because his friend Ellie had spent time with someone else.

She heard Brett's cool voice, describing his role in the household: '*I see myself as my mother's protector*.' Did that extend to covering up for the apple of her eye if he was responsible for a ghastly tragedy?

They had been out on Cober Pool together in a boat. There had been a 'secret'. Perhaps the 'secret' had been something heavy in a sack, needing two of them for balance while releasing it into the cold depths.

She closed her eyes. *Green darkness*...

In the small hours of Saturday morning Rowena arrived at her London flat, made a cup of weak tea and carried it into her chilly bedroom. Since the trip to Glastonbury she had done nothing but write; now she was three hundred and fifty miles away from Cornwall and forced to quell her surging impatience to revisit Cober Pool.

After a few hours' sleep she rose, showered and checked her mail over a scanty breakfast before telephoning her parents in Oman. Their conversation was, as ever, an exchange of superficial courtesies. She had never told them any details of her work in Cornwall – such explanations were best made in person – and they had not asked. June, she knew, would be discreet for the present.

That afternoon she drove to Haringey as arranged with Keith. He opened the door of his flat with a smile of welcome; in the background Harry loped about the floor, quite untrammelled.

'Hello, Keith. Harry won't escape, will he?'

'Hi. Good journey? Don't worry about Gordon. He's fully house-trained now. He wanders into everybody's room, chewing things...'

'You're giving him grass, I hope.'

'Everything on that diet sheet you left me. Carrots, bran, the lot.'

She picked up the rabbit and fondled the silky ears. 'He does seem to be in good condition,' she conceded. 'I'm not sure he knows me, though.'

'Perhaps they're not as bright as cats and dogs.'

She stared at him, sternly. 'Are you calling my rabbit – *limited*?' she asked.

He laughed as he led the way into the kitchen and made tea. The room was one of sticky disarray as befitted an all-male household, but was nevertheless infinitely more cheerful than the grey, life-sapping heart of Adrian Polzeath's farmstead. Highly coloured fridge magnets held various notes and shopping lists; one paper read: 'Keith – Chloe rang. 7.30 p.m.'

'Who is Chloe?' she asked.

'Oh – we've taken on a new junior reporter. I'm showing her the ropes. We went out for a drink the other night.'

'Ah. Do you think she'll be any good at the job?'

'It's too early to tell...' They spent a pleasant hour reviewing gossip and office politics, while Keith's flatmates passed back and forth injecting casual comments. Eventually, they both left and the house was quiet.

'Tell me what's been happening in Cornwall,' said Keith.

Rowena gave him an honest account of events since their last discussion, feeling unusually defensive and tense. Convictions which could thrive in the West Country's Celtic ambience seemed suddenly flimsier here in the happy chaos of this London flat. She watched Keith's face as she spoke; despite his expression of benign concentration, she sensed he was struggling to hide dismay.

'So...' he said lightly when she had finished. 'You think Ellie was killed locally and her body may be in Cober Pool, possibly dumped there by Daniel and Brett. Are you going to forget about Patrick, then?'

'No. Patrick could still have done it. Or maybe they were both killed. It depends very much on the reason... but I haven't yet been able to confirm if Ellie *was* seen alive the day after Patrick's disappearance, as the prevailing story goes.'

'I made some enquiries,' said Keith. 'One of Peter's detective pals checked to see if a Patrick Sullivan has any form. There were several of them, but all the wrong age and description.'

'It could be an alias anyway,' she said gloomily. 'Next week I'll pull out all the stops and try to get hold of a photograph. People are always taking snaps at village fêtes.'

'Good...' He lapsed into an uncomfortable silence, then glanced across the table at Rowena. 'Ro...' he began.

'I know what you're thinking.'

'What – another clairvoyant?' His genuine amusement momentarily cleared the air. 'Seriously, Ro,' he went on, 'you were obviously very impressed by this Mary in Glastonbury. You said she conjured Ellie's name out of nowhere... Did it occur to you that that could have been an innocent case of telepathy? Ellie was at the forefront of your mind.'

She shook her head firmly. 'I believe in Mary. That wasn't the way it happened.'

'I wasn't suggesting fraud, or anything. I'm sure she was trying to help. I just wondered whether the words of one psychic are enough reason to reach the hard conclusion that Ellie is dead.'

'She's dead. And she'll be found in Cober Pool.'

'You'll never persuade the police to drain it or send down divers on that evidence.'

'They do sometimes ask for psychic help themselves.'

'I know – but only when they've already got a case. Ellie is still just a missing adult who's done something similar before.'

'She's *dead*, Keith.'

He gave a mute nod. Conversation flagged; Keith opened the kitchen door and for a few minutes they watched Harry snuffling at the chair legs. Eventually Rowena broke the silence. 'You said you went to a medium, Keith.'

'Yes.'

'How did you feel?'

'You want the truth? She *got* to me, sitting with all these believers in a dark church hall. There was definitely an atmosphere... But afterwards, I analysed her tricks. "I have here someone who spent time away from this country but passed on after returning home." How many people *haven't* got some relative whose war service could be described in that way? And people who have died of heart or lung disease…twice she made a gesture of cupping her mouth and nose, saying, "There's something in front of his face," and the widow would nod enthusiastically and cry, "It's him!" All thanks to that rarity, the oxygen mask.'

'It made you angry,' observed Rowena.

'I'll say. It's a sham, Ro. A nasty, cynical sham perpetrated by con artists with a bit of a talent for psychology. There's even a jargon, faithfully parroted by the groupies…sorry, you did ask.'

'I know. I only wish you could spend some time with Caireen.'

After Glastonbury, Rowena had come very close to confiding in Caireen. It seemed perverse to be employed by arguably the best medium in the country, and not make use of her skills. Surely Ellie would come through…The possibility of Danny's involvement, however, forestalled her. Ruefully she realized that she may have joined forces with Brett in a tacit conspiracy of silence…

'…Italian, then?' she heard Keith saying.

'Er, yes.'

'I'll book it now.'

Keith clearly loved his pasta. In the vibrant scarlet confines of Tivoli that evening he demolished a Vesuvius-sized mountain of tagliatelli with rodent-like dedication, while discussing matters psychic with focused intelligence.

'I've been reading about your Eileen Garrett,' he said. 'Remarkable woman.'

Rowena sipped at her mellow Rosso di Puglia. 'She's more Caireen's heroine than mine, but you're right. She was a phenomenon in her time. Look at the airship disaster, when the R101 crashed in northern France in 1930 and burst into flames. At a seance three days later she spouted all kinds of technical jargon from the dead captain, explaining what had gone wrong. He also mentioned the airship almost scraping the roofs at Achy, and the people who analysed the transcript had no idea where this was. It took a special, enlarged railway map to show that Achy was a village near to Beauvais where the final crash occurred. I was all the more impressed because it was actually Conan Doyle she was trying to contact in that seance. He'd died not long before.'

'Ah, yes – Sir Arthur. He embraced spiritualism with fervour, didn't he – after all those years writing about the cold logic of Sherlock Holmes.'

She shot him a narrow glance. 'Doesn't that tell you something?'

'I think he's a prime example of the zeal of the proselyte. I think he was a decent, rather old-fashioned gentleman who took more things at face value than you might imagine. Unlike Harry Houdini, and the merciless psychic investigator Harry Price, I believe he simply didn't appreciate the *deviousness* of the fake mediums.'

'You *have* done your homework!'

He inclined his head graciously. 'It's an interesting subject,' he said. 'But Conan Doyle lost my vote when he endorsed the Cottingley fairies.'

Rowena knew about this hoax, when two young female Yorkshire cousins claimed to have met fairies at the bottom of their garden and photographed them. To their astonishment, they were believed, with even some individuals of the calibre of Sir Arthur Conan Doyle regarding the prints as genuine. She, too, found this particular episode difficult to justify. 'I think we're measuring the primitive technology of the era by our relatively sophisticated modern standards,' she said. 'People then were taken in by all kinds of images of mediums disgorging butter muslin "ectoplasm" which to us seem ridiculously obvious fakes... How about that famous "Nessie" photo from 1934? The one with an eel-like head and long neck poking above the water? Were you taken in?'

'I haven't given it much thought.'

'Well, thousands have, and accepted it as authentic. It's only just been established as a fake.'

'So you're saying that, given time, all apparently wondrous and unaccountable events will prove to have some dull, earthbound explanation,' he said cunningly.

'No, I wasn't. I was simply saying, don't judge Conan Doyle by modern criteria.'

*

Rowena was troubled by her inability to explain to Keith the basis for her increasing conviction about the legitimacy of spiritualism. The thin common ground of intelligent enquiry which she had thought they shared was becoming very shaky indeed as their viewpoints migrated unswervingly towards opposite poles. Healthy argument was one thing, but too much dissent could break up a friendship she was keen to preserve.

In Caireen's study the next week she tried to clarify her thoughts. The more she herself understood, the more she could explain to others. 'You must meet a lot of people who expect spiritualism to be black and white, and won't tolerate the shades of grey,' she said.

Caireen put down her notebook and leaned back in the easy chair. 'That's true. Mediums can be unlucky or incompetent, just like anybody else, yet someone might visit a single medium having a difficult session, and have their perception blighted for ever after. We are condemned for saying, "Edward – no, Edgar," but people don't realize that the sound is like a very distant telephone connection, faint and crackling with static. I have to concentrate ferociously to turn the impression of sound into something meaningful in my head. And sometimes several individuals are vying for my attention all at once.'

'Do you think mediums have a sensory apparatus that the rest of us lack?'

'I don't know. There are those who believe anyone can be a medium if they have the correct motivation and are properly trained. That would suggest we all have the "apparatus". I'm not so sure myself. I've seen a lot of amateurs, very giving people who provide much comfort within their community, whose accuracy nevertheless remains low throughout their ministry – and I've seen others who are stunningly gifted mediums even when they have barely begun any training.'

Rowena looked down at the rich fleecy rug between them. 'Do you see the spirit world as a kind of extra dimension co-existing with our own world?'

Caireen laughed. 'I'm afraid you've got the wrong person if you want to discuss the science of the afterlife... I view my work as more of an art.'

Only science would satisfy Keith, thought Rowena. Belief had no currency at all. 'I suppose I'm saying that if their form is simply a kind of *energy*, then they don't take up *space*, so there's room for them all...'

'Well, certainly their images seem to be transmitted on particular wavelengths which are not visible to most people...'

'Just mediums and animals!' burst out Rowena.

'Just mediums and animals.' Caireen smiled. 'And a few other susceptible individuals. We're back to apparatus, aren't we? Mallards can, I believe, see in the ultraviolet part of the spectrum.

Pigeons, too. What do they see? Supposing we could all "see" X-rays? How would they appear?'

Slowly they were creeping towards an explanation of sorts. Rowena remembered that Daniel had mentioned 'energy' in the context of auras. 'People who see auras must have special sensory perceptions,' she said. 'Danny was saying...' Abruptly Caireen's face clouded over. Damn, damn, damn, thought Rowena. '...he read about it once,' she finished up.

'Yes. It was a phase he went through. I sincerely hope he's not still pursuing that subject. Danny has special problems of his own. Being my son is one of them. However rudimentary his skills someone, somewhere, may well try to exploit them. Danny could both cause harm and be harmed.' She gave a small shake of the head, as if to shrug off the topic. 'It was good of you to take him to Somerset last week,' she said. 'I knew he was in safe hands...' Another well-meaning catechism on the historic heritage of Glastonbury followed, but Rowena was by now well prepared and fielded the questions confidently.

'Have lunch with me,' said Caireen, standing up. 'I'll take you to the Mount this afternoon. I've been promising ever since you came, and the tide will be just right. We'll leave the boys behind – this shall be our trip.'

Her protests about work overridden, Rowena thoroughly enjoyed the outing. Mount's Bay was wide and sunny, and the low calm waters had exposed the causeway to the island; she relished the sharp smell of seaweed as they walked across to the tiny harbour. Soon they were climbing the steep cobbled pathway up to the castle, once a priory, glimpsing blue sea through the dense canopy of trees. They paused on a rocky outcrop near the summit, where a battery of cannon pointed across the shimmering bay towards Penzance and Newlyn.

'This is one end of the Michael Line,' said Caireen. 'Apparently the Archangel Michael appeared to some fishermen on this side of the Mount in the fifth century. The actual Benedictine priory was built later, though – in the twelfth century. It's linked with the Mont St Michel in Normandy.'

Inside the castle they saw plaster friezes, Chippendale furniture and numerous pictures of the Mount through the ages, from military sieges to portraits of the resident family. The chapel seemed to underline the fact that this was a home as well as a national treasure.

'Thank you – it's been splendid!' said Rowena as they carefully descended the slippery cobbles.

'It's been nice for me, too; I saw everything through fresh eyes.'

Down in the harbour they caught sight of a plumpish woman in a bright print dress emerging from one of the terraced cottages. 'Isn't that Miss Granger?' murmured Rowena.

Madeleine came towards them, smiling sociably. 'Hello, Caireen... Rowena. Lovely day, isn't it? I was just visiting old Elsie Blackett. I shall ransack the National Trust shop for birthday gifts while I'm here. Have you been up to the castle, Rowena? Ah, good. You enjoyed it? Excellent...' She turned to Caireen, and it seemed to Rowena that there was a subtle cooling of her cordial tone. 'Charles has left a message on your answer-phone. He has an engagement tomorrow afternoon which may overrun, so he'd prefer to collect you at seven thirty, if that's convenient?'

'Tell him yes, that would be fine.'

Rowena pricked up her ears whilst overtly studying the tranquillity of the harbour. So Caireen would be out the following evening? That was helpful; she wanted to revisit Cober Pool as soon as possible, but on a night when her absence was least likely to be noticed. Unnecessary lies were best avoided...

When Madeleine had gone they returned to the shore across the causeway. The tide was rising; wavelets lapped the sides with increasing persistence, and Caireen gave a little shriek of excited laughter as water skimmed across the stones in front of them. 'Quick, Rowena! Before the next one!'

They were just in time to avoid removing their shoes, and soon ran chuckling on to the firm sand of Marazion beach. 'Let's have an ice-cream!' suggested Caireen.

Rowena was amused by this new, off-duty side to her employer's character. She suspected that Caireen spent much of her time locked into a part, fulfilling the expectations of those around her; now, just for once, she could let rip.

They strolled in the late afternoon sunshine eating strawberry ice-creams, laughed again as a very wet dog tried to seize Rowena's cone, and watched barefooted tourists paddling determinedly across the causeway, heading for the Mount. 'Don't worry,' said Caireen. 'They can come back by boat.'

Rowena sniffed the salty breeze which was rippling her hair. She felt as if she was on holiday with a benign adoptive mother;

strange, she couldn't remember feeling so relaxed with her own parents.

Caireen turned to her. 'I feel as if I've been lent a daughter,' she said. Rowena smiled.

Back at Uplands, the house was deserted. Rowena made tea and carried it into Caireen's study.

'Thank you,' said Caireen, accepting the cup. 'I hope you're happy with us, Rowena.'

'Oh, definitely.'

'I don't know... I've felt for a time that something has been bothering you, something isn't quite right. If I can help in any way...'

Rowena gave a small shrug. 'I might seem preoccupied sometimes when I'm working out descriptive phrases for the book or the articles... I do a lot in my head when I'm out walking, for instance.'

'Perhaps that's it. But if there's anything else, do let me know. I've sensed recently that someone is trying to contact you, someone from the spirit world, but maybe it's a false signal...'

Rowena's tea slopped into its saucer. 'Sorry,' she muttered. 'Do you – do you know who it is?'

'No. We'd have to sit quietly together and be properly receptive.'

Keith's voice seemed to hiss warnings in her ear, but Rowena was transfixed. You can't, she told herself. What if there's talk of murder? What if Danny is named?

Sooner or later, though, the truth was going to emerge. That was her entire reason for being here. If Ellie needed to make contact, and couldn't get through...

'Do you mean a proper sitting? A private one?' Her voice sounded thin.

'Yes. In the consulting-room. We're both free, and it's quiet just now. But only if you want, Rowena. Only if it would help.' Caireen gave an encouraging smile and waited.

A small upper window was open, and Rowena could hear the slow surge of the sea against the foot of Graw Head. Once... twice ... three times it swelled and faded. She tried to visualize Ellie's face, but it was indistinct.

'Yes,' she whispered.

9

The room with the purple curtains was cool with a faint, sweetly acrid smell like incense. The window was covered, and the only lighting came from the ceiling lamp's shaded bulb.

Caireen was sitting opposite Rowena in a high-backed Dralon chair. She had smilingly eschewed wearing her 'regalia' on this occasion, but her authority was tangible. After a quiet chat about what might or might not happen, and a few minutes' meditation, she was now staring intently at a spot just behind Rowena's left shoulder. 'Someone is with us,' she said softly. 'I can feel their presence, but I can't quite see... It's a person who used to know you well, but whom you haven't seen for some years...'

Three years, thought Rowena. If I hadn't been so damned busy with my job in London I'd have visited Ellie when she returned to the fold. I sent her a *fax*, for God's sake!

'Definitely family,' murmured Caireen. 'Passed over young... oh!' She sounded startled. 'It's that little boy!'

Rowena's heart seemed to give a great lurch. 'Oliver?' she whispered.

'Yes. He came suddenly. He says he was hiding. Young rascal! He's showing me a toy. An aeroplane – no, a helicopter. Quite a large helicopter.'

Rowena bit her lip as painful emotions flooded through her. 'I know that toy,' she said.

'It's blue.'

She nodded.

'It's all right, he's saying. He keeps repeating that.'

Still she nodded.

'I think he feels you've suffered for a long time, and there's no need. His actual words are, it's okay, it's okay. He's grinning. He keeps repeating the words. I think he's trying to put across some other meaning – is it a joke, perhaps? He seems very merry. "It's okay" – he's just said it again.'

'Oliver Kemp,' said Rowena. 'His initials were OK. He was always amused by that.'

'Oh. I see. He says you were naughty about the helicopter but he forgave you long ago.'

'I should have known better.'

'He says he was often naughty, too. You're to stop worrying about the things you did because you were young yourself at the time. It doesn't matter now. He's happy, and he wants you to be happy. He's going off to play now. Goodbye, little laddie...'

Once more Rowena's eyes pricked with tears. She drew her fingers across her cheek, and swallowed tenaciously.

Caireen seemed to be poised, waiting, listening. 'I thought...I thought there was someone else just then, but they've gone away. Everyone has gone. Yes...' She blinked and her face seemed to relax and become normal. 'Was that helpful?' she asked.

'Yes. Thank you, Caireen. That helped a lot.' She stumbled to her feet, blurted out more thanks and left the room. The house was beginning to hum with activity. She could hear Mrs Trelowan preparing dinner in the kitchen, and Brett was just entering through the front door. Behind him was Danny. Rowena fled up the stairs; she couldn't cope with Danny right now.

Upstairs she sat on her bed and stared out at the vivid evening sky. As her focus drifted to the farthest reaches, images seemed to gather at the edge of her vision, but as soon as she looked at them directly, they vanished.

'Oliver.' She spoke with her mind. 'You're out there somewhere...' She reviewed his short childhood, the outings, holidays and special Christmases. 'I felt excluded so much of the time,' she admitted. 'Father had always wanted a boy. I was jealous of you...'

Reluctantly she tore herself away to shower and prepare for dinner, because Caireen had particularly requested her presence. But afterwards, as the light slowly faded and a single star peeped out from behind the clouds, she sent special messages to a little boy with blond hair.

*

At eight thirty the following evening, Rowena stood on Cober Bar, her swimsuit beneath the outer slacks and shirt, and seethed with frustration. Her provisional plan, in which she would make repeated surface dives in the deepest part of the pool before dusk approached, seemed already doomed to failure. She had imagined that the area would be deserted by this time of the evening, with any tourists safely back at their hotels. Instead, couples were strolling along the seaward side of the bar, two men with backpacks had just emerged from the eastern lakeside walk, and another man was actually ensconced on a rug with his book opposite the very spot where she would need to enter the water.

Keith, at least, would be pleased, she thought – if he knew. She could well imagine his lecture on the hazards of diving alone to the obscure depths of an uncharted pool. He would expound on dangers both physical and microbiological – and he would be right.

With a sigh, she passed the lone reader and gained the western path to the tree plantation. If she walked the mile to the boathouse, she might just find some clue in the dinghy itself...

Once beyond the trees, she moved more carefully. Cober House was close by, and while Colonel Granger was with Caireen at a concert in Penzance (Mrs Trelowan was always well informed), Madeleine might conceivably be taking a post-prandial stroll along the lakeside. Out across the water, cat's paws of wind began to ruffle the smooth surface. She saw a branch wallowing sluggishly near the centre, something blue caught up with it. It seemed incongruous – the lake was otherwise immaculate.

Frowning, Rowena tried to identify the blue item, but it was too far away. This can't possibly be relevant, she told herself: not after all this time. Anything dropped on the water nine months ago would have drifted to the shore.

A man with a slouch hat and binoculars came past and murmured a greeting – a birdwatcher, presumably. She longed to snatch the field glasses from around his neck. As she cautiously approached Cober House she saw other people on the opposite side of the inlet, close to the boathouse itself. This is *hopeless*, she thought, gritting her teeth in frustration. Only after dark will it be safe to investigate, and then I shan't be able to see a thing myself! Heavily she plodded back to the Clio, which was parked near the bar. She climbed in and returned to Uplands.

The sound of a television reached her ears as she crept through the hall. Just as she passed the drawing-room door it opened, and Daniel appeared. 'I hoped it was you,' he said. 'Do you want to watch a video with me? Mother is out and Brett's not interested. He's no fun.'

'Er, thanks, Danny, but I've still a few things to sort out.'

'*Please*, Rowena. It's so boring on my own.'

She glanced at her watch. 'Not a whole film, if you don't mind, but perhaps a bit of television.'

He jigged up and down on the spot. 'Great! I'll get some toast and Marmite.'

She sat with him for an hour before making her excuses. Upstairs she changed her outer garments for darker ones, then padded out to the Clio with a bag containing a torch and a large screwdriver. As she opened the driver's door (why did it have to *creak* like that?) she realized that a towel might be a good idea. Leaving the door ajar, she glided back to the bedroom to fetch one. She could still hear the television as she returned to the car.

Brett's Mercedes, like Caireen's Golf, was still in its place as she drove slowly up the rocky headland track. Ten minutes later she was once more parking at Cober Pool, this time in the tree-shrouded public car-park behind Cober House. It was now eleven fifteen, and moonlight fitfully silvered the bushes as she negotiated the narrow, steeply sloping paths which led to the lake-side. Lights still shone in Cober House; she gave that vicinity as wide a berth as possible as she made her way to the boathouse.

The moon vanished behind a cloud just as she approached the structure: a mixed blessing. To the soft lap of breeze-blown water she hooded the torch with her hand, switched it on and commenced an external examination of the building.

It projected into the water, as befitted its function, and she had previously noted in daylight the double doors facing the lake. There was, however, an additional door at the side, secured by a rusting padlock. The padlock itself proved to be welded shut, but the hasp it embraced felt loose: with a little leverage from her screwdriver the attachment suddenly extruded from the rotting wood like a tooth from an unhealthy jaw. The door juddered open; she slipped inside and closed it behind her.

The wet, musty smell was all-enveloping. Immediately underfoot was a narrow jetty, its timbers dank and unstable; a short blind piece of rope hung from a post at the end. The dinghy she had glimpsed before was not floating in the foot or so of water at the distal end of the boathouse, but had been pulled bow-first on to the bank. Only the stern was lapped with water.

There *was* a painter, she noticed, but it hung down into the dinghy, unattached to any boathouse structure. The rowlocks and oars looked functional, but the dinghy itself seemed very elderly and dilapidated. Rowena experienced a stab of doubt; had Danny merely been spinning a tale to make himself sound mysterious?

She ran the torch-beam from end to end of the small boat, but saw nothing that might constitute a clue to his presence or Brett's. With a sigh, she made up her mind. Gingerly she clambered down from the jetty, pushed at the bow of the dinghy, and with effort refloated it. Scrambling inside, she used her hands and the jetty's wooden struts to edge the craft to the main double doors of the boathouse; if they were locked or silted up, her expedition would come to a premature end.

The play of the torch-beam revealed a two-foot length of timber bolting the doors together. There was nothing else... Stretching upwards, Rowena managed to lift out the wedge and place it on the jetty. Nudging at the left-hand door with the dinghy, she suddenly saw a shaft of moonlight.

As she emerged on to the lake, Rowena felt very exposed. The moon was merciless, a splendid pearl glowing in a large clear patch of sky. If she waited for the next obscuring cloud, there would be little to gain; the bright spotlight would reappear long before she had completed her task. Ignoring a sensation that the lakeside vegetation was bristling with observers, she swung the boat round with quiet strokes of the oars then set off decisively for the point at which she had seen the floating branch.

It was much further than she remembered. The shoreline landmarks she had carefully noted that evening were now lost in a dark, brooding coalescence of trees. As the moon made a sudden exit behind a cloud, the blackness seemed absolute. Rowena shipped the oars and paused to think; the same mild breeze that now slapped wavelets against the dinghy's hull could already have altered irrevocably the position of the branch. This could turn out to be the proverbial wild-goose chase...

Moonlight returned, a softer, more filtered glow. Unwilling to accept defeat, Rowena bent to the oars and continued sculling. The dinghy had now entered the narrower part of the pool, but the shoreline nevertheless appeared horribly distant. Something wasn't quite right... the horizon seemed higher, somehow, the water closer. Suddenly she realized why. Her feet were wet.

With a rush of dismay she turned her attention to the bottom of the boat. Some three inches of water had seeped inside through an unseen defect in the ancient planking. If it carried on at the same rate she must head back to shore now or be totally swamped.

Rowena searched in vain for a bailer; nothing remotely suitable presented itself. Torn by indecision she craned her neck in every direction to try to locate the branch – surely it couldn't be far away. It would be criminal to waste all this effort... Once more the moonlight vanished, this time with a brief smoky residue like a candle snuffed out. She willed herself to remain calm and patient. The lake in its dark shroud seemed infinitely long and wide, herself an insect perched on a flake of bark above its cold cryptic fathoms. Silence stretched across the valley, broken only by a faint moan from the plantation as the wind gathered momentum again. After ten minutes the light had not yet returned. Rowena pulled the torch from her pocket and scanned the pool's wind-ruffled surface to the limits of its beam. Nothing. She rowed a hundred yards and repeated the process. *Something* discrepant was wallowing off to starboard, low in the water... She bent to the oars and swung the boat on to a convergence course, feeling wetness slosh around her ankles.

As she approached the object she allowed herself to feel excited – it was definitely a branch. Nearer still, her torch-beam picked out the material caught up with it, no longer blue in the colour-bleached drabness of night but identifiable by shape as the scrap she had seen earlier...

She pulled alongside and grasped at the crumpled material as the bearer branch gently scraped the hull. It felt harsh, more like plastic. She shipped the oars and spread her find across the thwart in front of her, then snorted in self-mockery and deep disappointment. This had once been a child's beach ball, but was now merely a sad, punctured remnant. No blue dress, no overall, no clue – just a child's ruined toy.

Now she was forced to look to her own situation. The dinghy was becoming unwieldy, and it was a long way back to the boathouse. Reversing her course, she rowed as smoothly as possible to minimize the shifting of the water weight inside the boat. The leak had to be somewhere near the bows – the stern had floated freely in the boathouse – but knowing its general position was no help here: the entire craft was sinking, its gunwales now alarmingly close to the choppy surface of the lake. How long ago had Daniel ridden in this dinghy? Had it been watertight then? Questions hovered at the periphery of her brain, but she pushed them aside. Getting this leaden vessel back to shore was the current priority.

Her shoulders ached as she continued to row, glancing round periodically to check on distance and direction. She didn't know which was worse, darkness with its capacity to enlarge the lake to infinite proportions and make sinister each slap of water against the hull, or the intermittent silverings of moonshine which rekindled her impression of hidden watchers...

Supposing I meet Madeleine on the shore, she thought. How on *earth* am I to explain what I've been doing?

The dinghy was now canting, one gunwale almost underwater. To her relief the boathouse had just come into view, angular against the surrounding bushes. At all costs the dinghy must be saved... Shipping the oars again she slid over the side into the chest-high water and carefully steered the craft into the shallows. The double doors loomed; with a final burst of effort she manoeuvred the ponderous bulk inside and grounded it against the shoreline.

She paused, soaked and gasping for breath. It seemed colder now outside the water: she was sweating and shivering all at once. Torchlight revealed an empty paint tin lying in a nearby corner. She picked it up and began to bail water from the dinghy. As she bent for yet another tinful a sharp report sounded from just outside the boathouse.

She froze. That noise – surely it was a dry twig snapping under the weight of a foot...a human foot. Switching off the torch she ducked beneath the jetty at the shallow end, and waited.

A minute passed, then two, and she began to doubt her interpretation. Some other nocturnal creature, perhaps, crashing around in the undergrowth. A badger? They could be pretty heavy. Or –

A creak from the door above sent her theories into oblivion. For several suspended seconds she *knew* that someone was peering in, unable to identify much in the darkness, but wondering if anybody was there...

Blood pounded high in her chest as she gripped the nearest rotting stanchion. She heard a footfall and a distant rustle, then nothing further. Nevertheless, she remained motionless for another ten minutes.

Bailing furiously whilst trying to keep quiet – something of a paradox, she found – Rowena eventually managed to lighten the dinghy enough to push it back to its original position. The residual bit of water was just too bad.

At last she was back in the Clio, creeping away from the Cober estate. As she gained the main road she accelerated thankfully, anxious to put distance between herself and her latest fiasco. Only now was she able to consider the implications of the holed dinghy. 'We took it once,' Danny had said. That suggested lack of permission, as did his insistence that it was a 'secret' he shared with Brett. Forget Danny, she thought. Concentrate on Brett's motivation.

Caireen had only lived at Uplands for nine years, so Brett would have been an adult, as suave and sophisticated as he was currently. What would have induced him to seize a neighbour's ancient rowing boat for a covert trip with Danny when he could hire, buy or openly borrow a perfectly good one? Lack of time, perhaps. Some situation where he needed a boat and deep water in a big hurry and only one place fulfilled his criteria...

She turned off at the Anwith sign, and drove carefully through the village. Had Brett received the same shock as she had while out on the lake – a sinking dinghy made worse by the extra load of Danny (not to mention any other cargo)? Perhaps the hole had simply been smaller then, the leak a minor nuisance. Indeed, if her earlier speculations were correct and the two men had rowed the length of Cober Pool to the deepest part near the bar, the hole *must* have been smaller – or non-existent.

Rowena gave a wry smile in the darkness. She had a lot of respect for Brett's sharp brain. If the dinghy had been intact, though elderly, he may have deliberately made subtle damage to the planking *after* the trip. That way, no one would imagine that the boat could ever have been used for such a purpose.

The Mercedes was still parked outside Uplands. Rowena retrieved her bag from the Clio's front seat, locked the car then ran her hand over the Mercedes' bonnet. There was no discernible engine warmth. If the person who alarmed her in the boathouse had been Brett, he could have arrived back here no more than twenty minutes before her. Danny had no transport... Perhaps it had been Madeleine, or maybe Charles had spotted something on his return.

Her clothes were filthy and still damp; Rowena padded round to the side entrance which led to the utility passage. A low light burned in the kitchen, perhaps left on by Caireen after making a nightcap for Charles. Surely no one was about at this hour...

'Hello, Miss Kemp.' The tall shape of Brett appeared in the kitchen doorway.

'Mr Saunders.' This was ludicrous. Everyone else in the household called her Rowena.

He was holding a whisky glass in his hand. 'Would you care to join me? This is a very mellow single malt.'

'I – I'd better be going upstairs.'

'Oh, come on! You look as if you could do with a drink. You're soaking wet.'

She felt obliged to answer the unspoken question. 'I've been a bit reckless. I went for a moonlight swim in Graw Cove. Please don't tell Caireen.'

'I thought I just heard your car.'

'Well, yes. I drove to that public car-park near the National Trust mine. It's a long haul otherwise, climbing the cliff path and then crossing Graw Head.'

'So you're not a total fitness fanatic. That's a relief.' He moved to a kitchen counter and poured her a generous measure of the spirit. 'Here. Between you and me, though, I must ask you not to do this again. Graw doesn't have the undertow you get further along the coast, but it's still dangerous at night. We don't want our writer to drown – at least, not before the book's finished.'

She laughed dutifully, but his own smile was unreadable.

'Did Caireen enjoy her evening?' she asked.

'Yes. The Cornwall Chamber Orchestra was performing in St John's Hall. She and Charles are both fond of music.'

Affecting relaxation, Rowena finished her whisky and rinsed the glass. 'Thanks,' she said. 'I'll be off now. Goodnight.'

He stood between her and the door. Taking a backward step, he made an ushering motion of the hand, but as she drew level he sprang forwards with the silent grace of a panther and seized her by the shoulders. 'Goodnight,' he echoed before clamping his mouth firmly to hers.

For a few seconds she stood rigid, then as his grip tightened she found herself beginning to respond. It was several fallow months since Sebastian had left her, months of staving off a series of boorish males who assumed she was desperate. Brett Saunders was tall, good-looking, intelligent, generally fastidious . . . and possibly accessory to a murder.

She broke away, breathing heavily. '*Droit de seigneur*?' she asked him with contempt.

'I didn't know you were about to be married.'

'You know what I mean. A power play.'

'Actually, I thought you looked quite attractive. Your shirt is all plastered down.'

Rowena was angry, not least with herself. 'I suppose that's how you treated the last writer you had here?'

'The typist, Miss Drinkwater?' He gave a non-committal shrug. 'I think her preference was for children and hippies.'

Friendship with Daniel, goodness knows what with Patrick... 'I'm going to bed,' she told him sharply.

'Is that an invitation?'

'Certainly not.'

'Pity. I could have sworn you were interested. Ah well...'

She wiped the back of her hand against her mouth as she strode past him and climbed the stairs to her room. Peeling off the sodden clothes her unease increased. They reeked of mud and lake water, not salt and seaweed. Her hair wasn't even wet. Did Brett know she was lying? Was he playing cat and mouse all over again?

As she lay soaking in the bath she reprised her alarm when the boathouse door had creaked open. Perhaps that earlier feeling of being watched had been genuine, after all. If not one of the Grangers, could the watcher conceivably have been someone from Uplands?

With a stab of dismay, she realized that she had not checked the Golf for engine heat. Brett could easily have borrowed his mother's car, followed Rowena to Cober Pool and observed her amateur thrashings from the safety of the hide. He would have seen her clumsy return to the boathouse, allowed a few minutes for her to leave, then come along the path to ensure the dinghy was left in its previous position. (The attention of the Grangers must not be drawn to the boat.) As it was, Rowena was still inside, and so he had reached Uplands before her...

She soaped the length of her left arm, exhausted in body but mentally simmering. What about Danny? she thought. He can't drive. It *can't* have been him, unless...

She remembered returning to the house for the towel, leaving the Clio unlocked. Supposing Danny had been watching, bored, and crept into the back? It was dark, and he could have huddled under her tartan travelling rug... She had placed her bag and towel on the front passenger seat and driven away, preoccupied...

At Cober he could have given her a head start, relocked the Clio doors then tracked her to the boathouse. Her destination would have been obvious to him. And afterwards...

If it was Danny, she thought fiercely, then he's walking back from Cober right now! How far is it? Four miles, five? Hilly terrain. He wouldn't be back yet...

Galvanized, she rinsed the suds quickly under the shower and leapt out of the bath. Towelling herself dry she pulled on a bathrobe and padded out into the corridor. If Danny was not in his room...

A door opened. She half turned, but wasn't quick enough. There stood Brett (again!), wearing his own dressing-gown of silk with a rather fetching Liberty print design. 'Changed your mind?' he whispered, eyes glittering darkly above a wide grin.

'Of course not. I thought I heard a noise, that's all.'

'Must have been Brother having a nightmare. He does sometimes.'

She returned to her room with as much grace as she could muster and sat on the bed. Another notion had just occurred to her. If Danny had indeed stowed away in the Clio, that might not have been his first such venture. She had assumed that he had accompanied Brett in the dinghy either for practical purposes – necessary ballast, an extra pair of hands – or because it was a joint enterprise which his own activities had rendered necessary. But supposing Danny had been merely spying on his brother and been caught? Brett would have been forced to include him then, and swear him to secrecy...

Could the killer in fact be Brett himself?

At breakfast the next morning Caireen noticed nothing amiss. Brett was as cool and courteous as ever, and Danny ate with gusto, though he yawned continuously.

Rowena drank plenty of black coffee, furious with herself for falling asleep when she had intended to listen out for nocturnal doors. 'Was it a good concert?' she asked Caireen.

'Yes, thank you.' After a brief discussion of the programme she turned to Daniel. 'Danny, I do wish you'd remember to turn off the television when you go to bed. It wasn't very nice to find it blaring away when I invited Charles into the drawing-room.'

'Sorry, Mother,' he mumbled. He yawned again.

10

'I gather last year's fête was a good one,' said Rowena conversationally to Bill in the Tinner's Reach that evening.

'It was,' he agreed, pausing from polishing the glasses on a large tray. 'Lovely weather, lots of people and a general spirit of fun.'

The pub was deserted except for the two of them; Rowena had deliberately come early to catch him alone. 'I heard Daniel Malone won the boot-throwing contest,' she said. 'That must have been quite entertaining to watch!'

He chuckled. 'All those Young Farmers – my dear life, their faces! Here, see for yourself.' He came out from behind the bar and beckoned her into an alcove where a scattering of framed pictures hung so high on the wall as to be almost out of sight. 'That one there, Brian Pascoe, *he* expected to win, but young Daniel just seemed to have the technique.'

As he chatted about the tug-of-war, tombolas and Guessing the Weight of the Cake, Rowena's eyes flicked to each photograph in turn. On one, a blurred background figure stood rock-like with arms raised and a fiddle under his chin. There was an impression of untidy blond hair beneath the green floppy hat which obscured much of his face. 'You had live music?' she asked.

'Oh – him. Yes, he played for us, and very jolly it was, but nobody knew then what he was hatching. He's the one who robbed Adrian Polzeath.'

'Really? This man? He looks like a traveller. Did Adrian invite him to the fête?'

Bill frowned thoughtfully. 'Adrian never goes, and I'm not even sure they'd met at that point. No... I remember, Daniel Malone and Ellie, the girl who did your job last year, were helping Mrs Trelowan with the home produce stall. This feller walked over from Penzance and joined them. Ellie had asked him... that's right. People said Daniel wasn't best pleased. Perhaps he threw the boot to impress her...'

'Have you got any more pictures, Bill?'

'Sorry, just these few. Ginnie Carloose took a lot of photographs, I recall. Her husband may have scarpered, but he left his camera behind. She tried to sell them to the local press to make a bit of money, but they didn't buy any. There was only a small column of print in the paper.'

'Well, I must admit my editor keeps asking me for descriptions of rural life, and if Ginnie's pictures are any good, we might just make her an offer for one. I may have gone back to London by the time this year's fête comes around, and library pictures are always useful...Tell Ginnie if you see her. If she's interested, let me know next time I come in. There's no rush...'

Scarcely true, she thought, but she needed to play a cool hand with Ginette; the girl must not suspect that her prints were of any real importance. 'By the way,' she added, 'I'm playing chess with Adrian tomorrow. Thanks to you, we have the odd game.'

Bill's face cracked into a sincere beam of pleasure. 'Proper job!' he exclaimed. 'I'm really glad to hear that. He used to be such a different man...we want our Adrian back again.'

The following evening Rowena parked in the small widening of the lane outside Adrian's farm. In her bag she carried a bottle of Australian Shiraz.

As she walked past the deserted end cottage which had been Patrick Sullivan's temporary home, she heard the sound of a door opening behind her. Moments later Ginette drew alongside, out of breath from her short scamper.

'Bill at the pub says you want to look at my photographs,' she blared accusingly.

Rowena paused. 'He mentioned that you took some at the fête last year. I thought one might be useful to illustrate an article I'm writing, but obviously it depends on the quality.'

'It's a good camera! A Canon...You want to see them now?' Her manner was both eager and truculent in equal measure.

'There's no urgency,' said Rowena, beginning to walk again. 'I've got an engagement right now. How about tomorrow? Shall I come at lunch time?'

'I might be busy myself then,' pouted Ginette.

Pull the other one...'I'm considering several sources. If it's not convenient, we can leave it if you prefer.'

'Oh...I suppose I could be in. One o'clock?'

'That would be fine.'

As she knocked on Adrian's kitchen door, Rowena put Ginette to the back of her mind. Her hand tightened around the neck of the wine bottle: tonight she was going to get some answers from Farmer Polzeath!

After a short delay he let her in with a diffident greeting. Almost immediately she detected a change in his kitchen – it was cleaner, brighter. The musty smell had gone. Adrian himself had also undergone a smartening process. He wore an attractive bottle-green cotton jumper, and his shave was closer than before.

'I need all the help I can get with this game,' said Rowena, offering him the wine. 'I want us to drink this.'

'Oh – right. Yes. You've had supper?'

She nodded.

'Then, er – hang on.' He ferreted in a cupboard and returned with a packet of Ritz crackers. 'I haven't got any fancy savouries. Will these do?'

'Perfectly.'

As they settled on either side of the large pine table where the chess board and pieces were set out, she noticed that he had even changed the light bulb for one with a higher wattage. That seemed to symbolize a genuine attempt to climb out of the bleak chasm of depression where he had existed for so long. She hoped that was true.

Idly, she wondered why he did his entertaining in the kitchen. The reason was probably prosaic – a cold and unpresentable sitting-room, perhaps. She didn't mind. On this occasion the kitchen was actually displaying hints of cosiness. With some decent curtains and a rug in front of the range it could become quite a haven...

He had found two long-stemmed glasses and poured the wine. 'Cheers,' he said reticently, nudging the curve of her glass with his own.

'Cheers,' she replied. 'Now you're going to thrash me.'

Given the white pieces, she made a standard opening, and concentrated on the game. When she managed to capture his bishop with a subtle discovered check, she strove to capitalize on the one-piece advantage, but his careful positional play forestalled her. Eventually she fell foul of a clever knight fork, and was forced to resign.

'I'm getting closer,' she smiled after congratulating him. 'I'll win yet.'

'I think you will.' They had finished the wine and his cheeks were faintly flushed. The new shy awkwardness she had noticed had now mellowed into an easier, friendly demeanour.

She bit into another cracker. 'Mrs Trelowan told me you own the cottages outside,' she said. 'I was wondering...That end one is empty; it would make a good holiday let. Have you ever considered renting it out?'

His gaze fell to the table. 'I always kept it for casual labourers. It's small. It's empty now because Tom from the village is helping me harvest the cabbages.'

'The centre cottage is bigger.'

'That one used to be tied for a permanent labourer.'

'But Ginette's husband left, didn't he? Can't you persuade her to find somewhere else?'

He stood up, fists clenching, and strode across the kitchen to a distant cupboard. After a brief search he found what he was looking for, another bottle of red wine, this one filmed with dust. With agitated movements he wiped the neck, removed the cork and poured a thin carmine stream into both their glasses.

'She won't go,' he said, taking a gulp of the wine. 'Ryan Carloose left this area two years ago. He was fed up with her playing around, though in truth he was no better himself. They weren't actually married... Anyway, I felt sorry for her and allowed her to stay a few months until she was sorted out. Big mistake.'

'Surely she has no legal right to possession?'

'None at all. But public opinion's a funny thing. Everyone in the village knows what a scrounging bitch on heat she is, yet the moment I started asking her nicely what plans she'd made the word "eviction" went round like a rash of measles and I was vilified as the uncaring landlord kicking out the poor deserted wife.'

'That's not fair!'

'Whoever said life was fair?' His cynical look was back, and mention of Ginette had been the trigger.

'She isn't your responsibility.'

'Well...' He took another drink and eyed Rowena's face appraisingly. 'It's not quite as simple as that. There was an occasion, long after Ryan had gone, when...' He paused, peered at her even more intently, then continued, apparently satisfied. 'It was a party. I didn't want to go, but I had my arm twisted. Ginette was there. I got a bit drunk, and... well, you heard her the other day in the pub. She shouted it from the rooftops. So people think there's *that* kind of link between us, and that's another reason she should stay.'

'You did sleep with her, though?'

'Just the once. Never again.' He shuddered. 'I needed to know if I could... I needed to feel alive again.' Abruptly he turned away. 'Sorry. This isn't what you came for.'

'Please... I'm interested. Not as a journalist, just between the two of us.'

'She seduced me. Pathetic, isn't it? I think it was all to do with the cottage and someone to pay her bills. When I told her I didn't want a relationship, she turned vicious.'

When was all this? wondered Rowena. She couldn't bring herself to ask.

She stood up. 'Would you be willing to show me the end cottage? Your idea of small might be someone else's *bijou*. Think of all the people who holiday in caravans.'

'You mean now?'

'Why not?'

'Well...' His agitation seemed to be subsiding. Indeed, a glimmer of amusement rippled across his lean features. 'I wonder why my guest keeps pushing the idea of a holiday let at me? Could it *possibly* be because she imagines I'm skint, on my uppers, any similar term she cares to employ?'

'Frankly, yes. There's potential income in that cottage. This is a splendid area for holidays. Farmers diversify all the time now. They have to.'

'You're talking to an expert – at getting it wrong.'

'Show me anyway,' she urged.

'If you insist.' He took a key from a drawer and they crossed the yard together in the wan light of approaching dusk. Adrian unlocked the cottage door and paused in the entrance. 'This place was left in a bit of a state by the last occupant. I'm afraid I never got round to clearing it up...'

As they stepped inside and switched on the light, she saw that he hadn't exaggerated. Domestic order had clearly not been a priority for Patrick Sullivan: the cottage was filthy, its spartan furniture in careless disarray.

'The police didn't improve things when they searched in here for some stolen property,' muttered Adrian. 'I should have tidied up afterwards. I just couldn't face it.' He glanced at Rowena. 'You heard about last year, I should imagine.'

'Yes. Odd remarks from Bill and Mrs Trelowan. I'm sorry.' With reluctance she focused their attention on the structure of the cottage, the minor alterations which could be made. It was a simple two-up, two-down: sitting-room and old-fashioned kitchen below, bedroom and small bathroom above. The single bed was narrow, but the room was sizeable enough to take a double, she estimated. Each cottage had a modest square of garden across the lane; only Mrs Trelowan's had been neatly kept.

'Visitors could park where I am now,' she stated, pointing through the glass of the upper window.

Only when she felt she had established a bona fide interest in the building did Rowena feel it safe to return to the subject of Patrick Sullivan. 'Was this man Patrick a good worker?' she asked casually as they clattered down the wooden staircase.

'No. He was always late, lazy and sullen.'

'How did you come to engage him in the first place?'

'Ellie pleaded with me. She'd come across him begging in Penzance, and told him there was real work to be had if he wanted it. At least, that's what she said to me. I asked around: Bill said he'd met Patrick at the fête and he seemed a harmless enough lad – so I took him on.' He gave a snort of self-contempt.

'That was Ellie from Uplands, wasn't it? The girl you played chess with.'

'I was teaching her.' His jaw clenched. 'I was very fond of Ellie. I still can't believe I was such a rotten judge of character.' He locked the cottage and they walked slowly back across the farmyard.

'How did you find out about the robbery?' asked Rowena.

'Patrick didn't appear for work that morning. It was hardly unusual, but I was fed up with him. I came to give him a dressing-down and found the cottage door ajar and the place abandoned. It was a complete pigsty inside. I went back to the farmhouse and for the first time noticed that things didn't look quite normal in the kitchen. A tin where I keep petty cash, for instance, had been moved – and emptied. With a hollow sense of what I might find, I checked the sitting-room. Some miniature paintings had gone from the walls – heirlooms, not especially valuable. But he'd also ransacked the glass-fronted cabinet and taken some small antique items which *were* rare. Whatever he could carry in his rucksack, presumably. The television and music centre were untouched.

'He could have done this at any hour of the night. I started to look for evidence of a forced entry, then I saw the key. It was my spare – normally lives in that drawer. He'd simply taken it at some earlier stage. I never used to lock the farmhouse during the day.

'As you can imagine, the police weren't too impressed. I don't think they tried very hard. If Mrs Malone had agreed to publicize the loss of her silver we might have got somewhere, but she wanted to keep a low profile – she had an important client coming, a minor Royal, all very hush-hush, and she didn't want journalists crawling around.'

'"Crawling!"' sniffed Rowena.

'You know what I mean.'

'Yes...How did you find out about this client?'

'Ann Trelowan's a good friend of mine. She was bursting to tell *somebody*.'

Rowena nodded, desperate to ask more, afraid to dwell suspiciously long on events he clearly found unpleasant to relate. He settled the matter for her by changing the subject. 'Will you have some coffee, Rowena? I don't think we've got time for another game.'

'Thank you, yes.' She glanced at her watch; it was ten fifteen.

As he busied himself with the kettle they chatted about generalities, including her trips to St Michael's Mount and Cober House. Adrian knew the Grangers via his parents. 'My mother used to meet Madeleine at WI functions,' he explained. 'After Cathy went north with the children Madeleine would sometimes come this way, ostentatiously to visit Ann, but always ending up here in the kitchen. She'd comment on the weather, deliver a few brisk words about local events I might like to attend, plonk a jar of home-made jam or pickles on the table and leave. She never got much response from me, I'm afraid, but she kept on trying. Christian charity at its best.'

'The world would be poorer without it,' said Rowena. 'It's easier not to bother, you know.'

'You're right. Perhaps I'll take her a basket of cabbages,' he grinned.

They drank the coffee, a strong instant blend, then Rowena prepared to leave. 'I think I'd better walk back,' she said. 'That second bottle of wine...'

'Sorry. I wasn't thinking. You must let me escort you.'

He took a torch, but once again there was moonlight, and the air was cool and fresh. When they reached Graw Head, Rowena forestalled him at the stone gateway to Uplands. 'I'll be fine from here,' she said. 'Thank you for your company. Don't worry about the car – I'll pick it up tomorrow.'

He stood close by, his manner awkward again now the effects of the alcohol had worn off. 'Thank *you*,' he said after a moment. 'I've enjoyed this evening.'

'So have I. Goodnight, Adrian.' She held out her hand, feeling that some friendly gesture was appropriate.

He was slow to relinquish the grasp. 'Rowena...' he whispered. She lifted her face towards him enquiringly, and he bent his head to plant a gentle kiss on her lips. It was as unassuming as Brett's had been overpowering. She smiled.

'Thank you,' he repeated, but still didn't leave. He shuffled on the spot. 'I – I've been rather indiscreet tonight,' he murmured. 'I've told you things I've said to no one else...' For a moment he turned to stare broodingly down the granite peninsula at the dark shape of Uplands, limned against a wide silvery sea. 'I trust you,' he went on. 'You won't betray me, will you?'

It seemed an odd word to choose. 'Of course not,' she assured him, uncertain as to his exact meaning.

'I'm glad. Shall we play again soon?'

'I'd be disappointed if we didn't.'

Ginette had already laid the photographs out across a table when Rowena called the following day. They were an uneven collection, some sun-bleached and indistinct, others surprisingly sharp.

Both girls affected a nonchalance they did not feel, but when Rowena slid two prints aside from the rest Ginette abandoned her bored pose by the fireplace and arrowed to the table with avid eyes. 'They're a hundred pounds each,' she megaphoned.

'Forty. That's all I'm prepared to offer.'

'Each?'

Rowena pursed her lips and pretended to consider. 'Okay,' she said at length. As she paid out the money she sensed relief in Ginette's every limb. This girl has debts, she thought.

Outside in the Clio, she examined the prints more carefully. One was a general view of festive frolics, a tug-of-war with laughing spectators. The other appeared to be centred on a giant pasty displayed on a trestle table. Madeleine Granger was holding out a raffle ticket to Daniel Malone, while in the corner Ellie – a pretty, happy, carefree Ellie – was confiding something to Patrick Sullivan.

Sullivan's face was small, but raised so that his features were no longer obscured by the hat. It was a three-quarter view: enlargement would render it perfectly suitable to be offered to a private investigator.

Rowena studied Ellie's image with sadness and a renewed sense of loss. 'Hang on, Ellie,' she whispered to the air around her. 'I'm getting there. Really I am. Things are beginning to move at last.'

11

Mrs Trelowan was preparing lunch when Rowena entered the Uplands kitchen with the empty coffee jug from the dining-room sideboard. 'Someone's thirsty,' she remarked.

'Not guilty. I think it's Brett. I'll make some more. Caireen said she'd be wanting coffee for her eleven o'clock clients.'

'If you're sure? Thank you. How did your evening with Mr Polzeath go?'

Rowena had told Mrs Trelowan about the chess games. Initially lukewarm in her response – perhaps suspicious as to Rowena's motives – the housekeeper now seemed completely disarmed. Adrian must have said something. 'He won again, but I made it difficult for him.'

She smiled her approval as she grated carrots, and Rowena decided to seize the moment. 'He told me he taught Ellie to play chess,' she said. 'Just like you, he seemed very disappointed by the way she left. He told me all about Patrick and the antiques...' She stepped closer to the table. 'I was wondering, Ann... Do you think it's possible that Ellie was misjudged?'

The housekeeper's hands paused, still grasping the stump of carrot. 'I'd like to,' she said slowly, '– but I don't see how.'

'Well, as I understand it, the main reason people associate her with Patrick's crime is the loss of Mrs Malone's silver... but supposing someone else took it to discredit her?'

'Who would do a thing like that?'

'I wondered about Ginette.'

Now Ann Trelowan's whole body was motionless; only her eyes flicked back and forth under lowered brows as she assimilated this new idea.

'Adrian was obviously fond of Ellie,' continued Rowena. 'Ginette may have been jealous. Supposing Ellie heard what Patrick had done and tried to follow him to get Adrian's things back – or even left because she was ashamed and knew everyone would link her with the robbery because she'd got him the job... It was a perfect opportunity for someone to steal the silver and know she'd be blamed.'

The housekeeper seemed to recover. 'But Ginnie... I heard rumours, but – she's always so rude to Mr Polzeath in public!'

'It might be the rudeness of a woman scorned. Or her motive could have been simple opportunism... She used to work here. I wondered if she could have made herself a duplicate key?'

'She was sacked only two weeks before...' mused Ann Trelowan. 'She would have wanted to hurt Mrs Malone, as well... But how would she have known that Ellie had gone? We only discovered she was missing the morning after Mr Polzeath had called the police.'

Now Rowena was very close to the information she had been seeking. 'Had her bed been slept in?'

'No.'

'When was she last seen?'

'I saw her myself the previous morning. She'd got up late and come to make herself some tea. Mrs Malone had clients, I remember. Just like today... goodness! I'd better take them that coffee.'

'It's not quite ready,' said Rowena hastily. 'So when do you think Ellie ran away?'

'Nobody knows. Mrs Malone had given me the evening off because the various members of the family had plans to be out. I asked Ellie if she'd like me to leave her something to eat, but she said not to bother: she would either make beans on toast or go out herself. I was able to go home quite early that day, and it wasn't until I returned here the next morning that it became clear that she had gone, without a word to anybody. At first, they thought she'd simply slept in again, then Mrs Malone started to become impatient. She went up to Ellie's room to rouse her, and discovered she wasn't there...

'She could have left as soon as lunch time the previous day, though. I heard that Mrs Malone and Mr Brett were in Truro that afternoon, while Mr Daniel wandered off on one of his cliff walks. In the early evening a policeman – Detective-Sergeant Pendrea – came to the house asking to speak to Ellie. It seems that wasn't a good time – Mrs Malone was late back from Truro and she was in a rush to get ready for the evening. She was off to a National Trust meeting, while Mr Brett had promised to take Mr Daniel to the cinema. When they couldn't find Ellie, the detective wasn't too concerned and said he'd try again the next day.'

'Presumably no one noticed anything amiss with the silverware at that point.'

'It's kept in a cupboard – they had no call to look.'

'I see.' Rowena nodded thoughtfully as she prepared an artistic arrangement of biscuits on a plate. 'Let's just say for the sake of argument that Ellie heard that afternoon about the robbery at the farm – perhaps someone rang up to tell Mrs Malone, warn her to watch her valuables, whatever. She panics, packs a few clothes and walks across the headland to hitch a lift on the main road. She thinks she knows where Patrick may have gone. Ginette sees her, maybe even talks to her, suggesting everyone thinks she's implicated. Then she steals the silver while the house is empty, knowing Ellie will be blamed.'

'It's possible, I suppose.' Mrs Trelowan looked deeply doubtful. 'But why didn't Ellie leave a note, or write later, or telephone?'

'Perhaps she had an accident, or was ill, or something, and ended up having to stay with the travellers. I don't know, Ann. I just wondered if a girl that both you and Adrian seem to have been fond of could possibly be innocent after all... I'll take this coffee through.'

She picked up the silver tray (Caireen dispensed varying levels of hospitality, depending on the nature of her clients) and entered the small waiting-room behind a respectful knock. Caireen herself was there, wearing her 'regalia', seated close to two distinguished-looking gentlemen.

Rowena immediately identified one as a well-known character actor despite the anonymous diary entry 'Mr Stone, Mr Braithwaite'. She gave an involuntary beam of recognition to which he graciously responded. Idiot, she scolded herself. They must have to put up with this all the time.

'Ah, Rowena – thank you,' said Caireen, indicating the low table with a diamond-encircled wrist. Rowena gently lowered the tray and retreated.

'I've just seen Elliot Warman,' she hissed at Mrs Trelowan as she collected her own drink.

'You'll tell no one else, I trust. That's confidential information. Mrs Malone insists on complete discretion.'

'I'll be good,' promised Rowena. Back in her office she recalled that many famous names already featured in the draft of Caireen's autobiography, people who had given prior permission. These would vastly aid the saleability of the finished book.

She wondered if Keith would read the book when it was finished. Perhaps then he would finally appreciate that Caireen was one of the few genuinely excellent mediums and deserved her reputation. Right now, his mind seemed to be as closed as Kevin's.

He had seemed preoccupied the last time she had telephoned; his interest in her quest was subtly waning, she felt. It was her own fault: she had treated him as if he were on tap, altering arrangements at short notice and taking his understanding for granted. Now he wasn't quite so available – she was having to leave messages with his flatmates because he was out more. You never truly appreciate something until you've lost it, she thought sadly.

At lunch, Caireen asked Rowena if she would collect some items of stationery from Helston. 'I have more sittings this afternoon, and I need Brett to look after the clients. Would you mind very much?'

'Not at all.' Rowena was glad of another excuse to suspend work: she was getting close to completion already, despite the extra burden of articles for Kevin. Caireen had been so satisfied with her presentation of the material so far that few alterations had been necessary. Now only a handful of chapters remained. If the mystery of Ellie's disappearance was not solved soon, Rowena knew that she would have to devise some stalling tactics.

On Helston's steep main street she was unsurprised to see Madeleine, a plumply exotic flower amidst more drably attired pedestrians. A wicker basket hung over her arm, with celery stalks protruding.

'Rowena – how nice to see you! Shall we have a cup of tea together?'

She hesitated. 'That's very kind. I'm actually on an errand for Caireen, but...'

'Oh, a few minutes won't hurt!' She lowered her head and her voice. 'Actually, I'd appreciate a little chat with you, if you can spare the time?'

'Gladly.'

Inside a small, cramped tea shop Madeleine came gradually to the point. 'Caireen has told Charles you're making excellent progress with the book,' she stated. 'I should say she's delighted with your style – vivid yet restrained is her verdict. I'm very pleased. No one wants the work to end up a *melodrama.*'

'That's what I'm trying to avoid.'

'Quite. But even if the book is respectable, I must say I'd prefer to avoid the Granger name appearing within its pages. I was wondering, Rowena... has Caireen included descriptions of her sessions with Charles?' Despite her imperious tone, Madeleine's fingers betrayed her anxiety as they manipulated a paper napkin.

Rowena sipped the tea. This was a matter for Caireen and Charles. Yet she had the simple means to put Madeleine's mind at rest.

'I know Charles gave his permission,' went on Madeleine. 'But that was for Caireen's sake, to be agreeable. I just don't want him to regret it in later years...'

'Don't worry,' said Rowena, deciding that Madeleine's support could be useful. 'There's no mention of Charles.'

'Oh, that's a relief. It's not that I don't think Caireen's life is a remarkable story in itself, and her climb to fame, but...I view her powers rather differently from Charles. He may yet modify his own view...'

Another Keith, Rowena thought. She herself was moving ever closer to the conclusion that it was unfair to pronounce on a subject in the absence of study or personal experience.

'I'm sure she's a gifted psychologist,' went on Madeleine. 'If she just relied on that, I wouldn't mind, but...' She eyed Rowena assessingly. '...I rather think she cheated once.'

'What makes you say that?'

Madeleine hesitated. 'We are friends, aren't we, Rowena? May I speak about Caireen? Thank you...It was at the Spiritualist church some four or five years ago. Caireen was coming to give one of her "goodwill" sessions and Charles persuaded me to attend. She spoke at length to a lady in the front row, furnishing details of her life in South Africa before her husband Rory died...the woman couldn't confirm any of the story. Caireen was obviously puzzled, then another woman spoke up from the opposite end of the row and said that Rory had been *her* husband and everything fitted. She normally sat in the other seat, but had slipped out to collect some notices...

'Caireen was calm and gracious, and spoke of "residual energies" attracting her to the second woman's usual place, but I wasn't convinced. I think she had spoken to someone and had prior knowledge, but chance had led to an error. Charles, of course, would hear nothing against her.'

Madeleine tried hard to sound dispassionate, but her efforts were spoiled by the hostile set of her face. Rowena could sense not just reservations, but an active dislike of Caireen. She felt immediately protective. Perhaps Caireen *had* gilded the lily just this once. She had freely admitted doing so as a teenager, and even latterly acknowledged that there could be difficult times – stark days when nothing came through and people were waiting...'They forget, or don't realize, that the medium is a conduit rather than a controller of events, a hostage to circumstance,' she had sighed.

Rowena answered with platitudes. She knew it was hard for Madeleine to be neutral where Caireen was concerned; there had been gossip of county events which she had expected to attend with Charles, only to be supplanted by Caireen. It was a delicate situation.

'Of course,' said Madeleine telepathically with a rueful sigh, 'I observe Caireen with a critical eye because of Charles's affection for her. I don't want him to make a mistake. Her lifestyle is...glamorous, filled with travel and eminent people. We're much more staid here. I worry that she's attracted to the contrast, which would be a flimsy basis for any permanent union.'

Whether or not Madeleine's prime concern was for Charles or for herself, she was clearly perturbed enough to risk discussing her reservations with a relatively new acquaintance, and Caireen's employee to boot. Presumably she had to keep face in her own social circle, display an equanimity she did not feel out of loyalty to Charles.

'They seem very easy together,' Rowena said reassuringly. 'I would say there's genuine feeling.'

'You think so? You feel she's capable of that?'

'Oh, yes. Look at her devotion to Danny. She could have had him shut away in some expensive residential place, but she takes him everywhere, and gives him an active role in her work so he feels valued.'

Madeleine selected a cream horn from the plate in the centre of the table. 'I wonder if it's guilt?' she said slowly.

'I'm sorry, I don't understand.'

'Well, we heard about the illness that caused Danny's problems. Caireen had the virus first, so perhaps she feels responsible.'

Yet another blow, thought Rowena hollowly, recalling that Caireen had left that entire incident out of the book. She wondered how *she* would have coped with the nightmare of infecting a beloved child with such devastating consequences. It would have given rise to the guilt she felt about Oliver magnified a thousandfold...At least Danny was alive, to be treated and indulged in a poignant attempt at compensation...

'Anyway,' said Madeleine, with more perception than Rowena thought she possessed, 'we all have our guilt feelings, most of them quite unnecessary. We can't help Acts of God, and when we make mistakes ourselves, it's because we're human. Speaking of humanity, a little bird has told me that Adrian Polzeath is returning to our race thanks to a renewed interest in chess. You may well blush. We've been very worried about him. He lost his family and most of his livelihood, then shut himself off completely from his friends... none of us could reach him. We knew he was sitting for hours on end in that dreadful cold farmhouse just feet from a twelve-bore shotgun! He wouldn't see a doctor, and got angry if we suggested it. Not even Ann could persuade him, which greatly upset her. She would do anything for Adrian, anything at all – but he wouldn't let her. We're all grateful to you, Rowena, for pulling him out of the pit.'

After she and Madeleine had gone their separate ways in Helston, Rowena reflected on the strength of the 'grapevine' in small country areas where everyone knew their neighbour. It was fear of this network that hobbled her every movement. Question one person too intensely and they would all get to hear about it...

She opened her bag, pulled out her notebook and checked an address written there. As soon as Caireen had sanctioned this visit to Helston, she had scoured the Yellow Pages for private investigators. There was just one in the locality, Tanner and Associates; when she had rung in the name of Hillsworth he had agreed to see her at four o'clock.

The office was small and uninspiring, situated up a flight of stairs above a launderette in the least salubrious part of the town. Tanner, however, far from being the ferrety individual she had imagined, was large and florid, his West Country accent warmer in person. He motioned her to a vinyl-covered chair alongside the desk. 'Miss Hillsworth... sit down, my dear. You said you wanted help with a missing person. That's right up our street.'

Rowena gave a questioning glance towards a woman of forty or so who was typing in the background.

'Don't you go worrying about Mrs Tripp,' he said. 'She's with me, and we guarantee absolute discretion. Now, just give me an outline of the problem.'

'I'm trying to trace a young man in his twenties called Patrick Sullivan. He's a New Age traveller, and is probably in an encampment somewhere. He disappeared from this area on September the fifth last year after robbing a friend of mine. I need to trace him because he may have some information about another friend... I've got a photograph of him.'

'Good... good. Let me just take a few details about yourself, then we'll look into this more fully. You're Sarah Hillsworth... at what address?'

'I – I thought I could approach you periodically for progress reports.'

'I'm sorry, but we must have the basic details of our clients, even if only to protect our fee!' He guffawed.

'You could always follow me,' grinned Rowena.

'Waste of womanpower. Now... your address?'

'I really don't want you to send anything to where I'm staying, but just for your records I'm at Uplands, Graw Head, Anwith.'

His face seemed suddenly to smooth itself free of all expression. 'A New Age traveller,' he said. 'I think perhaps that's beyond our remit... I'm sorry, my dear; on reflection, I don't think we can take your case.'

She was astonished. 'You just said it was right up your street!'

'Tricky customers, New Age travellers. They go by funny names like "Mudbath", and drop so far out of normal society that we can't get a handle on them at all. No, I'm sorry, Miss Hillsworth, but this one's beyond our resources.' He opened a desk drawer and drew out a business card. 'These people might be able to help you.'

'Plymouth!' she read in dismay.

'It's not so far. Let me open the door for you. Sorry we weren't able to do business... goodbye.'

Scowling at the washing machines as she stalked past the big window at ground level, Rowena tried to rationalize what had just happened. She didn't believe a word of Tanner's thin excuse for rejecting the case. He had been affable and encouraging until the point where she gave her address – then his body language had completely changed.

What did it mean? Had someone from Uplands been in contact with the agency at some point, leading them to fear a conflict of interest? But if so, when... and why?

With a twist of unease she recalled the watcher at Cober Pool. All the evidence pointed to its being Danny... Supposing he had told Brett about her nocturnal rowing expedition? Brett was nobody's fool; he would want to know the motive behind such curious behaviour; he would want to know more about Miss Rowena Kemp.

Unlocking the Clio, she tried to quell this new feeling of alarm. People trusted her in her perceived role; slowly she was garnering the information she needed.

Now it looked as if her carefully nurtured façade might be about to crack wide open...

12

Keith's manner was distracted when she telephoned him the following evening, and he was unimpressed by her interpretation of Tanner's volte-face. 'I expect he simply changed his mind,' he said above a burst of background commotion. 'Decided tracking down a traveller was going to be more trouble than it was worth. I wouldn't read too much into this, Ro.'

'But he'd virtually agreed to take the case until I gave him my address,' she protested.

'So you said. You think the reason was a potential conflict of interest, and if you'd admitted to being Rowena Kemp earlier you wouldn't have even got that far... Let's say, though, that you're right and Brett is investigating your background. Can you imagine him using a rathole and corner agency in an office over a Helston launderette? With his money and London connections he'd get someone expensive and ultra discreet. And don't forget the focus of enquiries would be London and Amersham.'

Rowena was equally unconvinced. 'This is the electronic age,' she reminded him. 'Geography doesn't count any more. People can sit at their computer consoles and receive information from *anywhere*.'

There were further muffled background noises, including a female giggle, and Rowena knew she had caught Keith at a bad time. 'Look, I'd better hang up now,' she went on. 'I was thinking of coming up to Finchley this weekend... will you be around at all?'

'Saturday morning, if that's any good to you.'

'I'll see how things work out and let you know.'

'Okay. By the way, thanks for the photo of Sullivan you faxed to the office. We're exploring a few avenues.'

'Thanks. Bye, then, Keith...'

She replaced the heavy receiver and vacated the telephone box, still feeling that her long-held paranoia about using the mobile in the vicinity of Uplands was justified. As she walked back along Anwith's narrow pavements to the Clio, she tried to convince herself that Keith must be right. Certainly a London agency would be more appropriate for any legwork and face-to-face enquiries. Tanner's outfit was too small to have its own London satellite... But in that case, why *had* he turned her down?

She felt dispirited, cheated of the in-depth conversation with Keith she had been hoping for. Saturday morning was unlikely to be an improvement – a snatched hour, perhaps, squeezed in between his other priorities. Her time might be better employed here in Cornwall.

At least Keith had shown an interest in the Sullivan photograph. She had faxed a copy to Mick Vean, too, though her expectations of results were low. Now only one channel remained, an option she had hitherto been most reluctant to pursue: the police, namely Detective-Sergeant Pendrea.

Journalistic nosiness was unlikely to be accepted as sufficient reason for discussing the nine-month-old case. Rowena had always known that she would have to admit her full identity, approach them in the persona of family representative asking for news. So far it had seemed too risky; professional people were just as prone to gossip as anybody else. Now, however, she suspected she was already in danger of imminent exposure; there might be nothing to lose.

DS Pendrea was a heavy, lumbering man with a straggly moustache and a dull expression. Even his eyelids, dipping low over opaque grey eyes, seemed indolent. He sat opposite Rowena in a small bare interview room which smelt faintly of spent cigarettes. 'You said you're working locally, madam?' he asked in unenthusiastic tones.

'Yes. Near Anwith itself.' She had told him this while making the appointment.

'And you're Miss Drinkwater's cousin?'

'That's right. I'm here to represent her parents, Alan and June Drinkwater. They want to know if there has been any progress on the case.'

'Well...' A file lay in front of him but he didn't open it; presumably he had refreshed his memory before she arrived. 'Not a lot, really.'

'Did you find Patrick Sullivan?'

'No.'

'Or Mr Polzeath's antiques?'

'No.'

'We'd have heard if you'd found Ellie – so really you mean "nothing".'

'There are no new leads at present, madam,' he conceded in a maddeningly catatonic voice.

'Is anyone actively working on the case?'

The flicker in his eyes gave her the answer; Rowena strove to keep her temper. 'I've spoken to a few people about what happened last year,' she said, 'and certain aspects still puzzle me. Would you mind if I clarified one or two points with you?'

'Please do, madam.'

'Patrick Sullivan had gone by the morning of September the fifth, but Ellie herself was still at Uplands that day. She was seen in the morning by the housekeeper. What time did you visit the house?'

'Around six forty. There had been many things to arrange during the afternoon, and we had not been fully apprised of her relationship with Mr Sullivan. At that point we considered Miss Drinkwater as merely one witness among many.'

'What was her manner like when you saw her?'

'I didn't in fact see her. The household was in a state of bustle due to evening engagements; Mr Saunders undertook a brief search for Miss Drinkwater but concluded that she had already gone out herself. I warned them to lock all their doors and windows because Sullivan might still be on the loose in the area.'

'Did you see Ellie at all – later, perhaps?'

'No, madam. The next day she had gone, and it subsequently became clear that so had the silverware.'

'Was there any sign of a forced entry?' Rowena wasn't hopeful; Mrs Trelowan would surely have mentioned that.

'No. None at all.'

'How much silver was missing?'

He hesitated, and for a moment she thought she detected a faint gleam of sympathy in the bovine eyes. You don't get to be sergeant without *some* powers of perception, she thought.

'Just enough for a person to carry, madam. I'm sorry.'

She nodded ruefully. 'How did you interpret the timing, Sergeant Pendrea? The fact that Ellie left the day *after* Patrick?'

'We reckoned he'd left her behind, madam. Acted on his own initiative. But she decided to follow him, and took the silver as an offering of sorts, something to please him so's he'd let her stay.' He gave a benign shrug.

Another possible slant, thought Rowena. Even she hadn't considered that particular angle. 'Were you aware that Ginette Carloose from the farm cottages was sacked from her cleaning job at Uplands only a fortnight before all this?' she asked.

'Our enquiries did bring that to light, yes.'

'Did you ask her about the silver?'

He fingered his chin, as if deciding how much information he should reveal. 'Miss Carloose allowed us to examine her cottage as part of a general inspection of the area. Nothing was found to connect her with either Mr Polzeath's missing treasures or those of Mrs Malone.'

'Ellie had a platonic relationship with Mr Polzeath. He was teaching her to play chess. Ginette might have been jealous, and stolen the silver to discredit her.'

He made a non-committal face, and Rowena wondered how much he knew. Adrian's conviction that the whole village, not to mention the whole peninsula, was judging him probably boiled down to a few individuals in the pub...If this police officer knew nothing of Adrian's ill-advised night with Ginette, then it was not her place to tell him.

'What do you think?' she prompted.

He redistributed his weight on the chair. 'We heard about Miss Drinkwater's visits to the farm. We believe they were a cover for meetings with Mr Sullivan.'

'Ginette might not have known that.'

He leaned forward. 'If you don't mind my saying, madam, you seem obsessed by Miss Carloose. If you have any information which is germane to our enquiry, then I must ask you to divulge it. We can't let malice or gossip cloud the issue.'

'The issue' which in their books was as dead as last year's beached seaweed...'I'm sorry,' she said frankly. 'It's just that we're all very worried about Ellie. She hasn't been in contact with any of us. I was beginning to wonder if something – serious had happened to her, if she could possibly have met with an accident or something here.'

'I'm sure that's not the case, madam...' He went on to remind her about Ellie's previous travels, and that young people usually turned up in the end. With a heavy heart Rowena thanked him, handed over a picture of Patrick Sullivan and left. The rapport she had hoped for had simply not been there; it had been impossible to converse beyond the superficial.

Over and above the size of the silver haul, only one positive fact had emerged from their discussion: the police had not encountered Ellie directly. Had *anyone* seen her, apart from Mrs Trelowan, on that second day? Rowena knew she dared not ask Brett or his mother, but Danny in the right mood might respond to careful questions.

Back at Uplands, she found a message on her desk in Mrs Trelowan's unadorned handwriting: 'Mr Polzeath rang today. He asks if you can telephone him before the weekend.' This was Thursday evening. Rowena quickly went to the kitchen, where Ann Trelowan was stirring a tureen of casserole for the family, to ask for details.

'Mr Brett took the call,' stated the housekeeper. 'It was about half an hour ago. He asked me if I knew where you were, and I said no.'

As soon as she had eaten, Rowena called Adrian on her mobile; it seemed ludicrous to drive straight past his farm to the Anwith phone box. 'Adrian – it's Rowena.'

'Oh, good. I'm glad you called back. I – er, I was wondering... are you free on Saturday evening?'

'For chess?'

'Well, I thought perhaps... maybe... we might have a meal. I wondered about The Queen's in Penzance.'

Saturday... it took Rowena only seconds to conclude that this was a better prospect than kicking around uselessly in her Finchley flat. 'That's a lovely idea,' she told him warmly.

'So you'll come?'

'Yes, please.'

She arranged to meet him at seven by the gateway to Uplands, and emerged from the study with a lighter step than before.

Danny was standing in the hall. Solemnly he scrutinized her. 'You look happy,' he said.

The Queen's was Penzance's largest hotel. Its long frontage faced seawards across the promenade; inside, the plushly carpeted foyer contained glass display cases full of elegant gifts.

'I managed to book a window table,' smiled Adrian conspiratorially as they were led through the dining-room. Rowena was delighted with the wide view of Mount's Bay wearing its evening sparkle; the man sitting opposite her also seemed to glow. His dark lounge suit, though a little loose, was well tailored, and the shirt beneath shone intensely white. She noted cufflinks, a blue silk tie and smart black shoes, but most of all his neat haircut and the healthy colour in his face. He *was* good-looking, lean but not smoothly sculpted like Brett. The crow's feet were still prominent at the corners of his eyes (old laughter, or years of squinting in the sun?) but the other lines seemed fainter, lighter...

'You look beautiful,' he said, and she felt herself blush. She had vacillated for a full half-hour before choosing a deep emerald square-necked dress with elbow-length sleeves. A gemstone necklace encircled the base of her throat.

As they ate a mixed seafood salad, Adrian expounded on his love for Cornwall, especially its moorland and the coves of the Lizard. Unlike many other men she had known, he then encouraged her to describe her own favourite places. The evening flew by with more fish – this time Dover sole – and a raspberry Pavlova. After coffee, Rowena hesitantly suggested splitting the bill.

To her relief he was not offended. 'I may be skint, but I'm not that skint! It's been a pleasure dining out with such an attractive, well-informed companion.'

His nervousness seemed to have vanished, and Rowena knew she was meeting the man he had been before depression set in. When they crossed to the promenade in the mellowing light it seemed natural that he should take her hand. The sea surged idly against the granite bulwark beneath the railings as Adrian pointed out Newlyn's fishing harbour, and spoke of the excitement around Penzance years before when the aircraft carrier *Ark Royal* had visited the bay.

Swinging to the left he indicated a concrete wall leading to a low cluster of rocks. '*That* is a swimming pool,' he said with an edge of rancour. 'It's freezing whatever the season. My parents made me learn to swim there before they'd let me loose in Graw Cove.'

As they strolled towards the pool Rowena asked, 'Did your parents farm, as well?'

'Yes. I inherited Anwith Farm when Dad died. They had me late in life; in some ways I'm glad they're not around to see what became of the business they built up so lovingly over the decades...'

'Tell me more about this pool,' she invited as they drew level.

He grimaced. 'Stuff of nightmares ... but I must have been a wimp even then because there was an elderly gent who swam naked in the sea off Battery Rocks just along here every day!'

The rocks themselves were half submerged, but they stood by the War Memorial on the paved promontory above and viewed St Michael's Mount from a new angle. 'That island makes the bay special,' said Rowena. 'I can see Cudden Point, too. It looks just like a crouching mouse. And the Lizard ... but Graw Head is hidden.'

Veiled in mystery, she thought suddenly, and shivered.

'Are you cold?' he asked, concerned.

'No ... what's round here, the harbour? Isn't this where the *Scillonian* picks up passengers for the Scilly Isles?'

'That's right. Or you can fly there by helicopter ... look, you *are* cold. Let's go back. You don't want to catch a chill.'

As his ageing car travelled cautiously eastwards towards Anwith, Rowena found herself reluctant to end the evening. In direct riposte to her machinations with wine during their previous encounter, Adrian had ensured that she drank most of their Chardonnay at The Queen's. Away from sudden sharp sea breezes, she felt relaxed and slightly drowsy.

'Would you like me to take you straight to Uplands, or shall we have a brandy at the farm first?'

With a sense of inevitability she chose the brandy. Inside the farmhouse they didn't say much. Rowena stood by the kitchen table, feeling the warm spirit diffuse across her tongue, unwilling to sit down, unwilling to leave.

Adrian was beside her. Gently he removed the glass from her hand and kissed her face. She quivered and closed her eyes, feeling him draw her close. It shocked her how much she had missed this since Sebastian, so much so that she had almost made a bad mistake with Brett.

'Rowena ...' His voice was so low she could only just hear him. 'Shall we ... would you ...'

She thought of the contents of the side zipper pocket in her handbag. 'Yes,' she said.

He was kind and considerate, just as she had known he would be. For her part, she felt that warmth and trust were a more than adequate substitute for dangerous desires; the fleeting burst of raw passion she had felt for Brett almost certainly had much to do with his physical resemblance to Sebastian.

With a sigh she stretched, and heard Adrian's low chuckle beside her. 'We're all tangled up,' he said, 'like a pair of octopi. Just a moment...' He slid his leg from under her knee and turned on his side to hold her against him, curled up like a foetus. 'Not just a pretty face,' he said, planting a kiss on her shoulder.

'Who, you or me?'

'Me, of course.'

'Braggart.' She lay drowsily content as he pulled the patchwork quilt up the bed to cover her. Nearby on a Victorian chest-of-drawers shone a low-wattage lamp; the polished stone base interested her with its subtle swirl of colours – dark olive green, grey, thin glimpses of vermilion. 'This looks familiar,' she murmured.

'It's serpentine,' he said. 'Local stone from the Lizard. Craftsmen polish it up and make ornaments. Mrs Malone has a lamp like this.'

'Serpentine...' she repeated. 'Snake-like: they must call it that because the pattern is so sinuous and variegated.'

'Thus speaks the journalist.' He kissed her neck and the angle of her jaw, smoothing away her hair almost reverently. With a stifled sound of lazy pleasure she rolled on to her back and pulled his mouth down to hers. For several long minutes they continued to kiss, a slow and sensual exploration.

'Adrian...?' she said as he broke away for air. 'May I ask you something?'

He stroked the side of her face and his smile gleamed in the dim light. 'Anything.'

Rowena took a deep breath. 'Ellie,' she said. She felt his limbs stiffen, the hand become clumsy. 'Were you – and she... like this?' There. She had said it now. Some inner compulsion had demanded assuagement.

She looked up at the shadowed hollows of his eyes and sensed he was staring through her into the past.

'No,' he said after a pause. 'We weren't... but I wanted to. I was waiting. She was so young and fresh... innocent, somehow, despite the travelling life she told me about. I wanted to gain her trust... I was going to ask her to marry me.' He blinked and seemed suddenly to be aware of Rowena. 'I'm sorry,' he said contritely. 'I didn't mean to sound so insensitive.'

'You weren't. I asked. I'm glad you told me.' That was true. However blithely she had stated to others that Ellie's relationship with Adrian had been merely platonic, a tiny seed of doubt had persisted ever since Ginette's wild accusations in the pub.

Adrian's eyes were now focused on her face, and his expression was troubled. 'Rowena...' he said earnestly, 'sometimes you've reminded me of Ellie. A gesture you share, a quizzical look...But you are a separate person with your own identity. Ellie is in the past. It's you I'm with here and now, and you I want to think about.'

Somehow she had missed her cue. For a moment as he spoke it seemed that the time to confide her connection with Ellie had arrived, but now that he was silent she found that her ingrained caution had reasserted itself. Ambivalent, she slid from the bed with a murmured excuse.

'It's just along the corridor on the left,' he said as she padded to the doorway.

Outside in the passageway a thin shaft of moonlight sliced through the darkness from a small end window, providing just enough light for Rowena to grope her way forwards. Her fingertips brushed the panels of a door: she seized the handle but the door remained stubbornly closed. Further efforts were equally abortive; presumably this was a locked room or cupboard.

Finding the bathroom beyond, she soon returned to Adrian, who was sitting up in the bed. 'You're not upset?' he asked anxiously.

'Of course not. You obviously had honourable intentions towards my predecessor.'

Wordlessly he turned back the quilt and held out his arms; the old bed creaked and dipped as Rowena climbed inside. From the attic above came muffled chitters and a flapping of wings. 'Bats,' he whispered, leaning across her to turn out the lamp.

'Fellow creatures of the night,' she replied, and saw his wide smile in the moment before all became darkness, and movement, and heat...

Throughout Sunday, Rowena found it impossible to concentrate on her work. She was supposed to be writing up an account of the Mazey Day celebrations in Penzance, when all kinds of elaborate floats with marine connotations paraded through the streets for the festival of Golowan. 'A Cornish *Mardi Gras*,' she wrote, then paused, chewing her finger.

All she could think about was Adrian, the pressure of his body, the feel of his lips...It had been harder than she would have thought possible to leave him early that morning, and insist that they could not meet again until Tuesday. But she had put her journalistic responsibilities first... only to find now that she was wasting time.

'Help me,' she murmured half an hour later on rereading a nauseatingly turgid paragraph describing the procession. Danny had said something about the colour yellow stimulating the intellect. Right now she would try anything; she was tired and dreamy, and totally unable to function.

Half embarrassed despite her solitude, Rowena picked up the Yellow Pages and stared at the front cover, concentrating on the colour, 'breathing it in through every pore' as Danny had described. After five minutes she could take no more, but felt strangely alert. Remembering that orange was supposed to be a specific wake-up colour, she repeated the exercise with an amber book jacket.

Good Lord, she thought, astonished. It actually works!

She typed steadily for the next two hours, with only occasional lapses, before being distracted by voices in the hall.

'I *told* you about these books, Danny. You deliberately disobeyed me. I'm taking them away.'

Caireen sounded unusually angry. There was a pause before Rowena heard fragments of Danny's response. '... Not fair... always treat me like a child... I'm *not* a child!'

'I know... we only want what's best for you. You must understand that.'

Their voices faded, but Rowena had lost the mental link with her task. She found herself thinking about Glastonbury, and Lavinia's circle of students. Danny thought a lot of those people. Were they cranks and charlatans, or had they indeed recognized psychic skills in Danny? Would that be such a disaster? Caireen certainly thought so...

She stretched her arms and wandered to the window. The blue sky and fleecy clouds looked inviting; perhaps a walk would prove productive. Brett was out somewhere, she noted: his Mercedes was missing. Idly she wondered what he did for sexual gratification when he wasn't trying to pounce on members of staff. He probably had a girlfriend in London.

Clad in shirt, trousers and stout shoes Rowena set off along the cliff-line, guiltily relieved that Danny hadn't noticed her departure. She strode to the now familiar mines, pausing often to watch the creaming surf at the base of the cliff. With gull screams echoing in her head she turned inland, eager to create a new circular route. She struck a narrow lane and followed it for a few hundred yards, but it appeared to be veering unhelpfully eastwards. She was on the point of turning back when her gaze fell on a sleek black car parked alongside a farm gate.

It was Brett's Mercedes, and he was inside. Through the windscreen she could see him talking earnestly with a woman. Even as Rowena backed away she knew that the woman was familiar and was unlikely to be a girlfriend...

It was Mrs Tripp from the Tanner agency.

13

He knows who I am, Rowena thought frenziedly as she hurried back to the cliff path. Soon they'll all know – and then what?

Scrambling down to a rocky ledge, she sat and watched the restless surge of green water below. Somewhere nearby, where the water was dark and still, Ellie was lying, silent and alone... waiting with the unknowing patience of death for discovery...

Rowena ducked as a wave glided in with more height than the others, hit rock with a hollow thump and threw a soaring fantail of spray high into the air. It was no good panicking about this latest development, she scolded herself. Exposure had always been a possibility. She must decide on a sensible course of action.

Brushing a salty trickle from her forehead, she faced the fact that there were only two genuine alternatives: she could pack her bags and scuttle back to Finchley or bring the whole matter into the open, and bluff. While the latter would make demands on her courage, it was the only chance to allay their suspicions. She owed it to Ellie.

It was late that night before she was able to catch Brett on his own, helping himself to apple and cheese in the kitchen.

Rowena stepped inside and closed the door behind her. 'Have you a minute?' she asked. 'I'd like to discuss something with you.'

'Fire away.' He seemed his usual self, smooth and controlled. She felt no sense of his viewing her with different eyes.

She took a deep breath. 'You know who I am,' she stated.

'Miss Rowena Kemp, as far as I'm aware.'

'Don't play games, Brett. I saw you with Mrs Tripp today. You had me investigated.'

His eyelids flickered but he was otherwise unmoved. 'I see...' he said. 'Well, I'm sorry you found out, but I don't think you can blame us. I presume you're here to explain why you've kept quiet all this time about being Ellie's cousin?'

This was the difficult bit. She gave a loose shrug. 'There's no single reason,' she answered. 'It was more a chain of events... May I have a piece of apple? Thanks...' She took a bite, then faced him squarely. 'Ellie wasn't much of a correspondent, but when she wrote to me about Caireen last year she was brimming with enthusiasm. Later, when I discovered that Caireen was giving a demonstration at the Wimbledon Theatre I was curious. I wanted to see her, so I decided to ask for an interview for my paper.

'You remember what happened that evening... Danny told me about Caireen's search for a ghost writer and virtually *propelled* me into applying. That certainly hadn't been my intention, but I must admit when you accepted me I was delighted and – yes, flattered. There was only one fly in the ointment. I knew that Ellie had let Caireen down badly; I thought if I mentioned the family connection you'd assume that I might prove equally irresponsible, and you wouldn't want to take the risk.'

He nodded, his expression inscrutable. 'What about Tanner's?' he asked when she did not continue.

'Oh...' She hung her head. 'Since I came here I learned some very unpleasant things about Ellie and Patrick Sullivan. I'm only a distant member of the family, and I hadn't realized the full story, that both Adrian Polzeath and your mother had lost valuables. I don't think I'd have had the gall to take this job if I'd known... Anyway, I felt responsible. Adrian said the police had been pretty useless, so I thought it might be worth trying a private detective...' She looked up at him beseechingly. 'Are you going to tell Caireen?'

'She'll have to know.'

'She'll sack me.'

'Not necessarily. You've been doing a good job for her, and it's nearly finished. I don't think she'd want to spoil the ship...'

'She'll ask for your advice. Are you very angry with me, Mr Saunders?'

'Oh, we're back to that, are we? I was "Brett" a few minutes ago when you were animated. Listen – Rowena. We wanted a skilled writer and we got one. I'm a pragmatist and so is my mother. I'll talk to her tomorrow and I expect she'll see things my way.'

'Thank you, Brett.'

'That's better.'

She retreated to the door, then paused. 'Just one more thing...'

He raised interrogative eyebrows.

'Would it be possible to keep this information within the family? Local people might regret some of the things they've said to me about Ellie if they knew.' And Adrian might never forgive her lack of openness with him...

'We'll do our best,' said Brett.

Upstairs, Rowena concluded that she had escaped lightly. When Brett had used her Christian name a dark glitter had appeared in his eyes redolent of their last kitchen encounter. She had half expected him to attempt sexual blackmail.

Instead, questions had passed unasked on both sides. Why had she mentioned only Patrick Sullivan to Tanner? What had triggered Brett's visit to the agency?

Perhaps Tanner hadn't specified. Perhaps, like Adrian, Brett had seen Rowena echo some gesture of Ellie's and had his suspicions aroused. Perhaps...

Neither she nor Brett had mentioned Cober Pool.

'I do wish you'd told me,' said Caireen after breakfast the next day. 'There was nothing to worry about. We judge people on their own merits here – and we've always liked you.' She gave Rowena's arm a maternal pat and effortlessly moved on to a technical discussion concerning the book.

Later, Rowena telephoned Keith to test his reaction.

'Are you pulling out?' he asked bluntly.

'Definitely not...' With all the skill at her disposal she explained how Brett had accepted her story, and all was well; rehearsing the arguments helped to convince herself.

'All right,' he allowed when she had finished. 'But there's one thing you should consider. You don't know when they began investigating you. It could have been the day after you arrived. You've only Brett's word that Caireen didn't know. If you *have* been dabbling in spiritualist sessions with her, bear in mind that she might have had prior knowledge.'

Rowena felt sick. Oliver... Caireen could have been told about Oliver. That would be a monstrous exploitation... All that comfort a sham... Abruptly she relaxed. The helicopter. No living soul except herself knew about that. And she had *felt* Oliver's presence in the room. 'Kevin's been after you, hasn't he?' she accused.

'Well, he'd rather hassle *you*, but he understands the need for caution.'

'How many times, Keith? How many times do I have to tell you both that I'm not interested in cheap iconoclasm? Like tens of thousands of other people I believe in Caireen's powers, and I'm not about to start raking through her rare mistakes for material to cobble together some shabby "exposé".'

'Kevin said you were willing initially.'

'He wouldn't have let me go otherwise. But Keith – all this is a side issue. You know why I'm here. I'm going to find Ellie's killer – and there isn't much time left.'

There was a pause; clearly Keith had no comment to make. *He still doesn't believe Ellie's dead*, thought Rowena in despair.

Eventually he spoke. 'How's Farmer Giles?'

'I presume you mean Adrian. Fine, thanks. And Chloe?'

'Voracious,' he said drily.

'Good. Well, I won't keep you. Give Gordon a cuddle for me.'

Her acceptance of the rabbit's alternative name seemed to hold some depressing significance for Keith. 'You're not coming up next weekend.' His voice was flat.

'I can't, Keith. There's so much to do here. You do understand?'

'Yep,' he said lightly. 'Have fun with Farmer Giles.' He rang off.

Rowena could scarcely wait for Tuesday evening when she could see Adrian again. Nevertheless, it was with a slight pang of unease that she lifted the handle of the newly painted knocker. So far as she could tell, only Brett and Caireen knew her secret, but if there had been any kind of leak...

To her relief, Adrian's manner was quite normal. 'Welcome,' he said. As soon as the heavy door was closed he took her in a tight bear hug. 'I've missed you. Really missed you. I couldn't have lasted another day.'

Rowena clung on, relishing the strength of his lean limbs, his taut chest. When she pulled herself away, it was with enormous reluctance. 'Chess,' she said.

He pulled a wry face. 'You mean that?'

'We'd better... Anyway, I want to win.' She saw him smirk, and added, 'And I shall know if you let me win.'

'Seen through! Okay...' He led the way into his sitting-room, which wasn't mysterious at all but merely decorated in drab shades of brown. 'I thought you might wonder what I was hiding. It's also a more appropriate room for a guest.'

'But this *friend* prefers the kitchen.'

Accompanied by Merlot, crisps and the ticking of an elderly wall clock, Rowena played an inspired game, advancing her queen uncharacteristically early and creating havoc with doubled rooks on an open file.

'I submit,' laughed Adrian, laying down his king as his last useful piece was swept from the board.

'I like men who submit,' she said.

He stood up. 'That's a pity, because I intend to be masterful.' He seized her hand and led the way to the bedroom. They fell across the bed and he covered her neck with hot kisses. As she began to writhe, he paused and lifted his head. 'That was a long fifty minutes downstairs,' he said.

The following evening Rowena parked the Clio once again outside the farm. It had been impossible to resist Adrian's pleas that they meet again as soon as possible – they coincided so completely with her own inclinations. Engagements with Caireen were looming; this was her only chance before the weekend.

Adrian had promised her a light supper; as she approached the kitchen window she could see bread, cheese and fruit laid out on the table. Her knock on the door, however, met with no response. After repeating the tattoo she stepped back, peering at the upper windows for a clue to his presence. Two casements were ajar; curtains billowed sluggishly in the warm evening air.

A footfall behind caused her to swing round with a smile of greeting. To her disappointment, the figure swaggering towards her was not Adrian, but Ginette.

'Hello, Ginette,' said Rowena briskly.

'I know who 'e are.' The Cornish accent seemed harsher than ever, infused with a kind of bovine triumphalism.

With difficulty Rowena maintained a neutral expression while her stomach tightened with dismay. Who would have told this girl? Surely not Caireen or Brett. Mrs Trelowan had not been informed. Perhaps Danny had been listening at the door...?

'I'm not sure what you mean, Ginette.'

The girl tossed her head with a snort of contempt. 'Phh! You're Ellie Drinkwater's cousin. I thought maybe we could make a deal.'

'This must be some ridiculous rumour.'

'Tain't no rumour!' Now her eyes were narrow, and focused. 'I have it on *very good authority.*' When Rowena didn't reply she went on, 'A friend of mine's a police constable at Helston. He told me you're Ellie's cousin and you've been asking about her movements at the time of the robbery last year. See! So I thought I might be able to help you, seeing as I live here and I know something about that night...'

Rowena's thoughts whirled in hectic circles. Could Ginette be trusted...*had* she been involved herself? Was she just looking for an easy handout? 'I'd be grateful if you'd tell me anything that might have a bearing on Ellie's disappearance,' she said calmly, keeping her voice upbeat and pleasant.

'*How* grateful?'

'I thought you wanted to help.'

Ginette's overfull lips curled. 'We're talking valuable information here. I heard the argument – Ellie and old Romeo... that's right, Mr Polzeath. Talk about fierce! I could tell you what they said, if you were to persuade me proper, like. You can afford it.'

Rowena glanced towards the farmhouse, but it still seemed deserted. Ginette's story was a fabrication, she decided, a clumsy attempt to capitalize on her policeman friend's indiscreet blabbings. I shan't play her game, she thought. She can stew empty-handed. But Adrian must be told who I am tonight. If he hears it from someone else...'I'll listen to anything you feel I should know,' she said. 'Money's not a factor, though. You must realize that.'

'Suit yourself.' Ginette flounced away, but stopped after a few yards and turned round. 'Lover boy's not in,' she said. 'He's up the long field with Tom. If I were you I wouldn't bother... but if you're desperate and you want my leavings, then go right ahead.'

Bitch, thought Rowena angrily. The reminder of Adrian's dalliance with Ginette was unwelcome. Drink had a lot to answer for...

She angled across to the nearest barn in order to demonstrate a sense of purpose. She didn't believe that Adrian was as far away as the long field; he had known what time she was due to arrive. Stepping inside the wide doorway she called softly, 'Adrian?'

The barn was tall, with a cathedral-like gloom. Various pieces of machinery littered the floor near the entrance, but the darker reaches beyond seemed to have been created with livestock in mind. There were ageing timber stalls, and a corner area piled with old straw.

Rowena wandered forward, wondering if this was where Adrian's beloved cows had been quartered. Back here, despite the general air of mustiness and neglect, there were early signs of Adrian's new 'spring clean' mentality. The straw had been scraped to one side; a pitchfork and broom were propped against the partition wall.

Turning to leave, she paused. Some image had impinged on her retina just as her head had swung round: a vague rusty blemish on the wall, a splotch, a stain...

She returned to the straw-scattered area and looked more closely at the mark. It was a red-brown splash, a horizontal spray with downward-pointing runnels like a Portuguese man-o'-war in silhouette. Rowena stared, hollow with disbelief.

There was no doubt about it: this stain was blood.

14

Rowena went on staring as disjointed recollections chased each other across her brain. A locked door on Adrian's upper landing... Madeleine's anxiety about Adrian alone with a twelve-bore shotgun... the narrow dimensions of Patrick Sullivan's single bed... Like jigsaw pieces they began to meld together, but Rowena didn't like the picture. She backed away, shaking her head to make the images disperse.

A shadow fell across the doorway's patch of light. Adrian was there, his hair curling with sweat, wearing boots and working trousers. 'I'm *really* sorry,' he said to Rowena. 'Tom had a problem and I had to go back up the field. Just give me time for a shower and we'll have our supper. It's all ready.'

Rowena hardly took in the words. She was engaged in a mental struggle of trust against doubt. There *must* be an explanation, she told herself. There has to be…

She wished he had not appeared so promptly, giving her no time to think. Now she had to make a rapid decision that she might later regret…

She forced herself to smile. 'I was looking for you. Are you converting this barn, or just tidying it?'

'Bit of cleaning. That old straw serves no purpose.' He stepped closer and viewed the stalls with an assessing eye. 'I might pull these down and make better use of the space.'

Rowena swallowed. Her mouth was bone dry. 'There's a rather gruesome stain on this partition. What happened?'

Even in the dim light she saw his face change. His jaw clenched, and a tic jerked beneath the skin like a rodent squirming. 'You don't want to know about that,' he said roughly.

She held her ground. 'I do. Won't you tell me what it was?'

'I said, you don't want to know!' There was cold fury in his voice as he turned and stalked out to the yard. Rowena took a final look at the blood-spattered woodwork and followed him, feeling a sense of surprise as the mild evening air wrapped itself around her. The sky was a pale duck-egg blue; up near the farmhouse roof a pair of swallows were soaring, diving and calling to each other. Normal life – but all her senses felt trapped behind a glass wall.

Half-way to the house Adrian stopped and waited for her. 'I'm sorry,' he said. 'I didn't mean to sound angry with you. It's not something I can talk about, that's all. Don't let me spoil the evening. Let's forget it and start again. I'm glad you came.'

'Don't worry.' Rowena tried to project reassurance, but she had no idea how her voice sounded; everything was distorted. 'I've forgotten it already. But Adrian…' Furiously she cast around for an excuse to leave. '…I'm afraid I don't feel well tonight. Some sort of stomach ache. I thought it would go away, but unfortunately it seems to be getting worse. Would you be terribly upset if I give supper a miss? I'm really sorry.'

Immediately he was all concern. 'Poor you. Let me get you some paracetamol. We don't have to eat, or do anything…we could just sit quietly and listen to music.'

She couldn't bear another minute at the farm. 'I'd be rotten company. I'm sorry, but I think I'd better go back to Uplands and lie down. I'll ring you in a day or so…'

He kissed her cheek as she scrambled into the car; as the Clio bounced along the rutted lane she saw in the rear view mirror his tall figure standing by the gate, watching her. She accomplished the short journey to Uplands with dazed, automatic movements, but once upstairs in the safety of her room she found herself beginning to shake.

Rowena sat on the bed with her knees drawn up to her chest, held fast by the circle of her arms. That bloodstain had been old... Perhaps it had been hidden for some time by straw, and had only recently been re-exposed. It was three feet or so up the wall, but there was no telling where the floor level had been at the time the stain was made...

Wedging her chin into the notch between her knees, she closed her eyes. She had given Adrian a chance to explain. In fact, she had asked him twice. His negative response now seemed particularly sinister.

Against her will, scenarios flashed through her mind. Patrick Sullivan and Ellie together in the straw, muffled giggles... Adrian tall and dark with fury and a sense of betrayal... the flat report of a shotgun. Once? Twice? Blood in the straw, on the wall.

She rocked to and fro, hating the images. One half of her brain wanted to stop, to ignore it all and pretend she had never seen the stain. She would ring Adrian tomorrow and know the simple joy of hearing his voice...

The other half demanded that she analyse the situation.

She lay back on the bed and stared at the ceiling. Ellie and Patrick had both disappeared. Adrian had wanted to marry Ellie. Ginette had heard a quarrel between them 'that night'. She had made no mention of gunshots. Perhaps they had occurred later, when she had gone out, or...

With a jolt of horrified understanding Rowena grasped the key to Adrian and Ginette's strange antagonistic relationship. Supposing Ginette was blackmailing him? She liked her clubs and drinks and clothes, yet had no visible means of support. Free tenancy of the cottage, even if Adrian had nothing else to give, was well worth having.

She may even have helped him cover his tracks, by stealing the silver from Uplands or lending Adrian the door key. Someone like Ginette would have acquired a duplicate for her own ends during her short term as an employee of Caireen's.

With a mental groan, Rowena remembered Adrian's comment when she had spotted his serpentine lamp base that first time they had shared a bed. 'Mrs Malone has a lamp like this.' So Adrian himself had been inside Uplands on at least one occasion. And the lamp was in the room from which the silver had been taken...

Pain flooded her being, but she forced herself to carry on. Somehow the bitter conclusion had already been reached, but one of the facts was not quite consistent. Ellie... Ellie ... with a rush of hope she realized the flaw in her theory. *Ellie had been seen by a third party on the following day*. Mrs Trelowan, in fact. In the paralyzing horror of Rowena's discovery, that fact had slipped right out of her mind.

Even as she allowed her jangling muscles to relax in some semblance of relief, she realized that the awkward factor might prove to be nothing more than fool's gold. Visualizing the barn scene again, she made adjustments to the sequence of events. Once more the gun barrel pointed at the two terrified youngsters, but this time the man behind it was more in control of his fury. Ordering Ellie to get out and not come back, he waited as she ran wide-eyed and dishevelled out of the barn, past the gate and up the lane before turning his attention to Patrick...

The next day Ellie went back to brave Adrian's disgust and apologize. Patrick was nowhere to be seen. Adrian would tell her nothing about the end game of the previous evening. With mounting hysteria she insisted on being told. Their echoing argument was heard by Ginette...

Then what? wondered Rowena. Adrian knew the Grangers and their estate at Cober Pool. Had he strangled Ellie, and consigned her to the 'green darkness'?

Outside the window, the sky was a pearly lilac streaking to indigo. Somewhere out there, three hundred miles away, Keith was probably enjoying a jolly evening, the chaos of his flat, the girl Chloe, a lolloping rabbit called Gordon. All would be normal and wholesome, while here Rowena was stuck in a newly sinister isolation with only her febrile imagination for company.

'I need you, Keith,' she whispered. The darkening room provided no reply.

*

'Miss Kemp?' Detective-Sergeant Pendrea's voice sounded decidedly cautious. 'I understand you tried to ring me last night. I'm sorry I wasn't available. What can I do for you?'

Rowena clutched her mobile phone hard. She was glad to be in the privacy of the office but now faced the challenge of delivering a coherent and believable tale. 'It's, er, it's about the disappearance of my cousin and Patrick Sullivan. You remember when we spoke before I was concerned that Ellie might have had an accident, or even something worse? Well, yesterday I saw a very unpleasant bloodstain in a barn belonging to Mr Polzeath.'

'I see. You're aware he used to keep animals?'

'Of course. But this was a splatter, three feet up a wall. It looked as if blood had sprayed there, with force... I understand Mr Polzeath possesses a shotgun.'

'That's a very serious allegation, Miss Kemp.'

'I'm not making any allegation. I'm just recounting some facts. How they fit together isn't a matter for me to speculate. I just wondered whether you might be able to call round on some pretext and obtain a sample to test if it *is* human blood?'

'That might be possible. I'm sure, though, that this will have no bearing on the whereabouts of your cousin. Mr Polzeath is a citizen of some local standing.'

Unwilling to challenge such idiocy for fear of losing Pendrea's slender interest, Rowena pressed on. 'If your experts were to examine his gun, is it true that they would know if it had been fired within the last few months?'

'Let's not rush ahead, Miss Kemp. Let's wait and see what happens. Now, where did you say this bloodstain was located?'

Rowena described the partition wall. 'You'll let me know when you've examined it, won't you? You'll give me a call?'

'All in due course.'

She thought quickly. Would it help to mention Ginette's claim to have heard a quarrel? Probably not. That was double hearsay, and she suspected Ginette would not respond favourably to questions from the authorities. 'Thank you,' she said.

For the next forty-eight hours Rowena stayed indoors at Uplands and buried herself in work. Adrian had sent a message via Mrs Trelowan, saying he hoped she was feeling better, but on the Friday afternoon he asked to speak to her directly.

'He's on the domestic telephone,' said Mrs Trelowan.

Rowena had no choice but to take the call. 'Hello,' she said awkwardly.

'Hello. I hear you've been hard at work. Are you recovered now?' Despite the casual words his tone sounded guarded to her guilty ear.

'Yes. I'm sorry about Wednesday night.'

'No matter. There'll be other nights. I was wondering about this weekend... or are you off to London?'

'I – er, I've got a mountain of writing to do. I'm afraid I'll be in purdah.'

'Can't I see you just for an hour? You'll need a healthy cliff walk.'

'I'm really sorry, Adrian, but I can't commit to anything just at present. Caireen could want me at any point. We're pulling together the threads of the book now and it's all pretty intense.'

'Sorry. I didn't mean to be pushy. We'll talk again later.'

'Yes. Thanks for ringing. Goodbye for now...' She put down the receiver, aware that Mrs Trelowan had heard the gist of the conversation from her position at the sink and was wearing a look of disapproval. With a murmured platitude about life being all work Rowena turned to leave, but paused as a figure with unkempt dark hair angled in front of the kitchen window and walked away from them up the drive. 'Isn't that Ginette?' she asked.

'Yes. She came to the door ten minutes ago asking for Mrs Malone. Says she needs work. I told her she was wasting her time here, but she wouldn't take that from me. She insisted on bothering Mrs Malone.'

Ginette must be desperate, thought Rowena as she returned to her paper mountain in the study. Slumped unorthopaedically in the chair, she pondered the matter of Ginette. Since finding the bloodstain she had felt much more inclined to believe the girl's story and was now willing to pay for it. To visit Ginette's cottage, though, was to risk running into Adrian, a prospect she couldn't face.

'Is Ginette Carloose coming back here to work?' she asked Caireen guilelessly that afternoon. 'I heard she might be.'

Caireen's immaculately lipsticked mouth tightened. 'That little slut,' she said. 'What gall she has! Once was quite enough. She has no interest in doing a job well, just in being paid. I turned her down, of course.'

So Ginette wouldn't be returning to Uplands... on this occasion, Rowena felt that was unfortunate. She was now set on facilitating a full discussion with that young woman. To that end, she buttonholed Ann Trelowan when the housekeeper returned to prepare the evening meal. 'Is Ginette on the telephone?' she asked.

'None of the cottages has a line,' was the reply.

'Ah. You see, I bought a couple of pictures from her a few weeks ago for my paper, and I think I need some more. Could you ask her to give me a ring on the office telephone sometime?' Mrs Trelowan nodded mutely and carried on peeling potatoes.

A call *did* come through on the office telephone a bare hour later, but the speaker was DS Pendrea.

'Regarding the matter of the alleged bloodstain in the barn,' he said heavily after a halting introduction, 'we found no evidence of any such mark when we made an inspection today.'

Rowena felt all her muscles tighten as she tried to contain her incredulity. 'You went there *today*? Did you look where I described, on the partition wall?'

'There was no partition wall. Mr Polzeath told us he was in the process of converting the barn. He had dismantled the stalls and burnt them. We asked in casual conversation why he hadn't saved the timber, and he told us it was not suitable for reuse due to animal stains. So there's your answer, Miss Kemp. I hope that puts your mind at rest.'

Rowena thought her blood pressure was going to spurt out of the top of her head. She felt dizzy with the effort of attempting to sound calm. 'What about the shotgun?' she asked. 'Did you look at that?'

'Well, you'll appreciate that was no longer necessary. And enquiries along those lines would not have been consistent with our pretext for being there.'

'Which was?'

'A tourist lost a pedigree dog at Praa Sands yesterday. Colleagues of mine have been checking caravans, barns, outhouses... Mr Polzeath was happy to show us around.'

'Did you see the remnants of the bonfire?' she asked faintly.

'Yes, Miss Kemp. There was a pile of ash. I hope this has been helpful to you, and you have some news from your cousin soon.'

*

Rowena's sense of thwarted dismay persisted into the weekend. Every piece of apparent progress – a photograph of Sullivan, an ugly bloodstain in a barn – seemed to lead nowhere. In less than a month her job at Uplands would be finished. Was Ellie's disappearance never to be solved? She felt she couldn't face June again without an answer.

When Ginette telephoned late on the Saturday morning, Rowena acknowledged to herself the irony of the relief she felt. For some reason, the girl had not used the office number but had rung the domestic telephone; once again Mrs Trelowan was standing nearby, so Rowena was obliged to speak with circumspection.

'I heard you want something from me after all,' said Ginette when identities had been confirmed.

Rowena glanced at Ann Trelowan's rigid spine. 'That's right. I've been thinking about the last time we spoke, and I feel a financial agreement is possible, depending on the quality of the product. Perhaps we can meet again soon, somewhere mutually convenient?'

The girl seemed to catch on to the reason for Rowena's generalization. 'Is that old witch Trelowan still there?' she said. 'I get it. Come to my place tomorrow at four – no, best make it five. For the right price I'll tell you everything they said.'

'Tomorrow afternoon. Fine. But Ginette –' The dialling tone cut in and Rowena slowly replaced the receiver. That was annoying; she had wanted their rendezvous site to be well away from Anwith Farm. Now she would have to take great care to avoid Adrian.

That evening Rowena had no time to brood. Caireen was demonstrating mediumship in a Plymouth theatre; over a thousand tickets had been sold, and she needed both the 'regalia' and her full back-up team of Rowena, Brett and Daniel.

After a prolonged but highly successful session, Caireen sank exhausted in the dressing-room while Danny and Brett took bookings for private sittings in a front-of-house function room. Rowena watched as Brett guided Danny's lap-top computer efforts with an air of amused tolerance. 'I'm off up to London soon,' he said. 'Danny will have to be able to handle this. We've got the Duchess of Stour coming to consult Caireen in three weeks' time; I want to be sure he doesn't make any unfortunate double bookings.'

As the last eager client left the room, Brett stifled a yawn and prepared to follow, but Danny remained seated. He looked miserable and confused.

'What's wrong, Danny?' Rowena asked him kindly.

'I couldn't see the purple,' he muttered.

Brett rolled his eyes. 'Any more purple and she'd have resembled a Victoria plum! Are you colour blind, brother?'

'I couldn't see it,' persisted Danny, ignoring him. 'I should have been able to. I did once before. Roger can do it all the time. I'm no good...'

'Come on.' Brett helped him out of the chair. 'If you're talking about auras, don't let Mother hear you.' He gave Rowena a conspiratorial wink and escorted Danny backstage to Caireen.

Rowena had been pleasantly surprised by Brett's attitude towards her since the episode of the private detective. She had expected an atmosphere of strain and suspicion, but if anything, bringing her identity into the open had resolved underlying tensions. 'You're here to do a job,' he had told her, 'and you're doing it well. That's all we're interested in.' By mutual consent, Danny had not been informed. 'He might get mystical about you,' Brett had said frankly. 'He was very attached to Ellie. We're best not to stir that particular pond.'

The next day dawned hot and still. The office was stuffy, and after an intensive morning of writing Rowena found she was unable to eat much of the large roast meal Mrs Trelowan provided. By two thirty everyone had gone their separate ways: Brett to the drawing-room to read all the papers, Caireen to call on Charles Granger and Danny to wander down to Graw Cove with an adventure book.

Rowena wished she could have accompanied Danny and sat on a rock with her feet in cool water as the sea sucked and gurgled in the crevices beneath. Instead, she needed to give all her concentration to the forthcoming interview with Ginette. It was essential that the girl should not feel obliged to embellish her story in the hope of improving payment. Rowena wanted only the truth.

If Ginette *had* been in league with Adrian, that too raised potential complications. Would she try to play them off against each other in a 'highest bidder' situation, the price for silence versus that for information? Had she already told Adrian Rowena's identity?

The afternoon seemed to crawl. At four, Rowena knocked softly on the drawing-room door to find out if Brett would like tea. There was no reply. She made a cup for herself, then carried it upstairs to drink while she washed and changed. She had decided to walk to the cottages in order to obviate the problem of parking right in front of Anwith Farm.

As she set off past the parked Clio and Mercedes, she felt the hot sluggish air wrap round her like a stifling blanket. Even walking slowly up the peninsula triggered runnels of sweat down her face and back. At the summit she paused, panting, and brushed a lank piece of fringe to one side. Looking back at the stone gateposts of Uplands she thought briefly of Adrian, his first hesitant kiss at that very spot. Now all emotions were suspended, frozen into neutrality, a nothingness where even rage and pain were excluded. June lived with this every day.

She plodded on, her limbs feeling unusually leaden. Down through the lanes she walked, meeting neither vehicles nor people. Soon the cottages appeared, with their little square gardens across the lane. Mrs Trelowan's patch had neat dahlias and border shrubs. The lupins Rowena had given her were planted just outside the house. Ginette's garden, by contrast, was choked with weeds. Only a small area around her whirligig had been cleared.

With a furtive glance towards the farmhouse Rowena knocked on the door. There was no answer. She checked her watch: five o'clock exactly. She knocked again.

Increasingly anxious in case Adrian should emerge, she retreated around the corner of Mrs Trelowan's cottage to the narrow earthen track which separated the backs of the dwellings from a high hedgerow. Everything was very still. She padded to the back door at the centre of the terrace and found it was ajar.

'Ginette?' She kept her voice soft.

'Ginette?' Louder.

All she could hear was a vague droning of flies nearby. Angrily she turned to peer in through the window. If Ginette was attempting some heavy-handed one-upmanship...

The sight behind the glass startled her. Across the narrow, cluttered kitchen only a thin strip of the floor linoleum was visible, but she could see the dark stains defacing it. There were smears too on the cupboard above...

Heart hammering, Rowena elbowed open the door and stood on the threshold, appalled. Gouts and smudges and splashes of blood were scattered everywhere. The air was thick with the smell, and by the sink the largest pool of all crawled and heaved and buzzed with a crust of bluebottles.

15

Rowena backed clumsily against the door frame and stared wide-eyed around the room. So much blood. So many streaks and splashes... yet there was no sign of a body.

She retreated to the lane and took great gasps of air, then hurried round to the front to peer in at the window to Ginette's sitting-room. It was untidy, but not apparently ransacked. Much of the room was in shadow, but she could see no evidence here of bloodstains. Neither was there any human habitation...

After knocking fruitlessly at Mrs Trelowan's door, Rowena returned to the back lane, pulled the mobile out of her bag and rang 999. Tersely she described the locality and the scene she had found, before adding: 'Detective-Sergeant Pendrea knows the tenant of this cottage, and he knows me. I think he should be involved as soon as possible.'

She sat in a nearby field as the sun beat down, only climbing weakly to her feet as she heard a patrol car negotiating the lane. Two stocky police constables emerged from the car; she told her story again, then hung back dutifully as they entered the cottage.

'Is she in there?' she asked when one finally came out again. He shook his head and proceeded to radio his base for assistance.

During the next hour Rowena found herself both marginalized and central to the investigation, lurking at the periphery one minute, attentively questioned the next. It was with mixed feelings that she recognized DS Pendrea when he finally arrived; his glance towards her as he was briefed by the constable seemed infused with hostility.

After another long delay he strode towards her. 'We meet again, Miss Kemp. I understand you discovered this unpleasant scene.'

'Yes.'

'May I ask what you were doing here?'

'I told Constable Fry. Ginnie had invited me round for a discussion. She was expecting me at five. I walked over from Uplands and was here on the dot. No one answered my knock, so I went round the back. As soon as I saw the kitchen I rang your people. I didn't disturb anything.'

He pursed his lips and gave her a long, heavy-lidded stare. 'I thought Ginette Carloose was no friend of yours. I seem to remember you tried to suggest that she stole silverware from Uplands to discredit your cousin.'

'Sergeant Pendrea...' Rowena felt peculiar. It was all this standing in the sun. 'I came to you because my family has been worried about Ellie. You weren't able to tell me very much, so it seemed reasonable to make a few simple enquiries of my own. Ginnie indicated that she was willing to talk to me about the events of last year when Ellie and Patrick Sullivan disappeared. She telephoned me yesterday morning and asked me over today.'

'These cottages aren't on the phone. Did she say where she was ringing from?'

'No, but the nearest box is that one by the pub in the village.'

'Was anyone with you when you took the call?'

'Mrs Trelowan. She lives in that cottage.' She pointed. 'She's also the housekeeper at Uplands...sorry, you know all this, don't you? Ginnie rang through on the domestic phone, which is in the kitchen. Ann Trelowan answered.'

'Is she at Uplands now?'

'No. After cooking Sunday lunch she goes off duty. I don't know where she is. She's not at home.'

DS Pendrea wrote none of these details down, but Rowena had a new impression of data filed away for future use.

'We shall want a statement from you, Miss Kemp.'

'Today?'

'Tomorrow will do. Someone will come to Uplands to see you.'

'Oh – I'd rather it was another place. Mrs Malone is very protective of her clients. Some quite famous people come for private sittings. They wouldn't want to encounter police.'

'As you wish. We'll see you at the station, then. But we shall still need to interview all the local residents as possible witnesses, and that includes the occupants of Uplands.'

They moved to one side as another car drew up and official-looking passengers climbed out, and Rowena sensed a temporary reprieve. 'Sergeant,' she said hurriedly as he prepared to join them, 'do you now think as I do, that Ellie's disappearance is suspicious? Will you be reopening the file?'

He stroked his straggly moustache. 'The file, as you put it, has never been closed. And yes...I think you can say that we perceive a possible link between Miss Drinkwater and today's events.' His eyes were grey and wintry as he scrutinized her. Somehow, she felt, it was not the interpretation she had been hoping for.

Minutes later, Rowena stiffened as the figure of Adrian appeared on the scene. As soon as he saw her, he hurried to her side.

'Rowena, what's going on? All these police!'

'Something's happened in Ginette's cottage. Something horrible. There's blood everywhere, and no sign of Ginette.'

'Good God!' He looked shocked, but she found herself unable to assess whether the reaction was feigned. 'Were you on your way to see me?' This time the gleam of hope in his eye did seem genuine.

'Not exactly. That is... I was going to buy some photos from Ginette for my paper. She asked me round this afternoon, but nobody answered, and the kitchen is full of blood.'

'*You* found it? Oh, Rowena, you poor girl.' He flung his arm round her shoulders and squeezed tightly. Snakes of confusion coiled and plaited inside her.

'I think I'd better go back to Uplands now, or Caireen will be wondering what's happening. I expect the police will want to talk to you, as you live so near.'

He looked around vaguely. 'I suppose you're right. It's funny – they were here just the other day, searching for a dog. Where's your car? Do you need a lift?'

'Er, the police have said they'll take me.' She pulled away from him with a hesitant valedictory smile. Over by the cottages, DS Pendrea appeared to be looking her way.

She wondered how much he had seen.

Caireen's family seemed, like Adrian, duly shocked by the news, but within minutes they were discussing their own practicalities.

'This area will be swarming with Press soon,' said Brett with ill-concealed irritation. 'It's the sort of bizarre case they love. The Duchess is due in three weeks. She won't want to come here.'

Caireen sighed heavily. 'I'd see her in London but the house is closed up and there'll be no staff...'

Rowena drained her teacup. They were all gathered together in the drawing-room; despite the mid-evening hour, the day's heavy heat had robbed them of any appetite for an evening meal. Danny had made a plate of cucumber sandwiches. 'The police commented that whoever the blood came from couldn't have lived,' she said. 'If that was Ginette, who do you think could have done such a thing?'

Brett gave an elegant shrug. 'She was such a little trollop, it could have been any of her casuals. I wouldn't be too surprised if she took paying clients.'

'Oh... Do you think that's why the body has been hidden? To avoid DNA analysis?' That aspect had been puzzling Rowena ever since the discovery.

'Could be. These days, every bumpkin knows about DNA testing.'

Rowena remembered Ginette's voice on the telephone, discussing their arrangement to meet. 'Come... at four – no, best make it five,' she had said. Did that mean that she was expecting someone earlier in the afternoon?

She found herself fervently hoping that the truth lay along those lines. Because if it didn't, she herself was responsible. Her determined exhumation of a ten-month-old mystery had triggered this savage killing, and whatever kind of coarse, poor, ignorant country girl Ginette had been, she hadn't deserved to die.

It was late that night when she rang Keith. She sat on her bed with the mobile clamped to her ear, less paranoid about being electronically overheard now that Caireen and Brett knew who she was.

'Christ, Rowena, you've got to get out of there!' was Keith's reaction on hearing the gist of the day's events.

'It's not so simple. I have to give a statement tomorrow, and... let's just say I have a gut feeling the police won't let me go so easily.'

'There's a crazed killer on the loose. Even if today's bloodbath *isn't* linked with Ellie's disappearance, he might go for another young woman. *Please* be careful, Ro. Don't go walking out on your own.'

She was still reflecting on his second sentence. 'Do you believe me now about Ellie?' she asked quietly. 'Do you think she's probably dead?'

There was a long pause before his voice came over the line, compassionate and sad. 'Yes,' he said. 'Now I do.'

*

Rowena felt exhausted after a morning with the police in Helston. She had given her statement to a friendly woman police constable, but then Pendrea and a pale-eyed inspector had taken over and things had gone steadily downhill. What had been her real reason for mentioning the bloodstain in Adrian Polzeath's barn? Had there indeed been such a stain? Where had she heard about the shotgun? Had she seen it? Had she been trying to frame Polzeath... for some past *or* future crime?

They hadn't cautioned her, and much of their dialogue was veiled innuendo, but Rowena had been very afraid. 'I wouldn't frame Adrian,' she objected at last. 'We were friends. I played chess with him.'

It was impossible to know what was going on in their minds, but instantly she felt she had said the wrong thing. DS Pendrea's heavy features were slowly splitting open as he permitted himself a lop-sided, somewhat lupine smile.

A police officer decanted her from his patrol car at Uplands. She had been asked oh-so-politely if they might examine her own vehicle, and had felt it unwise to refuse.

Soon after her arrival, the doorbell rang and Madeleine Granger bustled in. Although it was almost midday, the family was soon gathered again in the west-facing drawing-room with coffee.

'This is all very shocking about Ginette,' said Madeleine, looking from one face to another.

'I didn't like her,' said Daniel, just as Brett was opening his mouth to reply. 'I thought I did, but I didn't. She was rude to me.'

Rowena saw a twisted, bittersweet expression pass fleetingly across Caireen's face.

'Did you have to run a gauntlet?' Brett asked Madeleine. 'I've heard Anwith is awash with Press. They've been telephoning us all morning hoping for a gory account from Rowena. It can only get worse. I'm thinking of engaging a security guard.'

'It will get worse,' said Rowena soberly. 'Just because I was first on the scene at Ginette's, the police seem to be treating me as more of a suspect than a witness. They've even impounded my car! I found myself having to justify my movements to them.' She leaned forward. 'I don't suppose anybody here saw me yesterday? I set off on foot about half-past four.'

Brett shook his head. 'Sorry. I was crashed out. I had too much wine with lunch and fell asleep over the papers.'

She scanned each face with the same earnestness as Madeleine, but there were no helpful responses, only apologetic murmurs from Caireen and Daniel. It struck her that Madeleine herself wouldn't meet her eye but was adjusting her plump body in the seat in obvious discomfort.

'What about Mrs Trelowan, dear?' asked Caireen. 'You said she didn't answer your knock, but she might have been in one of her odd moods. Perhaps she saw you arrive through her window.'

Rowena frowned. 'She never made herself known. I think I'll ask her, though, if you'll excuse me.'

Guiltily she paused outside the drawing-room door. Despite Madeleine's recent confidences, this morning she sensed a subtle closing of ranks against her as Madeleine rejoined her natural allies. There had to be a reason why.

Suddenly Madeleine was speaking. 'I don't know what to do,' she said in a rush. 'You see, I was driving past the farm cottages yesterday and I did spot a blonde woman standing on Ginette's doorstep. It might have been Rowena. But that was three o'clock, not five!'

'Are you sure?' The voice was Brett's.

'Positive. I was out delivering raffle tickets between two and four...'

A creak nearby made Rowena start and hasten away from the door. Ann Trelowan was emerging from the kitchen. Rowena glanced at her tight-lipped face: violent murder had occurred only yards away from her home, yet the family here were maintaining their precious upstairs/downstairs social distance. The matter had barely been mentioned at breakfast time. Perhaps Ann would like an opportunity to talk...

'Have you a minute?' she asked in a low voice. In the kitchen, she recounted the nature of her problem. 'It's silly, but I feel the need to prove myself to the police,' she finished up. 'I realize it may have been inconvenient for you to come to the door when I knocked, but did you by any chance see me through a window?' It was just possible that Mrs Trelowan had wanted no part of all the official fuss, and had kept a deliberate low profile late into the evening.

'I'm sorry,' the housekeeper said abruptly. 'I wasn't there.' Seeing Rowena's crestfallen expression she added, 'I walked over to Praa Sands and drank tea in that café on the front. I was watching the holiday-makers, admiring their energy in that muggy weather. Then I visited an elderly widower on behalf of the church on my way home.'

'Were the police still there when you got back?'

'Yes. Two constables asked me who I was and when I'd left and all kinds of things about Ginette – her family, her visitors, whatever.'

'Who do you think did it, Ann?'

'That's not for me to say.'

'Just an opinion...'

'I don't give opinions. These matters are best left in the hands of the authorities.'

Rowena wasn't at all sure she could agree with that sentiment.

True to Brett's prediction, the area did fill up with journalists. Rowena felt frustrated by the lack of her car; she would have liked to meet them as a fellow professional, find out what tips they had received from their police contacts. The best she could do was telephone Mick Vean and ask him to relay to her anything his crime-reporting colleague Jim could garner.

By the following day a strapping security guard was stationed at the gateway to Uplands, vetting all visitors and checking any doubtful individuals with Brett via his mobile.

'What a nightmare,' groaned Caireen that lunch time. 'We have many more clients from Thursday onwards – all those who booked in Plymouth. Nothing could be less conducive to a successful consultation than *this*!'

Rowena sat in her office throughout the afternoon, editing and polishing Caireen's autobiography. Periodically she stared through the front window to rest her eyes, and it was during one of these breaks that she saw the distant figure. It was shapeless in a red anorak and half buried beneath an enormous rucksack, yet Rowena thought she detected an air of familiarity about its physique. She watched as the stick-like legs marched steadily onwards, burden notwithstanding, crossing her line of vision from right to left. There was definitely something recognizable about the gait. In other circumstances, she would have had no doubt, but *here*...

Whoever it was, this person had somehow circumvented Brett's security cordon. He (for it looked like a he) must have come along the coastal path above Graw Cove, missed the National Trust sign and strayed on to the private headland.

Still ambivalent, she hurried through into the hall. It seemed to be deserted, but just as she left through the front door she glimpsed Brett on the stairs.

Keeping up the pace in case he was following, she angled towards the highly coloured intruder. 'Excuse me,' she called. He didn't seem to hear, so she covered a few more yards and tried again. 'Excuse me!'

He stopped, and turned. With a rush of gladness she saw that what she had suspected in the office was true – the 'hiker' was Keith.

'What are you *doing* here?' she hissed.

He kept his own voice low. 'That dark-haired chap's watching us. Pretend to give me some directions.'

Rowena gestured towards Penzance. 'I can't believe you're here. Are you mad? What does Kevin think?'

'Kevin didn't have any choice.'

'Keith, you . . . you anorak!'

'It's a cagoule, actually. And don't worry. I haven't got myself sacked. I'm on holiday, somewhat short notice, coincidentally in this area. I thought you might need some help.'

Mixed emotions flooded Rowena's chest; both irritation and profound gratitude fought for precedence. 'Quickly,' she said, waving her arm in the air once more. 'Tell me where you're staying.'

'I'm booked into a Bed and Breakfast for the next fortnight. It's in Penzance: Chy-Growyn on Alexandra Road. Can you come tonight?'

'Tonight's impossible. And my car's out of action. I'll explain later. Have you got wheels down here?'

'Yes.'

'Then can you meet me in the National Trust car-park above Graw Cove tomorrow around seven?'

'Yes. We'll eat together if you like.'

'Yes, please. Now *go* – and Keith . . . thanks.'

He plodded towards Praa Sands as she returned to Uplands.

'I saw that specimen from upstairs,' commented Brett. 'Thought he might be a photographer trying it on.'

'No,' she said. 'Just a hiker who'd got a bit lost. He's walking the coastal path . . . wanted to know if he was far from the youth hostel in Penzance.'

'You took your time explaining.'

'He's French,' she lied.

Just before supper Rowena's mobile rang. It was Mick Vean. 'Listen, doll,' he said. 'Jim has passed on some gen for you, but he wants an exclusive in return. Can you give him an account of your discovery of the scene at the Carloose cottage? Five hundred words should do.'

'I suppose so,' she conceded with distaste.

'Good. Well – you asked about the farmer's shotgun. It was actually licensed for his father, Richard Polzeath. This gun is missing, and Adrian Polzeath claims he has no idea when it disappeared. I don't know what your angle is on this, but the incident at the cottage was a stabbing: the forensic people are confident of that.'

'I see. Thanks, Mick.'

'Any time. There's something else you might like to know, but it's strictly hush-hush. Apparently the place was quite a tip upstairs. Not done over, or anything, but untidy, squalid. Grubby make-up bags, clothes strewn around . . . There was an overflowing waste bin in the bathroom. Down among the tissues and the hair they found something interesting.'

'Go on!'

'It was the dipstick from a pregnancy test. The cops think that's the motive. They reckon young Ginnie was up the spout.'

16

'I can't decide whether I'm glad you're here, or angry,' said Rowena to Keith. They were sitting in a harbourside pub in the tiny fishing village of Mousehole. This part of the coast, to the west of Penzance, would hopefully be safe from the presence of other Uplands residents.

'"Glad" sounds better,' he said. 'I don't intend to get in the way, but I have been worried about you. I crossed Graw Head partly to take a look at Uplands, and partly hoping you'd spot me. You said your office faced the front.'

'It was risky. Brett might have got to you first. He'd have chewed you up and spat you out. They're paranoid about trespassers just at present.' She collected their glasses to take to the bar for a refill. 'Who's looking after my rabbit, by the way?'

'The chaps in the flat. He's fine.'

'Won't Chloe miss you – or is she coming down?'

He tried, and failed, to suppress a knowing glance. 'No,' he said. 'She's latched on to somebody else now, thank God. It was never particularly serious.' He grinned. 'I was just trying to make you jealous.'

'Pull the other one,' she laughed, turning to the bar to hide her face. She didn't know if he was serious or not, but he had caught her on the raw. She *had* felt jealous – or piqued, or neglected, or whatever – and that had led straight to the fire pit with Adrian Polzeath.

Over renewed glasses of cider she gave Keith a detailed review of all the recent events around Anwith. He didn't interrupt but nodded periodically, his eyes sharp behind the rounded spectacle frames. 'What are your thoughts now on Ellie's disappearance?' he asked when she had finished.

'Well... if that bloodstain in the barn *is* significant, then I think Patrick was shot there, and Ellie killed the next day.'

'By Adrian?'

'So it appears.' She looked down at the table. 'That supposedly missing shotgun – it's so convenient.'

'True... I'm sorry about your Farmer Giles. I got the impression that you were fond of him.'

'I was.' A red-hot lance seemed to tear through her stomach; abruptly she raised her head. 'To continue – Ginette was an accessory after the fact, and may have blackmailed him.'

'You say that by reason of access to the silver?'

'Yes. It had to have been Ginette... or Ellie.'

'Mm. You know these people, Ro; you've been living among them. To me, though, they're just names, so I feel more free to consider alternative scenarios. I think no one can be ruled out. We should assess motive and opportunity for every person in the immediate locality – starting with Mrs Trelowan.'

'Ann Trelowan?' Suddenly out of nowhere a comment of Madeleine's came winging into her brain. *'She would do anything for Adrian – anything at all.'*

While Rowena baulked at the logical extrapolation Keith continued. 'She could have taken the silver from Uplands. She could even have done the murders – all of them. You said Adrian's key drawer was common knowledge, so she could have unlocked the gun cupboard and taken the shotgun.'

'I've only got Ann's word that Ellie was alive at Uplands on that second day,' said Rowena slowly. 'Nobody else saw her.'

'So she *could* have been killed with Patrick. That makes more sense. But motive's tricky for your housekeeper.'

'Blind loyalty... protecting Adrian somehow? It's just conceivable.'

'Let's keep going. We'll concentrate on Ellie and Patrick's deaths at present. Who else might have wanted to kill them? You had suspicions about Daniel at one point.'

'He's possessive and emotionally labile. If Ann isn't involved then her story stands and Ellie *was* alive at Uplands on September the fifth. Daniel had a perfect chance to kill her because everybody else was out that afternoon...but why? Did she say Patrick had left and she was going to follow him? Did he catch her taking the silver?' She paused as the cold blue-green depths of Cober Pool once more materialized in her mind. 'There's a problem, Keith. Danny doesn't drive. At least, I'm told he doesn't, and I've never seen him do it. Perhaps he hid the body in the house and confessed to Brett that evening when they set off together for the cinema. Brett decided to keep it dark. He's a fixer: he knew it would destroy Caireen if Danny had to face the judicial process.

'They doubled back, knowing they had very little time to dispose of Ellie more definitively...Caireen would be back from her National Trust meeting by ten thirty or so. They had to use whatever means were to hand, namely a deep lake and a neighbour's ancient rowing boat.'

'And Brett took the silver in order to provide a believable explanation for Ellie's sudden disappearance,' added Keith.

'Yes. It's possible, isn't it? But I don't know where the missing shotgun fits in.'

'It might not. What about Brett as a prime suspect? Can you think of any motive for him?'

Rowena twined her fingers together. 'He did, er, try to jump me the night I rowed out across Cober Pool.'

'*Did* he indeed?'

'Yes – it was rather nice.' She flashed him a naughty look. 'You don't have to wear that disapproving face. Nothing much happened. But I wonder – seriously – whether he tried it on with Ellie.'

'Jealousy again?'

'No...that doesn't fit. The spirit was very much that of a light dalliance, a meaningless fling. Unless...' She found that she couldn't go on.

'Pregnancy?' prompted Keith gently. 'Like Ginette?'

'I suppose it can't be ruled out. But it feels all wrong. Someone like Brett wouldn't be careless in that department. And I don't believe Ellie would have got involved in that way with him.' (*Was* Adrian's testimony of Ellie's purity worth the candle now? she wondered. Had he merely been sowing insurance for the future?)

'Right. So motive doubtful for Brett. Also opportunity, if your schedule of the family's movements that day is correct.'

'Perhaps she caught him late at night when everyone was in bed. She said she was pregnant, he lost his head and strangled her, and the rest is as we outlined except that Danny stowed away in the car and Brett had to swear him to secrecy. But again... I can't envisage Brett panicking in that way. I *can*, though, imagine him doing something unpleasant out of necessity, in a calculating manner.'

'Let's leave Brett for now. Who else? Caireen?'

She shrugged. 'Like Brett, Caireen's only chance would have been late at night. And why? Ellie had a lot of affection for her, and I think it was reciprocated.'

'The Grangers?'

'Hm. Madeleine maybe, in some obscure Machiavellian plot to bring discredit upon Caireen. Charles, though, would do nothing to rock the boat at Uplands.'

'There!' Keith drained his cider glass. 'The answers so far are clear as mud. Are you ready to talk about Ginette?'

'If you can stand it. I don't know when we'll next get a chance.'

'I'll kick off, then. From what you've told me, Ginette was murdered in her own kitchen some time on Sunday, probably in the afternoon. Possible motives range from an argument with a casual lover or client, a declaration of pregnancy that went down rather badly, or someone determined to stop her talking to you...' His eyes flicked to her face as she gave an unhappy grimace of guilt. 'Did you tell anybody at all about your appointment with Ginette?'

'No. But Ann Trelowan knew I wanted to contact her – she acted as intermediary. And she was on the scene when Ginette rang...' She bit her lip. 'In fact, I was expecting Ginette's call on the office phone, but she came through on the domestic line, which meant that Ann answered first. I wonder...'

'Yes, so do I.'

'It could have been an innocent mistake. Either way, Ann must have heard me confirm Sunday afternoon with Ginette. I'd told her I was buying pictures, though.'

'Perhaps she didn't believe you. Perhaps Ginette had started teasing her, dropping hints about how much she would reveal. Maybe there was point-blank blackmail. A lot of this could equally apply to Polzeath.'

'I know nothing of Adrian's movements that afternoon,' Rowena said, 'but Ann spoke of drinking tea alone at Praa Sands, before visiting some elderly man. It's a poor alibi. You'd have thought she could have done better.'

'If the murder was planned, yes. But this has all the hallmarks of a spur-of-the-moment killing. Let's assume that it was, just for now.

We have Ann Trelowan standing in Ginette's kitchen with a dead body...'

'Ann can't drive,' burst out Rowena. 'She goes everywhere by bike. She couldn't have disposed of Ellie on her own, and Ellie was small and slender. Ginette was quite well built.'

'Then she had an accomplice. Polzeath's the most likely candidate. Maybe he simply became involved afterwards, in the role you were suggesting for Brett. He could be protecting Mrs Trelowan because she insisted she did the deed for him.'

Rowena peered round to ensure that no one else was listening. 'It all seems so speculative, but I suppose we've no choice. Let's go through the rest of the list... Brett: he claimed to be asleep that afternoon but no one saw him. His car, though, was parked in front of my office window at least until I set off walking myself. Motive is difficult. Brett's fastidious – I can't imagine him embroiling himself with Ginette.' (But Adrian did, came a silent reminder. In the right circumstances, when a party night was steaming and brains glowed slow with alcohol, Ginette had the capacity to dazzle and ensnare.)

'Caireen,' she went on: 'she was at Uplands in the morning and with Charles Granger that afternoon. Motive: I can't imagine. She disliked Ginette, I could tell, but so did a lot of people, including Daniel. Daniel himself: the transport problem again. The Grangers: Charles Granger has an alibi, Madeleine doesn't. Motive a complete mystery.'

'So that's the list,' said Keith.

'Not quite. There's one more suspect, at least in the police's book.'

He raised his eyebrows.

'One Rowena Kemp. This is the girl who appeared out of the blue asking awkward questions about her cousin Ellie, and about Ginette. Within weeks Ginette is violently murdered. Lo and behold, that same girl claims to have stumbled upon the scene. Is she telling the truth, or has she just indulged in an orgy of misguided vigilante justice? There is some evidence to implicate her, though the motive may not wash with a jury. What about her trying to point the finger at Adrian Polzeath with talk of bloodstains in barns, and shotguns? An elegant case of killing two birds with one stone, or a farrago of idiocy that said jury would find even harder to swallow?'

Keith was watching her tensely; she couldn't continue out loud. But Pendrea's mental processes had moved on from there, she was sure. He had seen Adrian's affectionate gesture, heard, perhaps from Mrs Trelowan, that they were close. A much simpler motive was at hand. What if Ginette had pronounced Adrian the father of her child and refused to get rid of it? Miss Kemp may well have murdered her in a possessive rage. The shotgun story? Either a mistake, or a clever attempt to put distance between herself and Polzeath in the minds of detectives...

'You spoke of evidence,' said Keith.

'Circumstantial only. Why did Miss Kemp, who on previous visits to Anwith Farm had always taken her car, leave it behind this time? Who was the blonde woman spotted by Madeleine Granger in the vicinity of the cottages at three o'clock? I reckon the police think I went twice, the first time by car. After hiding Ginette's body I felt obliged to go back because Mrs Trelowan had known about my appointment. I went on foot so no one would want to examine my car. It also meant that any stains on my clothes could be attributed to my so-called discovery of the scene.'

'That's daft,' said Keith. 'Forensic people know all about the direction of blood splashes and the like. They can tell the difference. If the cops seriously suspected you, they'd have asked for your clothes by now.'

Rowena fingered the outside of her glass, making a line in the thin haze of condensation. 'Yesterday,' she said quietly, 'they did.'

An hour later, she stood with Keith on one arm of Mousehole's stout harbour wall, next to the narrow entrance where boats came and went in daylight. It was now dark, and lights from a restaurant across the harbour were reflected in the tranquil water. They had eaten hearty food in their pub, and knew that soon Rowena would have to return to Uplands.

'You don't really mind my coming?' asked Keith as a light breeze skimmed around their shoulders.

'No. I'm glad. Thank you, Keith.'

'I thought I might offer moral support, as it were. Even immoral support if you wanted...no, perhaps not. But someone to talk to, anyway. Someone nearby. I've got two weeks, and my arrangements are flexible.'

She gave his hand a light squeeze of gratitude.

'I've been reading some more about Eileen Garrett,' he said, studiously avoiding any attempt to capitalize on her gesture.

'You were right, she had an excellent reputation as a medium. But some of those claims about the R101 seances have been disputed.'

'How so? The transcripts showed pages and pages of technical information about the airship that could only have come from members of the dead crew.'

He shook his head. 'Not necessarily. The myth is that of a refined woman articulating all kinds of scientific jargon she had no experience of whilst in a trance. But she had been worried about the airship *before* the disaster. She had seen precognitive flashes of a dirigible crashing in flames some months earlier. She had discussed this in depth with Sir Sefton Brandon, the Director of Civil Aviation, who knew plenty about the R101's construction. After the crash, the newspapers printed all the details they could. Eileen Garrett was a prominent member of London society, but she wasn't a brainless Sloane-type or a dotty Madam Zingara. She's been described as a "visceral intellectual". I think that in all good faith she was regurgitating things that she'd picked up before, either consciously or subliminally, believing that they emanated from Captain Irwin via her spirit guide Uvani. That, plus a bit of telepathy from the relevant sitters.'

'How do you explain Irwin's comment that the airship "almost scraped the roofs at Achy", and no one knew where Achy was? They had to find a special large-scale railway map before anyone identified the hamlet.'

Keith cleared his throat. A few feet below where they stood, the dark water surged gently in the harbour mouth. Right across the bay shone a faint twinkle of lights on St Michael's Mount. 'It seems Mrs Garrett used to motor frequently between Calais and Paris, and there was an obvious signpost to Achy on that road . . . Sceptics think she subconsciously retained the name. There's no actual evidence that the airship *did* pass over Achy . . .'

'I see.' Rowena tried to keep the snap out of her voice. His apologetic manner irritated her; was he expecting her to shoot the messenger? 'There's another dimension, though. Mrs Garrett had been receiving seance warnings about the R101 a full year before the crash from another dead pilot.'

'Hinchliffe.'

'Yes: he'd drowned during an attempted east-west Atlantic crossing in a small two-seater plane against the headwinds. He kept telling Mrs Garrett how anxious he was about the construction of the R101.'

'So she would be alert even then to newspaper articles on the subject – and there were plenty. A lot of national prestige was riding on the project. Many of the technical choices – like the heavy new diesel engines – had been well aired in the papers.'

Rowena sighed. 'I accept what you're saying. Mrs Garrett imbibed these things in good faith and imagined they came from Hinchliffe and Irwin. But how do you account for this: Hinchliffe pinpointed the location of missing documents for his widow via Eileen Garrett. The widow herself, over a long series of sessions, changed from total sceptic to believer.'

He gave an enigmatic smile. 'I must read about that. For now, though, we'd better agree to differ. I had a theory to put to you about Caireen Malone's Wimbledon Theatre success, but perhaps it's a bit too late for that tonight. Let's head back.'

She nodded her approval and they strolled amiably around the picturesque harbour to the steep road leading out of the village. Keith's car, an elderly Mini, was parked in a lay-by on the coast road. He said little as they drove back to Anwith, but as Uplands approached he expressed concern. 'Are you sure I can't take you to the door?' he asked. 'I don't like leaving you here. There's half the headland to cover, and that maniac may be on the loose.'

'"That maniac" may live at Uplands,' she said drily. 'Don't worry. The security guard stays at the gate till twelve. I'm sure he'll escort me if I ask him nicely. He'll assume I've been to the village pub.'

'Well... take care.'

'I shall.' She paused just before climbing out. 'You know, Keith, in all this awfulness there's one thing I consider as positive. It sounds grotesque, but – for the first time the authorities are actively combing this area for a woman's body. There's a chance they might find Ellie. I do hope they will.'

'Now *there*'s an interesting motive for the dispatch of Ginette,' said Keith. 'Don't tell your friend DS Pendrea, will you?'

She grinned.

Two days later the household at Uplands was clearly ruffled. Rowena left the office to take a light lunch only to find a thunderous-looking Brett deep in conversation with his mother over the salad. 'What infernal gall!' he was saying. 'You aren't going to go get involved, surely?'

'Sorry,' muttered Rowena from the doorway, preparing to retreat.

'Come in, Rowena.' Caireen gave her a warm smile. 'You might as well know what's going on. Tell her, Brett.'

Brett's scowl momentarily darkened, then he shrugged. 'I've just heard from a journalist. Ryan Carloose has come back to Anwith. He's badgering all the reporters to make him an offer for a "My Life With Ginnie" brand of story. Suddenly, it seems she wasn't so bad after all. Just a high-spirited country girl.'

'I trust he has an alibi,' said Rowena.

'Oh, yes. He was in Bodmin with a clutch of eyewitnesses. But that's not the problem. He's whipping up synthetic outrage because Ginette hasn't been found yet. He claims all the evidence will disappear. He points out that the famous medium Caireen Malone is right on the spot. In a nutshell, he wants some newspaper to organize a public seance.'

'I wouldn't have minded if he'd come to me privately,' said Caireen, 'but this is all so tacky. He's only interested in enhancing public awareness so his story will be worth more. To the best of my knowledge, he and Ginette never exchanged a civil word while she was alive.'

'It's putting us more in the goldfish bowl than ever,' said Brett. 'Several clients have cancelled.'

'We'll have to hope this blows over,' said Caireen.

Brett shook his head gloomily. 'Some hope.'

Rowena was still ruminating over the complication of a loose-cannon-former-common-law husband when her mobile rang that evening. She was in the bedroom, stretched out with a copy of the *Telegraph* graciously donated by Brett. 'Hello,' she said idly into the mouthpiece.

'Rowena? It's Keith here.'

'Hi. How's your holiday going?'

'Listen. You won't believe what I've got to tell you. Are you alone? Good...

'I've just seen Patrick Sullivan.'

17

The ageing Mini was making strange clunking noises as Keith guided it eastwards along the A30 past Exeter. 'Remind me,' he said to Rowena. 'The police have asked you not to leave Cornwall – yes?'

'I got lost,' she replied solemnly.

He nodded. 'Right.'

Rowena scribbled a few *aides-mémoire* in an official-looking notebook. Patrick Sullivan was lying low at the A30 road protestors' camp. But not low enough, it seemed: Keith had spotted him in the background of a local TV news broadcast, complete with fiddle, stringy blond hair – and tattooed forearm. He had always possessed a good memory for faces, and was confident that this man matched the individual in Ginette's photograph.

'It's funny,' she said as they came closer to Honiton. 'I got held up around here on my first trip down the peninsula. I saw a tatty-looking camp across the fields. I was probably only a mile or so away from Patrick then, but was totally unaware!' She had decided her identity would be that of sympathetic journalist. If and when she reached Sullivan himself, she would judge whether or not to disclose her relationship with Ellie.

'You're sure you don't want me to come with you into the camp?' asked Keith for the third time that day.

'Thanks, but I don't want them to feel threatened. Even by you.'

'Fair enough. I wonder if the police will regard this as interference in their investigation?'

Rowena felt her blood pressure soaring as it did every time she thought of DS Pendrea. '*What* investigation? Did *they* find Patrick Sullivan? Did they even look for him? If we'd gone to the detectives like good little citizens when you saw that transmission, they'd have found a way to botch things up. I'm sorry, Keith, but it's my turn now. I shall talk to Sullivan about the things that interest *me*, and I shall know if he's telling the truth.'

Keith smirked, but nevertheless warned her to be careful. 'There's just an outside chance that *he*'s the one who took that shotgun,' he commented.

'We've been through this before. Adrian would surely have checked the gun cupboard when the robbery was discovered.'

'Probably... oops, I think we should have turned off there. I need a navigator.'

Keith eventually parked at the side of a rutted track, beneath a canopy of tree branches. 'Good luck,' he said as Rowena slid out of the passenger seat. She thanked him, squared her shoulders and set off with a determined tread for the camp.

The atmosphere was one of slovenly *ennui*, of people marking time. Rowena knew all about the tunnels, tree houses and redoubts, but here was a more general sprawl of tents, makeshift furniture and weathered-looking occupants. A blackened kettle mingled steam with the rising woodsmoke from their fire; a young man idly strummed chords on his guitar while beside him a girl chewed vacantly on a pipe stem.

Rowena approached the most alert-looking individual, a man with a bared chest and hair set in a solid sculpture of grease and dust. She stated her business; he appraised her consideringly. 'It's Jethro you want,' he said. 'He gives the interviews.'

'Fine. Where should I find him?'

'I'll take you.' He led her through crackling undergrowth to another part of the camp where an enormous bearded man sat on a log with a tin mug of tea. Covertly she glanced at every face she passed, but none was that of Patrick Sullivan.

'Were you at Twycross?' asked Jethro in a gravelly voice when she had repeated her explanation.

'No. My paper has only recently started doing an "out and about" page. Important issues affecting the countryside.'

'You won't get much more important than this. This is government vandalism. Make sure you mention Twycross and Newbury. And the Okehampton bypass. We weren't awake then; we weren't organized. But we are now...' He reeled off details of strategy which she dutifully recorded in the notebook. 'We made 'em pay out at Twycross,' he finished up with a reminiscent twinkle. 'Sued the cops for unlawful arrest. We got thousands of pounds for the fund.'

'How would you answer those who say that it's not the police who pay, but the taxpayer, whose sympathy you would presumably prefer to court?'

'Oh, if you hit 'em in the pocket it focuses minds. We hit 'em with legal aid, compensation, cost of policing – and our Social Security.' He grinned. 'It makes them all personally involved. They can't ignore the issue then.'

She nodded, discussed the new offence of aggravated trespass and Jethro's hope that Devon and Cornwall police would make mistakes in their law enforcement, then moved to more general topics. 'Your camp's quite cosy,' she said. 'I was wondering if I might run into a friend of a friend here – Patrick Sullivan.'

'Fiddler Pat? He's here. He was at Newbury, too. He can give you some more details.' Jethro levered his huge bulk into a standing position, and stretched. 'Follow me.' He tramped further into the woodland and stopped below a tall tree. 'Hey, Pat – visitor for you.'

Rowena smiled and lifted a hand as a hairy blond head peered over the edge of a platform high in the branches, but she made no attempt to introduce herself until he had abseiled down a rope to ground level.

He stood there, his breathing slightly accelerated, and she saw that he was muscular beneath the green sleeveless jerkin he wore. The trellis tattoo on his left arm was unmistakable.

'Hi,' she said. 'I'm Rowena – Ellie's cousin. Ellie Drinkwater.'

Intently she watched his face. Now was the moment for a flash of alarm, or guilt: involuntary reactions in response to her unexpected statement. But nothing of the sort ensued. His blue eyes gleamed with pleasure, and the lids crinkled at the corners. 'Ellie! No kidding! How's she doing?'

'I haven't seen her for a while, actually. I was hoping you might be able to tell me where to find her...?'

He made a vague gesture of acknowledgement to Jethro, who was sloping off back to his log, before frowning in concentration. 'Must be nearly a year since I saw Ellie. We were in Cornwall – did she tell you she got me a job? Yeah, well, perhaps I am a bit ashamed. Ellie said, like, I ought to find the self-respect of work again, like she had, but...' He shrugged with a winsome grimace. 'It wasn't my bag. I decided to split: took a few things the farmer didn't need and hitch-hiked up the county. I reckoned if I didn't tell Ellie no one would blame her.'

'Mm. Did you know that some silver vanished from Uplands around the same time?'

His surprise seemed genuine. 'No kidding?' he said again. 'I never went near the place myself. Too toffee-nosed for me.'

She nodded absently. 'You know, there's something I've been curious about. Were you and Ellie an "item"?'

'No. She's a sweet kid, but not my type. I think Farmer Adrian had the hots for her, and maybe that weird boy Danny. I'll say one thing for Danny, though – he's a nature lover...' The conversation strayed into the realms of threatened badger setts and other habitats, but Rowena already knew she would get little else of value from Patrick. Clearly he had not been blasted to death in a barn; other misconceptions, too, were now cracking apart. She believed his assertion that he had not been Ellie's boyfriend. She also felt he was innocent of any hand in Ellie's disappearance.

So who *had* killed Ellie, and what had been their motivation?

At lunch time the next day, Rowena walked the two miles to the Tinner's Reach. She needed to speak to people; time was getting shorter and she would learn nothing new incarcerated at Uplands.

The bar was very quiet. Accepting a pint of cider from Bill, she leaned against the nearest stool and began to chat with him. 'I thought you might be packed out with journalists,' she commented.

'We were...but they've all gone to Porthleven now, because that's where Ryan Carloose is lodging.'

'He seems to be enjoying his "fifteen minutes of fame",' she said.

'What about you?' asked Bill with an odd look.

'Oh – it's horrible. I wish it had been anyone but me who had gone into Ginette's cottage last Sunday. I've been hounded ever since by police and reporters, so I've kept my profile low. Today, though, I got fed up with isolation.'

Bill nodded slowly. 'That's what Adrian reckoned. I think he's just a mite hurt because you haven't phoned. Perhaps a nice game of chess will make you both feel better.'

'Er...yes, later, when things are a bit closer to normal.'

She waited as a smartly dressed woman with bouffant blonde hair entered the pub and caught Bill's eye. 'Did you manage the collection, Bill?' she asked cheerfully. 'Or perhaps just the envelope?'

'Now, Tina – need you ask? Here's the jar. Forty-seven pounds, fifteen pence. I counted it.'

'Seamen's Family Trust.' Rowena read the label out loud. 'Is that for widows and children? Ah... Just a moment, I'd like to give something.' As she dug in her bag for a contribution, she learned from the gist of their conversation that Tina collected for the charity over a wide area, mainly via envelopes through letterboxes.

Suddenly an idea struck her. 'I don't suppose you delivered any envelopes around Anwith last Sunday?' she asked casually.

'Delivered – no. But I did call at a few houses to collect the donations, places where people had been out during the week.'

'Anwith Farm?'

'Yes.'

'Was that in the morning?'

'No, the afternoon.'

'How about the adjacent cottages?'

Tina was beginning to look puzzled. 'Well, I tried, but no one was at home.'

Bill leaned forward, understanding Rowena's purpose. 'Tina, my dear, where've you been burying your head? Didn't you know the middle of that terrace was Ginette Carloose's place?'

'No, I didn't. Stan and I have been away to Dorset these last few days. I've only read one paper, and it didn't mention her address.'

'Detective-Sergeant Pendrea at Helston would be very pleased to hear from you,' Rowena told her earnestly. 'They're collating information from anyone who was in the area that afternoon.'

As Tina left the pub minutes later, Rowena was convinced that she was the blonde Madeleine had seen. The concept was a relief for two reasons: not only would it help to exonerate her in Pendrea's eyes, but it laid to rest a tiny niggle of doubt about Madeleine herself – she had not lied.

She put down her glass, and sighed. 'I've got to trek back now, Bill. Those detectives even took my car. I must say, I don't know how Mrs Trelowan manages around here with just her bike. It's a long way to the supermarkets.'

'Oh, her! She *did* drive, while her husband was alive. They had an old Ford Escort but she had to sell it when he died.' He rubbed his chin reminiscently. 'Yes...' he said. 'She was woefully slow, and didn't have much sense of direction – but it was driving of a kind...'

Rowena wasted little time in contacting DS Pendrea. She didn't want to leave her fate in the hands of Tina, who might have second thoughts and decide not to get involved.

'I see,' he said when she had finished. 'Well, we'll check into this, of course.' He sounded generally more forthcoming than on previous occasions. 'We'll be returning your car shortly, Miss Kemp. We're grateful for your co-operation.'

So you didn't find anything, she thought sourly. I could have told you that. 'Have there been any developments?' she asked.

'I'm afraid I'm not at liberty to say.'

'I was wondering... since nothing has washed up at the coast so far, have you any plans to drain Cober Pool?'

He gave a hollow chuckle. 'Are you asking as a journalist?'

'Partly... and also as an interested party. I'm as keen as you are that this mystery should be solved.'

'Draining the pool would be a major undertaking, Miss Kemp. Divers, now... that might be possible. Do you have any special reason for enquiring about Cober Pool?'

'Only that it's within a five-mile radius from Ginette's cottage, and I understand its depth reaches thirty feet in places.'

It occurred to her that he might attribute her suggestion to revenge against Madeleine, an attempt to cause her inconvenience and embarrassment. His manner, however, remained unnaturally friendly. 'I was meaning,' he went on, 'have you had some *guidance* from Mrs Malone?'

'Guidance... oh, nothing like that. She's trying to distance herself from this incident in case it upsets her clients.'

'Come now,' he chided. 'We all have our professional discretion. But "distance" isn't what your colleagues have been suggesting. The papers all say Mrs Malone is preparing to hold a public seance. I thought perhaps she had already undertaken a preliminary session...'

'Those people aren't my colleagues,' said Rowena firmly. 'They're exerting moral blackmail against Caireen by printing all kinds of outrageous things. You can take it from me that she hasn't agreed to any seance. You'll find Ryan Carloose is behind this nonsense.'

'I note what you say,' he answered ponderously; Rowena thought she detected an edge of regret to his tone. They *want* Caireen to try, she realized with shock. They're floundering. They have no idea where to search next for Ginette...

It was only after she had rung off that she began to speculate as to whether they had actually examined Mrs Trelowan's cottage.

'Just look at these papers!' exploded Brett later that day, arriving home with an armful of newsprint. Caireen and Rowena had been working in Caireen's study; they drew alongside as he spread the relevant pages out along the desk.

'Oh, dear,' said Caireen, biting her lip. 'They're making such *assumptions*!'

Rowena read the lurid stories with dismay. Caireen, they claimed, would hold a satin underskirt of Ginette's, and through 'spiritual vibrations' would receive a detailed picture of the girl's burial place.

'That's not what you do,' she said to Caireen with a grimace.

'No. I was never very successful at that. I can't understand –'

'*I* can!' interrupted Brett savagely. 'They're trying to pretend they have a concrete arrangement with us. They're raising public expectation, so if we try to say no it'll look as if we're backing out of a commitment. Just wait till I speak to those editors!' He stormed out of the room, and Caireen and Rowena exchanged rueful glances.

A door thumped in the background. 'Is that Danny?' asked Caireen. 'Would you go and see?'

Daniel was in the hall, looking tanned and dishevelled; Rowena beckoned him into the study.

'Where have you been?' asked Caireen.

'Oh – out along the cliffs.'

'I thought I asked you to stay close to the house just at present?'

He hung his head. 'I wasn't doing any harm. I was by myself most of the time, then I met a really nice man who'd read about you in the papers and wanted to know when you were going to hold the seance. I told him you hadn't decided yet. He asked all about your work...'

'Danny, that was probably a reporter. I *specifically* warned you not to speak to them.'

His face began to pucker. 'He wasn't. He's on holiday here in a caravan. He comes from Norfolk.'

Caireen rolled her eyes in exasperation. 'Go and clean yourself up while we decide what to do with you.' He left and she picked up one of the papers, reading the account with an anxious frown. With a murmured apology to Rowena, she disappeared next door to Brett's office.

The nature of their decision became apparent the next day. Rowena met Daniel on the stairs, descending with a loosely wrapped parcel.

Caireen's voice floated across the hall, 'Danny, are you there?' and he instantly showed alarm. 'Please, take these for me,' he hissed. 'Get rid of them. I was going to throw them away.'

She felt the shape of books sliding across each other under the thin brown paper. Thrusting the package under her bed she returned to the ground floor to find Caireen and Daniel together.

'Danny is going to spend a couple of weeks with his cousins in Ireland,' she told Rowena. 'We all think that's best, in view of the current situation.' She put her arm around him and gave an affectionate squeeze. 'I'm sorry, darling. I know you're not keen. But we'll all be together again soon in London. It's just that I have work to finish here first.'

'Can't I go out at *all* now?'

'Well...' Her eyes flicked to Rowena. 'If one of us is with you, and you don't talk to strangers.'

'This afternoon,' he beseeched Rowena, 'would you come out to the mines with me? Please?' In the background, Caireen was nodding approval.

'Of course,' she replied.

'Incognito!' chuckled Daniel as they strode along the cliff path wearing sunglasses and wide-brimmed hats.

'That's right.' Rowena was determined that he should enjoy his afternoon. She had a rucksack of fruit, crisps and drinks, plus books to read and a pack of cards. 'You're sure you don't want to swim in Graw Cove?'

'It's too crowded today,' he said, indicating laughing figures on the beach far below them. 'I want *our* place – it'll be peaceful there.'

Eventually they flopped down in the grass beside the ruined engine houses. There had only been one suspicious-looking person on the path, a man staring intently at Uplands, but they had passed him without incident.

'I don't want to go to Cork,' said Daniel, tearing at grass stalks as he watched a fishing smack bobbing in the topaz water while the Lizard peninsula shimmered in the distance.

'I've heard it's very beautiful there,' said Rowena.

'But my cousins live inland. I like the sea. We were due to stay here another fortnight, and I had plans.'

'Tell me, Danny.'

He lay back, arms behind his head, but continued to watch her as he spoke. 'I wanted another day in Glastonbury. We could have managed it. I wanted to talk about the purple with Lavinia and Roger.' Suddenly he shot upright. 'I *did* see it once, you know. It was a Polish medium visiting London. She hardly charged people anything, and somehow you could *sense* her goodness across the room... She spoke of tuning into a collective consciousness, of all the knowledge and feelings of people who have passed on being in a kind of cloud above her head. An energy cloud... Roger has seen one. I couldn't identify it myself, but I saw the link – great bands of violet, and gold, and white *pouring* into her head... Her entire aura went violet. And everything she said was accurate.'

Rowena nodded, only just listening. She was wondering whether she could create an opportunity to ask Daniel about Ellie's last day.

A chance cropped up an hour later, after they had lolled about and eaten grapes. 'You were going to show me a secret place along here once,' she said. 'I was too busy to come. I'd love to see it now, if you'll let me.'

'It's no good,' he said. 'It's all blocked up. I think the roof must have fallen in.'

'Show me anyway,' she said brightly, standing up and swinging the rucksack across her shoulders. This suggestion of a tunnel sounded promising – there might even be some sign of Ginette.

He began to scramble down a hollow near the main cliff edge. Hidden beneath an overhang of sea-thrift and weeds was the mouth of a small passageway. Immediately she could see that he was right: whatever its original depth, this tunnel was now no longer patent. A tumble of rocks and soil had obstructed it completely. Her intuitive flash that she might be about to discover Ginette's last resting place was way off beam; the soil had weathered and weeded over. This tunnel had been blocked for months.

Ellie...? she wondered briefly. No. Mary's message had been quite distinct. Ellie was lying in still water, within earshot of the sea. Green darkness...

'Did you show Ellie this tunnel last year?' she asked.

'Yes. We didn't go in far, though. She was frightened.'

'I was wondering, Danny... You remember that day when Ellie went missing? The day you went to the cinema with Brett? Well, I've been interested in Ellie because she did a job like mine, and people say she was a nice girl. They seem quite surprised that she ran away. It appears that only Mrs Trelowan saw her that day, in the morning. Did you see her yourself? Did she come out here with you?'

It occurred to Rowena that a cliff-edge location was not the best place to ask this sort of question, but it could be her last chance. Daniel seemed quite calm; only his jaw tightened a little, but he evinced no desire to rush back up the hill and kick the engine house wall.

'I saw her the evening before,' he said, 'but that was all. I still think she should have left me a note.'

Rowena stared idly out to sea. 'Do you like Mrs Trelowan, Danny?'

'Yes. She gives me ginger biscuits.'

'What about Farmer Polzeath?'

'I don't really know him all that well.'

'He told me he was invited to Uplands once, but I think he was spinning a tale.'

Daniel screwed up his face, considering. 'No... he's right. Mother held a cocktail party here years ago – about eighteen months after she bought the house. It was a kind of "thank you" to all the local people who had been friendly, or shown her hospitality. Farmer Polzeath came with his wife.'

Rowena went on staring at the water. *'Don't betray me,'* Adrian had pleaded. So what did I do? Just that... and I still don't know whether I was right or wrong.

18

When they tramped back to Uplands in the early evening, Rowena was surprised to see Colonel Granger emerging from the front door. He tipped his hat and murmured a greeting, but did not linger to converse. Rowena knew Caireen had not been expecting him; as he climbed slowly into his Volvo, she found herself speculating about his visit.

Caireen soon confided the reason. 'You won't believe this,' she said when Daniel was safely upstairs. 'Charles has just proposed to me. I'm afraid his sense of timing is abysmal.'

'Oh. Did you... demur?'

'Yes. His main reason for springing this now is one of chivalry. He came to offer "sanctuary" for the boys and myself at Cober

House. Quite apart from the fact that security there would be even worse than here, with all those woodlands flanking the property, I would never leave Uplands under these circumstances.'

'Marriage seems a bit drastic.'

Caireen gave a strained smile. 'Charles is old-fashioned. It's part of his charm. He felt we shouldn't reside under the same roof without an understanding, as he called it. But this just highlights the long-term problem. He *does* want us to marry, and live together permanently at Cober House. It's out of the question. I'll never give up Uplands. Not for anybody. This home is all I've ever worked for and wanted!'

Her face had sharpened with vehemence, the violet eyes glowing passionately. Noticing Rowena's scrutiny, she relaxed with a rueful little shake of the head. 'You'll understand one day,' she said.

'I think I do now. If this house was mine, I wouldn't want to give it up.'

They walked together to the wide, south-facing window; Caireen opened the small upper windows and the curtains billowed lazily as the drone of surf filtered into the room. 'I don't feel I can concentrate on Charles just now,' she said. 'This matter of the seance for Ginette just won't go away. Brett told me today that Ryan Carloose says if I won't do it, he'll invite another medium. Linda Vivaldi's name was mentioned. That would be a huge publicity coup for her – and death to my reputation.' She turned round, intent once more, and met Rowena's gaze. 'I'm beginning to think perhaps I should accept,' she said. 'What is your opinion, Rowena?'

'I don't know,' she said frankly. 'They've put you in an awful spot. It could be argued that failure in front of an array of the Press wouldn't do too much for your reputation, either.'

'Nice to know you have such faith in my abilities!' Caireen was laughing, her teeth a sparkle of pearl. 'You'll be pleased to hear that your opinion coincides exactly with that of Brett...but I've been thinking about this whole question. All night, in fact. The manuscript we've produced between us: it's good – very good, but there's no specific end point. We risk anticlimax. Supposing, though, I accept this very public opportunity to assist the police, and it succeeds? Then we have a perfect climax. We could start with that, and flash back to the rest ...'

She pulled a wry face. 'Brett will take some convincing. But this could be a career high-spot, and perhaps I shouldn't relinquish the chance so readily.'

Brett was indeed hard to convince, and spent much of the evening in earnest, low-voiced conversation with his mother. The next morning, he set off for Exeter airport with Daniel, and despite the presence of Mrs Trelowan in the kitchen, and the intermittent hum of the vacuum cleaner upstairs, Rowena felt that the house was much emptier.

Just before lunch time, as she completed a section of desultory editing, her office telephone rang. She answered crisply, as Keith tended to ring on the mobile.

'Rowena – it's Adrian.'

Her heart lurched, and all her hard-won neutrality seemed to fracture. An emotion – fear, desire? – seized her innards at the sound of his voice.

'I know you're having a difficult time, but I really miss you,' he said. 'I wondered if we could meet sometime – in the pub, say, or here at the farm?'

She swallowed, gripping the receiver tightly. *Did you do it?* she wanted to shriek. *Just tell me.*

'I... I'm so sorry, Adrian, but I have to go back to London very soon now, and there's still a lot of work to do. I think if we stir things up again, it'll be even harder to leave.'

'Are you saying what I think you're saying?'

'Yes. For a short time we were close, but we knew it would have to end. Ginette's death just brought that end sooner than we expected, that's all. I'm a city girl, and you're a country man.' She couldn't believe those cold, measured tones were her own.

'I saw a future for us,' he said after several seconds of silence.

'No,' she replied. 'Ellie was your future. I just reminded you of her. I'm sorry. Goodbye.' Deliberately she replaced the receiver, then lifted it off again and laid it on the polished desk top.

She was trembling all over.

At the end of an afternoon of zombie-like work, Rowena padded upstairs for a shower before dinner. She had been invited to dine with the family, and had heard Brett's car return, so they would be three at table.

As she slipped out of her skirt and blouse, her toe grazed against something under the bed. Bending down, she found Daniel's parcel.

The brown paper split even as she lifted it on to the coverlet; books and magazines cascaded out, and she saw immediately that they were not the expected abstruse tomes on auras, and such. Soft pornographic images leered up at her, and she realized with a sigh that Daniel not only had the body of a man, but the mind of a normal, prurient adolescent boy.

Caireen had chastised him recently about books, she remembered. In all likelihood they were more of this ilk. Without further ado, Rowena buried them again in brown paper and replaced them under the bed. She would honour Daniel's request and destroy them. When she went down for dinner, Brett was already in the drawing-room. He, too, looked freshly showered, and wore an attractive sage-green shirt. He greeted her suavely. 'Sherry, Rowena?'

'Yes – thank you.'

They chatted about Daniel's departure and the arrangements for him in Cork before Caireen joined them and they strolled through to the dining-room. 'Thank you, Mrs Trelowan,' she directed through the serving-hatch.

When the parsnip soup was steaming in three bowls on the table and Mrs Trelowan had withdrawn, Caireen smiled brightly at each of her companions. 'I have something to tell you,' she said. Her eyes were lustrous; her whole expression was aglow and yet serene.

Brett's head snapped upwards suspiciously and he abandoned his bread roll.

'Indecision is always the most nerve-racking state,' went on Caireen. 'These last few days we have found ourselves the innocent victims of Ryan Carloose's machinations. Not only is it impossible to retreat with grace, but after much thought I can see merit in his plan. I've made up my mind – I shall indeed perform the seance.'

She turned to Brett as if awaiting his reaction, but Brett was dumb. With precise movements he broke a fragment of bread from his roll and added a sliver of butter.

Rowena was not distracted. She was watching his face. All the blood had drained from his cheeks leaving the skin a dead, pasty white.

'I'll have to leave you now,' whispered Rowena after leading Keith to the extra chair she had placed at the very back of the hall. He gave a thumbs-up gesture as she flitted through the crowds to return to Caireen and the elaborate preparations.

It was difficult to believe that this event had been organized in a matter of three days. Caireen and her entourage, six police officers, a score of Press and around a hundred local people were squeezed into Anwith village hall. All national dailies except the *Dispatch,* who had arranged and publicized the event, were excluded, but local representation was permitted since they would go to print days later.

Brett had tried to downgrade the occasion, suggesting that Caireen hold out for a private sitting, but it was no good – Ryan Carloose was revelling in the attention. As she assisted Caireen with her *toilette,* Rowena remained acutely aware of Brett's demeanour. He was taciturn tonight, devoid of his usual professional charm. Pernickety and pedantic, he was clearly uneasy in a situation where Brett Saunders was not gripping all the reins. His anxiety was understandable to a large extent, of course: she felt nervous herself. They had specified no television cameras, video or tape recorders, no flash photography while the psychic communication was in progress, and various other safeguards, but in these gatherings there was always *somebody* who deemed themselves above all regulations. Brett, however, had more on his mind than these factors, she was sure. Fear that Caireen would fail, perhaps...or was he more afraid that she would succeed?

'Thank you, my dear,' said Caireen as Rowena carefully secured an elegant diamond choker around her neck. She was dressed in the violet gown Rowena had first seen at the Wimbledon Theatre, but her coiffure was more elaborate, and the jewellery almost regal. Her manner was calm and gracious, but beneath the careful make-up the muscles of her face were tight, and Rowena detected a faint tremor in the hands that smoothed the shimmering skirt folds when Caireen rose to her feet.

'Danny will be disappointed,' Caireen went on, 'but I must confess I'm glad he's not here tonight. This is difficult enough.'

Rowena caught her hand. 'Good luck,' she said. 'I'll be sending all the right vibes.'

Caireen summoned a brave smile then stayed on alone in the backstage room as Rowena and Brett made their way to the side of the stage. Rowena side-stepped along the front row until she reached the seat Madeleine Granger had been guarding for her; Brett whispered a few words to the *Dispatch* representative who was due to act as Master of Ceremonies, then disappeared.

As the *Dispatch* man stepped forward to speak, Rowena viewed the stage with mixed feelings. There were no large candlesticks this time, just a plain wooden chair and an enormous poster-sized picture of Ginette looking irritatingly unassuming and girlish. 'The *Dispatch* is the paper that cares,' declaimed the man forcefully after his introduction. 'A lovely young girl is brutally butchered in her own home on a drowsy Sunday afternoon...' He went on to state that Caireen Malone cared, and was offering her services for no reward except for that of finding the killer...

Rowena glanced around. There was no sign of Brett, but Mrs Trelowan was sitting rigidly at the other end of the row, her mouth a sharp line.

Suddenly the lights dimmed. As the *Dispatch* man retreated, Caireen softly stepped on to the stage from the other side. Her expression was vague and drowsy, as if she were already in a partial trance. With a sober nod towards the audience, she sat carefully on the chair. 'Come forward, Ryan,' she said pleasantly.

Rowena had already been introduced to Ryan Carloose that evening. He was a wiry, dark-haired man with a broken tooth and a pronounced five o'clock shadow. He shuffled on to the stage and wordlessly handed over a beige satin garment.

There was a sudden incandescence as a flash unit fired.

'*No* photography, ladies and gentlemen,' protested the *Dispatch* man. 'Mrs Malone has agreed to co-operate later, as we explained.'

Ryan backed away clumsily and silence once more descended. Caireen closed her eyes, visibly breathing deeply, and held the garment on her lap with both hands. Rowena was reminded of Mary in Glastonbury, her thin bony fingers manipulating Ellie's nightshirt, facilitating that elusive psychic link... If Caireen had continued to refuse, she had considered proposing Mary herself.

Minutes ticked away, and Rowena felt her stomach tighten in empathy with Caireen. That wretched photographer – had he destroyed the crucial focus she had achieved in the dressing-room? Madeleine, statue-still by her side, was wearing too much perfume, a heavy floral scent which swamped the senses.

Slowly Caireen's eyes opened. She looked bewildered, unsure. 'Ladies and gentlemen,' she said huskily, 'I feel I need some assistance here. Please will you all concentrate – picture Ginette as you knew her in life. Thank you.'

Another white-light flash lit up the stage. Brett leapt out of nowhere, an avenging fury, and roughly seized the arm of the offending photographer. 'Out!' he spat, and ejected him from the premises.

There was a murmuring as the audience released their accumulated tensions. Rowena heard Charles Granger mutter, 'Moron!' and further minutes passed before tranquillity was once more restored. She strained to focus on Ginette, even the misleadingly demure photograph. Caireen was in trouble... she was breathing more quickly but nothing in her face indicated a connection, and she was not articulating visions. Against her will Rowena thought of Keith in the back corner, his regretful 'I told you so.' He had been keen to come and see the legendary Caireen Malone in action, but tonight Caireen was mute.

Suddenly the woman on stage stood up and cast the garment to the chair in one liquid movement. She peered into the middle distance above the heads of the audience, her face alert. 'Who are you?' she said clearly. 'Don't play games. Oliver – is that you?'

Rowena felt her scalp crawl, and an icy chill scuttle across the back of her neck. In the past she had suspected Brett of assisting events by opening outside doors at strategic points in the evening, but tonight she knew such stratagems were unnecessary. There was a prickling in the air, a coalescence of expectation from all the people present. The awed gaze of each person was locked to Caireen's face as her own features relaxed into a mobile play of expression. 'Can you find Ginette for us?' she asked in the tone of voice one would use for a child. 'No – you can play later. We need to speak to Ginette... Yes, you can.'

She waited calmly, hands clasped in front of her waist, and once again there was silence. It seemed interminable; Rowena heard a great gusty sigh at her elbow and realized that Madeleine had forgotten to breathe.

Once again, Caireen was abruptly alert. The direction of her gaze swung down to Ryan Carloose and rested just behind him. He cringed, terrified, as her mouth began to move, whispering words, words more imagined than heard...

'Ginette is with us.'

19

'Don't be afraid,' said Caireen in a normal voice, though whether to Ryan or to the spectre of Ginette Rowena was uncertain. 'Ryan needs to know where you are lying – your mortal shell. He'd like to lay you properly to rest...' She stood, apparently listening on some psychic wavelength, while a hundred and thirty people again suspended their breathing. 'Can you show me?' she said at last.

There was another pause before she half turned towards the police complement. 'I see a hillside...a hollow stone...another stone, tall with strange writing...moorland heather...bracken and bramble. There's an old engine house...shafts nearby...wire fencing...down, down like a well. She's curled up. Black bags. She's in black bin bags, far from the light.'

Ryan's face was twisted now. 'Cat and dog,' said Caireen to him. 'She tells me cat and dog, but there was also love.'

'Our fights,' he muttered, and blew his nose fiercely.

'Ginette...Oliver, don't let her go. Why is she still afraid? It's all over now. I understand. Do come back...please ...'

She had held out her arms, but dropped them with a gesture of frustration to stand pale and wilted in everybody's sight. Swaying, she took a step backwards and sat heavily on the chair. Charles attempted to spring to his feet; Madeleine restrained him.

The *Dispatch* man was looking stunned and helpless, so it fell to Brett to end the session formally. After his closing words the audience filed out in silence, casting strange, fearful glances towards Caireen and the stage.

Rowena caught a glimpse of Adrian among the crowd, and hurried backstage to join Caireen.

She looked ill.

'You were superb,' said Rowena. 'You did your very best.' She wanted to ask about Oliver, but knew the timing was wrong.

Caireen sipped at a glass of water. 'It was horrible,' she said. 'Her face was covered with blood. I didn't tell them everything she said...she wouldn't stay. Rowena...'

'Yes?'

'She said the killer was there – in the hall.'

Again the icy trickle. 'We must tell the police!'

Caireen shook her head wearily. 'No. It was all confused. They wouldn't believe me... too melodramatic. Everything I've told them might be wrong.'

'But surely –'

'No – please. Let's wait and see if they find her first. It's all academic if they don't.'

Brett entered the room, grim-faced. 'Well, that's that,' he said roughly to his mother. 'The Press are waiting for the picture we promised them, and the interview.'

She nodded. 'Danny and his teapot would be welcome right now. Just a minute...' She sipped again at the water, then rose, squaring her shoulders. 'Lead on.'

For the next half-hour Rowena lurked on the sidelines while the Press photographed Caireen and bombarded her with questions. Adrian had gone; the hall was almost empty now, except for police and the overexcited group by the stage.

'Who is Oliver?' Caireen was asked. 'Is he your familiar?'

She managed to summon up a smile. 'That sounds like something from *Macbeth*! I prefer the term "spirit guide". Oliver is a young boy who seems eager to adopt that role, but I don't normally have a spirit guide. My contacts are usually direct.'

Rowena was glad that Caireen made no attempt to clarify Oliver's own situation and relationships. She listened as Caireen politely answered a battery of questions, including details of Ginette's appearance, which she described merely as 'dishevelled' – Ginette's normal state in life.

At length Brett called a halt to the Press interrogation, and the police moved in to ask for further details of the burial site. Pendrea and his cold-eyed inspector were keen that Caireen should accompany them on their search, but Brett stepped in again before she could reply. 'My mother is exhausted,' he said. 'She's given you the best description she can. It may or may not prove to be of value. I suggest you look first, and only enlist her help again if nothing is found.'

He was tired as well, thought Rowena. More than that, she could tell he was suppressing an inner agitation which threatened to boil over at one more foolish or unacceptable question. She had never known him so tense. For a second time she was obliged to wonder: was he afraid that Caireen had just wrecked all they had worked for – or did he need Ginette's body to remain concealed?

Rowena swung the Clio into an off-road parking space just outside the coastal village of Marazion. Keith was sitting astride a wall which separated the road from the wide sweep of Mount's Bay. Behind him, the tide was low, and a flat expanse of sand led all the way to the land-facing harbour of St Michael's Mount.

'Hi,' she said, leaning her elbows against the wall. 'I'm afraid I haven't got long. What did you think of last night?'

He grimaced. 'Creepy... and impressive. But, of course, the proof of the pudding...'

'That's what Caireen says. She and Brett are both acting very calmly today, but underneath I can tell they're jumpy as hell. One phone call from the police is going to alter Caireen's professional life irrevocably.' She climbed up alongside him and let the wind ruffle her hair. 'Brett wanted to go to London this weekend. That's why he was training Danny. But everything's all in the air now, anyway. It's very difficult to get any work done.'

'I can imagine. Are you writing a report for Kevin?'

'Well...'

'If you don't, I'll have to. This is too big to let slip.'

'Kevin wanted an exposé, if I remember correctly.'

'He may yet receive one...'

He ducked away as if he imagined she might strike him, but Rowena was contemplative. 'That part seems less important now,' she said. 'All I can think about when I look at these people is "Which one of you killed my cousin?" If Caireen's powers can throw light on that question, then so be it.' She looked down at the wall. 'I have some reservations about Brett. He's not himself at all... If he *does* go to London I might try and examine his things. The police have heard enough of my speculations; nothing less than evidence will make them act.'

'Do be careful. Can I help?'

'I'll let you know. Must get back now...' She scrambled down. 'Thanks for listening.'

It was late that afternoon when the call came. Rowena, debating adjectives with Caireen in her employer's study, heard the muffled ringing tones from Brett's adjacent room. A long silence ensued before he tapped on their door.

'Come in,' called Caireen, her voice suddenly strained.

He stood on the threshold, seemingly unwilling to enter. 'That was DI Lovatt,' he said. 'They found Ginette an hour ago, in one of the old shafts at Ding Dong mine. You did it, Mother. Congratulations.'

Rowena felt a rush of emotion, not all of it pleasant. Brett's delivery had been deadpan as a droid's and his face was a glassy marble white.

'Excuse me,' he said abruptly, and vanished into the hall.

Caireen was dabbing uselessly at the tears which were coursing down her cheeks. 'I'm sorry,' she said. 'Such a relief... I think I need a drink.'

'I'll get you something. Brandy?'

Caireen nodded, and Rowena smartly left the room herself. She had heard a distant door-creak she recognized. Ignoring drinks for the moment, she glided past the consultation room and her own office to the small front cloakroom and listened at the door.

Inside, cool, sophisticated Brett was retching his guts out.

Two days of sheer chaos followed the discovery of Ginette's body, with national dailies clamouring for interviews with Ryan Carloose, Caireen, Rowena herself and anyone even remotely connected with the case.

'I *must* go to London,' Brett insisted in exasperation. 'There's a deal I've got to handle myself.'

'You go,' said Caireen.

'I can't leave you with these wolves, even with three security guards at the boundary. Come with me. Let's pack up here altogether.'

'You know we can't do that. The police want me around just at present. Rowena and I will be fine.'

'You won't. You'll be hounded to distraction.'

At that point Rowena had her brainwave. Eagerly she turned to Caireen. 'Tell everyone you're going with Brett, just for the weekend,' she said. 'Release Mrs Trelowan from her duties. I can cook for us, and you'll have a respite.' She was well aware that the quiet life didn't suit Caireen; with luck Caireen might go out, leaving her alone in the house...

On the Saturday evening she got her wish. Brett had left that morning in the Mercedes along with his own master-stroke: Mrs Tripp from the Tanner agency. Smuggled into the Uplands grounds lying flat on the back seat, she was then driven out openly but at speed, wearing a convincing Caireen-like russet wig.

'Now, Rowena,' said Caireen after an uneventful day of editing, 'you won't mind if I leave you this evening? A family in Helston who recently lost their father have been wanting a consultation for some time, and they've been afraid to come here because of all the publicity. I've agreed to visit them instead, at seven thirty.'

'Would you like my company?'

Caireen smiled. 'Frankly, yes. But they seem very shy, so I think I'll build up a better rapport alone. Have a nice quiet evening. You're welcome to watch the television.'

They shared a light meal in the kitchen before Caireen left – another pleasing chink in her carapace of grandness. Rowena left the house for a breath of air as the Golf's rear lights climbed the rutted headland track and slowly faded to pinpoints. After so much sunshine this was a grey, uneasy evening with scudding clouds and occasional splatters of rain. Brett had retained the security guards in case Press or souvenir hunters tried to break into Uplands, but they were sitting in their own cars out of sight over the hill.

As she turned back towards the welcoming glow of the hallway, Rowena could hear the spill of surf on the rocks below. The visible sea beyond was lumpy and menacing, with a high swell and waves breaking well out in the bay.

She estimated that Caireen would not return for at least an hour and a half. That would be time enough to examine Brett's papers and personal effects. It was hard to know exactly what she was looking for – anything resembling blood on clothes or shoes, any communication from Ginette, especially if blackmail was hinted – but here was her best chance to try. Brett knew something, she was absolutely certain. If he was the killer, her heart bled for Caireen and Danny, but Adrian would be exonerated... not to mention Ann Trelowan.

Rowena wondered if Brett had any intention at all of returning from London... Determinedly she turned the handle to his office door, but it was locked. She turned it again, thumping her shoulder against the woodwork, but nothing yielded.

How *frustrating*! she thought furiously. That room was a general office for the household. How dared he turn it into Fort Knox!

Caireen would have a key somewhere, but much precious time might be lost trying to find it. The windows were double glazed and very secure, but she felt it might just be worth checking from the outside that nothing had been left ajar.

The weather was deteriorating fast. As she picked her way across the terrace and round to the south-facing seaward façade, Rowena felt the wind gusting more strongly, plucking at her clothes and demanding ever more caution. Just as she had expected, the windows were secure. Over her shoulder the sea was a hostile, heaving indigo.

Back inside, she hurried up to Brett's bedroom, and this time gained entry. With only a fleeting surge of distaste for her actions she began to ransack his wardrobe. Brett had a penchant for dark navy Italian suits in fine wool; almost a dozen were hanging there. On the rack beneath were various highly polished black shoes, loafers in soft leather and a pair of Gucci slippers. These she ignored – her search was for casual country wear.

A door flush with the opposite wall proved to be another wardrobe, this one much more promising. After a thorough exploration, however, Rowena was no further forwards. He might have got rid of incriminating garments, of course, but she was hoping for subtle signs on some item whose absence Caireen would query.

She rifled his sock drawer, but once more drew a blank. Swallowing back a few resurgent guilt feelings she checked the objects on his chest-of-drawers: a carved wooden box with mother-of-pearl inlay, an antique cigar box. Only cufflinks, coins and tie pins lay within: no keys.

Caireen's own bedroom was nearby. Rowena had never seen the interior, and for a moment she was overwhelmed by curiosity. Caireen had such beautiful dresses and jewels... Almost as if the house were occupied she tiptoed to the door, turned the handle and pushed it open. The room was decorated in pale shades of apricot, though the furniture was white-painted wood with patterns in gilded relief. Rain lashed against the windows; Rowena switched on the light.

She crept further inside, telling her now lively conscience that the keys might just be lying around on the dressing-table. Her footsteps, however, led her inexorably past the bed to an alcoved dressing-room. Here, behind a curtain, hung Caireen's most ravishing gowns, all in shades of lavender and purple. Above were stacked hat-boxes, handbags wrapped in tissue, weekend cases...

Rowena had seen people reach out to touch the hem of Caireen's gown after some of her more convincing sessions, an almost blasphemous echo of the New Testament. Certainly people believed in her, and benefited from her skills. Nervously she stretched to touch the silken hem herself before backing away and crossing briskly to the dressing-table.

An ivory box lay on an oval lace mat. It had a tiny keyhole, but Rowena found she could lift the lid easily. Inside nestled the ostentatious crystal ear-rings Caireen wore with her 'regalia' – even for the consultations inside Uplands. People expected it, she had claimed, and she was probably right.

These gems were paste, Rowena could see. No doubt Caireen's diamond necklace and bracelet resided in a safe somewhere nearby. Responding again to impulse, she picked up the trinkets and held them against her own ear-lobes, leaning forward to view her reflection in the mirror.

As she lowered them once more to the box, she noticed that the right-hand ear-ring was shaped differently to its fellow. There was something metallic on the back, and a shaped portion like an ear-piece...

Her heart began to thud palpably against her sternum, deep funereal beats to mark the dying of all illusions. She sank down on the dressing-stool and stared. This was a radio receiver. Wearing this device, Caireen could receive messages from fifty yards away. Information overheard and relayed from an audience, for instance ...or her own waiting-room.

Greatly perturbed, Rowena recalled Caireen's practice of separating clients, seeing members of a family one at a time to 'assess the individual focus' before seeing them all together. The members outside would talk in low voices, perhaps discuss the deceased loved ones they hoped would 'come through'. If Brett was listening from Caireen's study, he could transmit valuable snippets to Caireen right in the middle of a consultation.

Brett...Rowena could imagine now why his office was locked. There would be files there, probably on computer, covering all their regular and prospective clients – information gathered by the Tanner agency, whom they had doubtless retained for years.

She wanted to think everything through, but there wasn't time. The bitter knowledge of fraud was one thing, but evidence of murder still remained to be found. Carefully replacing the ear-rings,

Rowena decided to check the lilac gown briefly for gimmicks then resume her search for the key downstairs.

As she pulled out the gown, still wrapped in its polythene dust jacket, its trailing skirt caught against a box hidden beneath, and dis- lodged the cardboard lid. Rowena laid the gown across the bed and turned to replace the lid. She found herself staring at a blonde wig.

The nightmare of Ginette's kitchen flooded her brain: crimson smears, that stifling smell, the voracious buzzing of bluebottles ... What sort of person had stabbed and stabbed and stabbed again? Someone who couldn't control their emotions... someone who had suffered in the past from severe encephalitis?

Madeleine had seen a blonde woman on Ginette's doorstep at three o'clock that Sunday. Had it really been Tina, attempting to collect charity envelopes? Or could it have been Caireen?

Rowena replaced the box and gown, and numbly began to rifle Caireen's dressing-table drawer. She took an emerald brooch shaped like a feather, checked that the room was exactly as she had found it and glided through to her own bedroom.

Picking up her mobile phone she rang Directory Enquiries, obtained Charles and Madeleine's number then made a call to Cober House. By good luck, Charles himself answered.

'Hello,' said Rowena brightly. 'I'm really sorry to disturb you. It's Rowena, Caireen's assistant. Caireen's out just now, but she's been concerned about a lost brooch. It's green, about two inches long and shaped like a feather... It just occurred to me that she might have dropped it when she visited your home the other weekend – that Sunday afternoon.'

'Hm. I don't recall seeing her wear it. I wasn't at my best, though. Another blasted summer cold. She didn't stay very long... maybe half an hour. I shall ask our housekeeper tomorrow if anything has come to light.'

'Thank you so much. Sorry to have bothered you, colonel.'

'Think nothing of it. I hope the brooch turns up.'

When she had rung off Rowena sat dazed with horror. Half an hour, he had said... Caireen had left Uplands just after two o'clock. Her alibi had been academic, anyway. The police had never even asked her for it. Caireen Malone had been secure in the knowledge that she was above suspicion.

Rowena glanced at her watch and calculated that she had at least forty minutes before Caireen was likely to return. There was time to thrust all her belongings into the Clio and flee to Alexandra Road... but Caireen would instantly be alerted. She would destroy all evidence, and justice would never be served.

On the other hand, thought Rowena, can I look her in the face again without signalling what I feel? Am I capable of that degree of dissimulation?

Her fingers hovered over the phone again before moving away. If she called Keith, he would come blundering over to Uplands and ruin everything. No... she must keep her nerve, carry on searching for hard evidence, put every item back in its place, and be watching television when Caireen came home. That way, conversation would be kept to a minimum.

She descended to the utility passage, but none of the keys hanging there looked appropriate for Brett's office door. Creeping into Caireen's study, she made a further brief fruitless search for the keys, then turned her attention to the wall adjoining the clients' waiting-room. Several gilt-framed pictures hung there; she lifted off a central frame which hung at eye level; a spy-hole was immediately revealed.

After peering through, she carefully rehung the picture and moved along to the next one. Just as she had lowered it on to the chair she heard the creak of a door.

Panic-stricken, she tried to engage the horizontal wire with the picture hook, and missed. She tried again; it hung at a crazy angle. Rowena had only partially straightened it when the study door flew open.

Caireen stood on the threshold, her eyes glittering with an evil rage.

20

'Brett told me it would be unwise to engage you.' Caireen's tone was almost conversational, but the malice radiating from deep behind her eyes was terrifying. She stood in the doorway, her coat splotched with rain, her hair and cheeks glistening. 'I overruled him. You were a good writer; I was confident we could keep you on side.'

She stepped into the room. 'You *were* happy with us, weren't you? Just like Ellie, you were satisfied. You believed in my work. But then you had to meddle. You both had to meddle.'

Rowena fought to produce some sound. 'You've lost me,' she croaked. 'I don't know what you're talking about.'

Caireen's glare darkened. 'I will *not* be taken for a fool. I saw my clients in Helston . . . then I called on Charles and Madeleine.'

'I see.'

'Presumably you've hidden my emerald brooch somewhere.'

'I found it on the floor in the hall, just after I rang.'

'Don't *lie* to me! I never told you it was missing. I haven't worn that brooch once this summer.'

Rowena stood poised for flight by the corner of the desk as Caireen's nostrils flared and her chest heaved with agitation. She was acutely aware of the crooked picture, and even as she determinedly avoided glancing towards it herself, Caireen's gaze homed in and rested there that very moment.

'We'd better have a talk,' said Caireen. 'A proper one.' She shrugged off the coat and slung it over her arm. Reaching into her bag, she withdrew a clutch of keys and deftly unlocked the door to Brett's office, where she disappeared inside. Rowena heard the scrape of a drawer. Before she had even decided to sprint down the hall, Caireen had emerged. 'The drawing-room,' she said. 'We may as well be comfortable.'

With cool precision Caireen switched on lamps around the room, including the lamp with the serpentine base. While her back was turned, Rowena released the catch to the heavy sliding terrace door, but knew she lacked time to pull it open. Instead, she took the armchair Caireen offered with an airy hand, and attempted to compose her features into an enquiring, non-hostile expression. 'Madeleine accused you once of gilding the lily,' she said as Caireen sat down. 'I defended you. I've seen how people benefit from your perceived skills. You give them what they're seeking.'

Caireen watched her steadily. 'Go on.'

Rowena adopted a more relaxed posture. 'I found a few of your props tonight, quite by accident. That doesn't make any difference. You can't afford to fail when for some people it's their only visit.' Suddenly she leaned forward. 'It was that illness, wasn't it? It robbed you of some of your powers. But you were carrying everybody's expectations by then. You had responsibilities – you couldn't admit what had happened.'

The violet eyes opposite were now peering back into the past. 'Everything disappeared,' Caireen said. 'I was grappling in the dark. Yet Danny... that was when he started to display signs himself of psychic ability. Never before had he done so – never. First I gave thanks because he hadn't died. Then slowly I realized he would always be a child. Finally, I began to perceive his new gifts...'

'You wanted to protect him,' said Rowena soothingly. 'You didn't want him exploited, so it was better that he didn't study and develop those gifts.' The truth was much harsher, she now knew. Danny had 'seen the purple' surrounding a genuine medium, and was becoming increasingly upset because he was unable to discern any such aura around his mother. At each trip to Glastonbury he received confirmation of his abilities; it was only a matter of time before he challenged Caireen to explain.

'I've always protected Danny,' said Caireen. 'From life, from disillusionment... from being made a pawn. Ginette wanted to make him a pawn... I wouldn't let her.'

Rowena felt a new *frisson* of horror. Much as she wanted to hear Caireen's confession and know all the facts, that way lay dreadful danger. What would happen when Caireen came to her senses and realized what she had been saying? Perhaps she already did know. That meant she felt secure... Rowena flicked an uneasy glance around the room. They were alone, as far as she knew. Caireen was a little heavier than she, but older and shorter in stature. If matters became suddenly physical, Rowena might be expected to prevail. Why then was Caireen unworried? Was she simply out of touch with reality, or did she possess some hidden advantage?

Caireen was looking at her quizzically, as if expecting a comment.

'I never liked Ginette,' said Rowena carefully. 'I believed her capable of blackmail.'

Her employer nodded slowly. 'She wanted Uplands.'

'*What*?'

'I thought that would shock you. I felt just the same. She used Danny, poor Danny with the mind of a child and the body of a handsome young man. She told me she was pregnant and refused point-blank to have an abortion. In fact, she mocked my Catholic background and said I shouldn't ask such a thing.

'She said she would marry Danny and "take him off my hands", but the price was Uplands and an annuity. If I refused she would name Danny as the father anyway and make sure we reaped the very worst publicity for abandoning her.'

'You believed she was pregnant?' Rowena was only going through the motions. She knew it must be true. She could even guess the day it had taken place – that afternoon weeks before when Danny had begged for her company on his cliff walk but she had been too busy. He had run off over the headland in a froth of emotion, to return hours later exhibiting a kind of rebellious smugness... Sometime that afternoon Ginette had seduced him, and even insulted him when it was all over.

'I believed her,' said Caireen sharply. 'She came here to the house to tell me, gloating, very sure of herself. She suggested I check with Danny... I did.'

Rowena wondered what Caireen's initial intentions had been that following Sunday afternoon, but dared not rekindle her fury. Instead, she swung the scene away from that scarlet-spattered kitchen. 'You sent Danny to Ireland so the police couldn't question him or ask for tests,' she said.

'Yes. He may well have talked himself into trouble, and while I didn't really expect them to request samples they might have decided to test every young male within a certain radius.'

And once Danny was safely out of Cornwall, you felt free to dazzle people with your remarkable corpse-locating powers, thought Rowena. She understood Brett's reaction now all too well. His mother had not confided in him. He had fought to stop her undertaking the challenge on the grounds of certain failure; when she insisted, his suspicions grew, and when she succeeded, he understood the appalling truth. Why? *Because she had killed before.*

Tell me about Ellie, she wanted to plead, but Caireen's equilibrium was too precarious for that risk. 'Ginette played with fire,' she said steadily. 'The police knew about her chequered history as far as men were concerned. I'm sure this will all blow over now they've got the body and Ryan has milked his story for all it's worth.'

'What about *our* story?' asked Caireen. 'What about our book?'

'I've drafted the final chapter. I don't see any reason to change it.'

'Let me see... we'll collect it together.' Side by side they walked to Rowena's office, waited while hard copy was run off from the printer, and returned with the sheaf of papers. Silently Caireen read the dramatic account of the gathering in the village hall, her face intent. 'This is good,' she said at the end. 'You've captured the atmosphere perfectly.'

'I just have to change the beginning now,' said Rowena. 'Perhaps some of this material can be a preface...'

'I dare say I can manage that,' answered Caireen. 'I'm afraid your services, valuable as they are, have suddenly become too expensive.'

Fear leapt into Rowena's heart. All this frankness...Caireen had needed to talk, but she had done so in the knowledge that she could control the consequences. In what way? This still remained to be seen. 'You don't need to worry,' she said as levelly as she could manage. 'I know how to be discreet. It's not for me to judge how you handled the problem of Ginette...I shall keep quiet about it.'

'So you say.' Caireen shook her head regretfully. 'Unfortunately I don't believe you. You're one of those pious people who view life in terms of moral absolutes. You see only black and white, because it's simple and comforting – not the fifty shades of grey which constitute reality. Ellie was just the same. So I'm sorry, Rowena, but I can't afford to accept what you say.'

You're wrong, thought Rowena. I'm the one who first acknowledged the grey. And when Madeleine accused you of cheating, I trusted your reasons.

Caireen was still speaking. 'I liked you. I liked you a lot. If only you'd stuck to your brief we wouldn't be in this ghastly position, but –' she gave a sad shrug – 'we are.' As Rowena watched in a state of numbness Caireen snaked one beautifully manicured hand into her bag and drew out a small pistol. Instantly she cocked it. 'Brett bought this for me in New York,' she said. 'He taught me how to use it. You meet such strange people...'

Rowena remembered the scrape of the office drawer. She was unable to speak or move.

Across the luxurious carpet Caireen was raising her arms, still clutching the gun, but with an air of uncertainty...perhaps she was contemplating the same carpet irrevocably stained, the perils of attempting to explain.

Rowena licked her lips. 'Please...' she whispered. 'If you're going to do that, at least tell me about Ellie first. I need to know.'

Caireen lowered the gun, but kept it on her lap. 'Ellie...' she said musingly. 'It was similar, really. Just the two of us in the house. I'd gone out that evening for a National Trust meeting, but I had a headache and half-way there I decided to return. Uplands should have been empty. The boys were out at the cinema, and I knew Ellie herself had left earlier because there had been no sign of her when the police called...' A small frown puckered her brow. 'I must have entered quietly, because when I opened my bedroom I caught Ellie with one of my ear-rings in her hand. I began to remonstrate, but to my astonishment she rounded on me, calling me a cheat and a fraud. It's true it was a special ear-ring, one of my "props", to use your description, but she was disproportionately upset, quite hysterical... I couldn't calm her down. I tried, but she shrieked at me that she would tell the world I was a sham, a criminal, a parasite battening on the desperate. I seized her shoulders to try to reason with her, then her neck. We fell against the bed; the more she thrashed that blonde hair back and forth, the tighter I squeezed. Then suddenly... she was limp and there was no life, and I *felt* her spirit recede from the room. Yes...' Caireen's own shoulders sagged and her eyes seemed to glaze. She still held the gun, though, and as Rowena made as if to move she tightened her grasp and began to lift the barrel.

'Brett...' said Rowena hurriedly. 'He helped you, didn't he?'

The gun dipped again. 'Yes,' said Caireen. 'When Danny was fast asleep he helped me take the body away. We hid some silver near the house, as well. I thought when the robbery investigations had blown over I could take it back to London, but Brett disagreed strongly. He said the pieces could be traced and soon afterwards he disposed of them for good. I haven't seen them since, which is a pity.' Abruptly she raised the gun and sighted down the barrel. 'This is a pity, too. Stand up.'

Rowena did so. Her limbs felt tremulous and clumsy; there was a distant ringing in her ears.

'We'll go to the kitchen,' instructed Caireen.

The ringing stopped, then started again. Through her fog of terror Rowena identified it as the doorbell.

Caireen, suddenly tense, assumed a listening attitude. 'Not a sound,' she hissed, 'or I shoot right now!'

A third ring followed, this one very long. Both women stood statue-still as the reverberation went on and on. When it fell silent Rowena could still imagine the summons in her brain.

Caireen was irritated, distracted. 'The security men are supposed to telephone,' she said, 'and no one else should have access.' She peered from side to side, as if uncertain whether or not to proceed.

'You were telling me about Ellie,' said Rowena. 'Where is she, Caireen? I must know. You can tell me...'

Caireen stared at her in suspicion, then her gaze was jerked as if by a string to the terrace door. There, equally startled, stood Keith on the rain-lashed paving, his red cagoule a lurid beacon in the gloom. 'Who…?'

'*Run*, Keith!' bellowed Rowena, but instead he began to pull on the door. Spinning away from Caireen she dashed towards the gap. An ear-splitting report sounded in the room behind her; something punched against her arm.

The nearest house corner was immediately to the left, the seaward side, and instinctively they veered towards it. Broad bands of light shone outwards from Brett's office windows and from Caireen's, but beyond these the darkness was almost absolute. The cliff edge was obscured; Rowena could hear the shuddering crash of surf against the granite headland, but the boundary between land and sea was lost in the twilight. 'Stay close to the house!' she gasped.

Even as she called to him, she saw Keith slip on the wet grass and fling his arms in the air. Tumbling down the slope with a crackling of cagoule his shape became indefinable, inhuman – then it disappeared.

'Keith!' The word was torn out of her mouth and fragmented in the wind. A faint noise momentarily overlay the sound of surf and driving rain, but it was a flat crack, not Keith. In the same moment she staggered forward as something kicked her in the ribs.

Rowena's hands hit the wet grass. Crawling to her feet, she glanced over her shoulder to see Caireen silhouetted against the office windows, her arms raised for another shot.

'Oh, God,' she muttered as she lumbered towards the cliff edge where Keith had vanished. Another report spurred her steps, then suddenly the ground was shelving away from her, swooping down into nothingness. She was losing her balance. As she clutched at a tussock of grass on the very edge, she saw with a sick heartsink that no ledges stretched below, no crumbling paths…just a drop into surging black water.

'Keith!' she called again. As a wave creamed against rocks over to the right she saw something bobbing in the unbroken water directly below.

'Keith!'

Was that an arm? She couldn't hear him call. With a last despairing look towards Uplands she saw Caireen making a careful progress down the grass slope, a mere handful of yards behind.

There was no choice. Sucking in a huge lungful of air, Rowena jumped feet-first over the granite lip and plummeted through the darkness.

The impact was heavy and jarring; pain shot through her ankle as she hit an underwater rock, then she found herself on her back, rising with a wall of water as it reared towards the black cliff-face.

She had just time to curl her body into a 'chair' shape when she was slammed against rock; as the water receded, carrying her with it, she turned and tried to swim away from the danger with clumsy strokes.

A faint cough gave her a surge of hope. Somewhere ahead, though out of sight, was Keith. Weathering another roller-coaster wave, she struck out as strongly as she could to seaward. Suddenly her flailing overarm arc hit something solid.

'Rowena – thank God!'

She glimpsed a pale gleam of face, still wearing its spectacles, and dark plastered-down hair. He appeared to be treading water and was weighed down with outdoor gear.

'We've got to get away from here,' she gasped. 'I don't know which way the tide's going, but it's close to high. We must get clear of these rocks, then try to stay parallel with the shore.'

A worrying maelstrom of white water was visible to the left of the looming cliff-face, but some sort of current seemed to be pulling them the other way. Any relief Rowena felt was tinged with the knowledge that Praa Sands, the closest beach, could not be reached. Graw Cove would be covered at this state of the tide, and to the east there was nothing but rocks...

Keith coughed again, then spoke in a light, strained voice. 'You go ahead, Ro. I don't think I can...'

She waited as they bobbed like corks in another huge swell, then berated him with vigour. 'It's just those clothes, Keith. You've got to shed them. I'll help you.'

'No.' He spluttered weakly. 'I'm a lousy swimmer. Always have been. You go – please.'

'Certainly not. Get that top off!'

In the end she held his head in a lifesaver's grip while he struggled out of his boots and outer layers of clothes.

'Now we swim together,' she instructed. 'One, two...'

For an hour they battled, sometimes swimming, sometimes just staying afloat. Rowena's vague idea that they might eventually come ashore at Cober Bar was overtaken by reality; from what little she could discern, they had not yet passed the large headland east of Graw, and their leaden flounderings were keeping them just out of reach of the rocky shoreline below the mines.

The water, only slightly chilly at first, now seemed to have sapped all the warmth from their bodies. Keith was clearly exhausted, and she felt scarcely better. They were still fighting the tide, but she knew it would change at any time now. And when it did...

Keith voiced her worst fear. 'If the tide starts going out, we won't make landfall anywhere, will we?'

France, she thought wryly. 'There are lots of boats in this region,' she said. 'Once it's light...'

They both knew they couldn't possibly hang on for the seven or so hours before dawn.

Wordlessly Keith turned on his back to float again. His limbs were dipping below the surface; he gave a low, resigned sigh.

'Keith?'

'I've had it, Ro,' he said softly. 'I can't do any more. I'm sorry.'

'Yes, you can!'

'I can't... You swim for shore. You can make it.'

Shore... she could hear the sinister sound of breaking waves over to the left, and could readily visualize in her mind the tumbled rocks and inlets of that particular headland. They would be smashed to pieces... yet surely anything was better than allowing themselves to drown out here in the bay...

'You're right,' she said urgently. 'We must strike for shore. It's our only chance. Just relax, and I'll take you in.'

'Ro... I've no energy to argue. Just go.'

Overriding his objections, she gripped the sides of his face once more in a lifesaver's hold and pulled him backwards behind her, kicking rhythmically with her legs. Her ankle felt both heavy and painful, but her hips and knees were moving freely, for which she was grateful. Her arms, too, were functioning well; whatever had hit her as she fled from Caireen had not proved crippling.

Rowena murmured words of encouragement to keep Keith awake, but as she neared the shoreline she was temporarily silenced by a qualm of fear. The surf here was very active; one wave made a sound like a pistol shot as it slapped against a rocky outcrop. For a moment she was reminded of Caireen, then brushed aside the image to concentrate on survival.

'Keith?'

There was no reply; she pinched his cheek.

He groaned.

'Keith – we're getting close now. Can you be ready to protect yourself?' She had to shout above the crashing waves.

'Yes...' Feebly he kicked his legs then craned round in the water to see the source of the noise. 'Christ!'

'Exactly. Get ready...'

A swell caught them, lifted them up and dashed them down against a slab of rock. Rowena scrabbled to maintain a hold, but she was sucked backwards beneath the surface. Salt water shot up her nose and sinuses; as she broke free to the air she coughed and spluttered.

There was no sign of Keith. Barely had she time to gather her wits when another wave came thundering in. Buffeted and helpless, she glanced off several rocks before she found herself wedged in a V-shaped crevice. As the wave receded she hung on, then levered herself up over the edge just before the next mill race rushed towards her. Water seethed all around, but she gripped tightly and was not pulled back with the ebb.

'Rowena!'

Keith was calling from somewhere nearby.

'I'm here. I'm okay.'

'I'll come to you.'

'No – stay put. Let's get our strength back.'

Her nose stung as she sat gasping on the rock. Although water swilled over her legs at one point, it came no higher, and she dared to hope that high tide had just passed.

The blackness was not quite absolute. She had an impression of the cliff rearing above her, which would mean they were not clinging to an isolated outcrop. The poor visibility, however, meant it could be lethal to climb around in this gully.

'I think we're stuck until dawn!' she called to Keith.

'You sound so near... let me try...'

'*No!*'

She heard a splash and a muffled curse, and knew she was being ignored. 'Just a rockpool,' he reassured her. A minute later he was sitting squelchily alongside.

'Eventful holidays you have,' she murmured.

He chuckled, and she was relieved to hear that he sounded almost normal. She had been very concerned about him in the water.

The night passed slowly with wind gusting around the rocky crevices and the constant swish of the retreating water. Rowena clamped her teeth tightly to stop them from chattering, but she could do little to control the shivers that racked her body. Awkwardly Keith put his arm around her, but he was in a similar state of sodden misery.

'Thank you,' said Rowena suddenly after they had exchanged desultory remarks about tides and cliffs and lifeboats. 'You saved my life tonight.'

'Funny, I was just about to say the same thing to you.'

'But I was responsible. You, though, you appeared out of the blue, just when...' She tailed off, unable to continue.

He shrugged, embarrassed. 'There must be something in this telepathy lark after all. You told me you planned to do some snooping this weekend; I had a feeling you were in trouble. I drove out here to that National Trust car-park and phoned your mobile. You didn't answer, but I could just make out your car still at the front. And the Golf. I decided it wouldn't hurt to pull the "lost tourist" trick again, or even come clean as a friend of yours, just to make sure you were okay. It was easy enough to outflank those guards at the top: they were smoking in their cars, reading the paper.'

She gave his hand a grateful squeeze. 'When we were in Mousehole, there was something you wanted to tell me about Caireen,' she said.

'Oh, it was just a theory. You recounted her performance at the Wimbledon Theatre, how a young man was stunned that she had described his house, the plant in the window, his dead father, his cat... It occurred to me that there would have been some credit-card bookings, with tickets sent through the post. Brett, or one of his detective friends, could have wandered into the box-office under the guise of finding out how the tickets were selling, and taken a gander at a couple of addresses. The rest would be easy. A look at the house, a few discreet local enquiries... then on the night Caireen would know exactly where that individual would be sitting and could direct her miracles with accuracy.'

'I'm sure you're right.' Rowena felt drained and empty. 'There's something I *didn't* tell you, though – and I'd like to now.' She described the unexpected advent of Oliver, and his subsequent visits. 'I don't know how she did it,' she said. 'I haven't got the energy to hate her just now, but I need to know how she conjured up Oliver, his nickname and that helicopter!'

'Telepathy again?' Keith said doubtfully.

'No. I wasn't thinking of him at all. I was expecting Ellie...' She paused. 'Ellie knew about the helicopter. It was her idea. But she's loyal; she wouldn't have said anything to Caireen.'

'That incident seems to worry you.'

Restlessly she knitted her fingers together. 'I'm ashamed of what I did. I was a teenager; I should have known better. Oliver was just a little pest to me – I didn't know he was about to die.' She stared out into the darkness. 'It was the end of the summer holidays, and Ellie was staying for a few days. We were sitting on a rug on the lawn reading. Oliver kept running between us with his helicopter, making loud noises and trampling on our books. The more annoyed we got, the more of a pain he became.

'Eventually Ellie suggested we confiscate the helicopter, and when he went inside for tea I hid it in a bag in the garden shed. He made a great fuss, but we wouldn't relent and after a while he started playing with something else. Two days later Ellie went home and I found to my horror that the bag from the shed had been thrown out. Oliver kept asking for his toy, but I told him he had to earn it by good behaviour and searched the shops frantically for another one. He was killed in a road accident before I succeeded...'

'That was bad luck – the whole thing,' said Keith. 'I'm sure you were a great sister to Oliver. You've just let that incident stick in your mind.'

'I was jealous of the attention my parents gave him,' she admitted. 'I did some petty things, and – yes, they have stuck in my mind ever since.'

'You mustn't let them.'

She gave a rueful huff. 'I thought Caireen had released me... gullible, aren't I?'

'Rubbish.' He recaptured her hand and held it firmly.

'I wonder what time it is?' she mused as they continued to shiver on their ledge.

'Not late enough.' He peered at his fluorescent watch face. 'Two fifteen.'

'God!'

They talked all night. Rowena learned about Keith, his family, his own boyhood in the shadow of a golden elder brother. At last, faint cracks of light appeared in the dark shroud of sky to the east. Slowly the streaks grew and coalesced until a pearly grey dawn illuminated their gully.

The rock where they were huddled was wedged against a steep cliff-face. The sea, several feet below, swilled about the base in a relatively peaceful manner. 'I think I know this place,' said Rowena. 'I looked down once from Danny's mine... I think we're just round the corner from that inlet the visitors get trapped in.'

Keith climbed to his feet, shivering, and rubbed his upper arms furiously. 'We might as well be on Mars,' he said. 'No one's going to see us from above: we're too near the cliff. And this gully is so narrow, a boat would have to be just in the right place to spot us.'

'Caireen must think we drowned,' said Rowena. 'She'll be desperately hoping she missed us with those pistol shots.'

Keith turned to her in alarm as she stood up stiffly and stretched her arms. 'Ro – there's blood on your shirt. Round here at the back. *And* your arm!'

She ached all over, and her ankle was giving her the most pain, but his words confirmed what she had suspected – that Caireen's .22 had made its mark.

'Let me look!' he said urgently.

'I'm sure it's nothing. I wouldn't have been able to swim if it was serious.'

Patiently she waited as he rolled up the shirt and examined her ribs and arm with much clucking of tongue against teeth. 'The arm's just a scratch,' he said at length, 'but your back – I'm not certain. There may be something still lodged there.'

'I suppose it's not bleeding badly because I'm so cold,' she laughed.

'Yes – but it might start up again later. We need to get out of here.' He looked out to sea, then scanned the steep cliff above. 'It's either another swim, or a climb. You'd better stay, and I'll get help.'

Gingerly, she tried to put weight on her ankle. 'I can't walk too well,' she said apologetically. 'I hurt my ankle when I jumped off Graw Head. Perhaps we should just wait for a boat...'

Keith's eyes had narrowed as he scanned the cliffside for ledges. 'Over there,' he said, pointing across the gully. 'Just behind that conical rock. Is that a cave entrance?'

'Could be.'

'I don't suppose it leads anywhere.' He fell silent, and Rowena knew he was weighing up the unappealing options: more swimming, albeit in a calmer sea at low tide, a steep and dangerous climb, or more chilly waiting with no guarantee that a boat would pass within hailing distance.

'I think I'll go and check it out,' he said. 'There might just be some sort of tunnel.'

She watched as he edged his way along the adjacent cliff-face without too much difficulty and crossed the gully. He crawled across a sloping rock, then disappeared behind the conical marker rock.

The sky grew silvery. Rowena chafed at her hands and tried to feel optimistic: he had been gone a long time.

When he reappeared he didn't shout, but retraced his steps with wooden deliberation. As he regained the rock where she stood, Rowena could see his face was white and set. 'Ro...' He took her hand. 'There's something I think you should see. Do you feel you can manage?'

He didn't need to explain what it was: instinctively she knew. She nodded, feeling the cold thin blood drain from her own cheeks. Only her ankle was on fire, but with gritted teeth she followed him and was able to gain the other side of the inlet safely.

The cave entrance was about ten feet wide, but it soon narrowed to six and curved round a corner. The walls were damp, and bore traces of seaweed; evidently the spring tides surged in and flooded the passageway.

Just as the light was becoming dim, Keith stopped. He pointed to a rocky hollow which was filled with still water. The inside of the pool was grey-green with marine flora but just beneath the surface they could see another green: a rolled-up cylinder of carpet from which a few strands of pale hair protruded, like slender sproutings of weed.

They had found Ellie.

21

Rowena sat at the cave mouth as Keith stood tensely nearby. She had sent a few silent thoughts to Ellie; now she wanted to see

Caireen brought to justice before the evidence at Uplands was destroyed.

Despite pitch blackness Keith had attempted to follow the tunnel as it sloped gently upwards and into the cliff, but he had been obliged to turn back. 'I think you would have found it blocked anyway,' she reassured him. 'Danny showed me an obstructed tunnel mouth up on the headland last week – Brett must have done that after he'd carried Ellie down to the level part.' Surely he hadn't deliberately placed her in water? Perhaps the hollow had been merely cave-moist at the time, tempting with its offer of additional concealment. Brine from an extra-high tide may have found its usual drainage route blocked by seaweed and debris...

Green darkness...

Her fingers clenched; Keith sought to distract her. 'Why did Caireen claim Ginette told her the killer was in that village hall?' he mused. 'Surely that was a piece of truth she could have done without?'

Rowena picked up a small pebble lying loose on the rock beside her and doggedly examined its contours as she considered her reply. 'I think it was an extra move to keep Danny out of people's minds,' she said at length. 'He was the link with Ginette, and the weak link in Caireen's armour. Two minutes of persuasive questioning and Danny would spill all he knew. Caireen might even have hoped I would mention her comment to Sergeant Pendrea, so he would concentrate on the locals.'

'You could be right. Or perhaps she was responding to subliminal feelings of arrogance. I dare say – *hey*!' Keith suddenly swung round and waved furiously as a small craft puttered past the entrance to the gully just a hundred yards out to sea. He jumped up and down, cupping his hands into a megaphone, shouting out across the glassy water. Rowena also waved and shrieked. For several heart-stopping moments the vessel stayed on course, then to their joy it began to swing to starboard.

'They've seen us!' Keith leapt to embrace her before they scrambled as far as they dared down the glistening rock-face and waited as salvation drew closer.

Detective-Sergeant Pendrea's face twitched with something approaching eagerness as he peered down the peninsula from the National Trust car-park at the brooding hulk of Uplands. 'The Golf's there, at any rate,' he said quietly, before returning with Rowena to the unmarked police car where DI Lovatt and Keith sat in the back. A reserve vehicle was parked alongside.

Rowena edged herself stiffly into the passenger seat and prayed that Caireen had felt secure enough to bluff it out, remain in residence and later express sadness over her employee's unfortunate accident.

It was eight thirty on a Sunday morning. Earlier she and Keith had been rescued from the rocks without recourse to the inshore lifeboat; the craft they had hailed, a small wooden boat heading for a day's fishing from the harbour village of Porthleven, had managed to negotiate a safe channel and pick them up directly.

At first the police had been unwilling to believe Keith's wild story, but one sight of Rowena's back had been enough to convince them. A bleary police surgeon – a local GP – was called in, delved with forceps and emerged triumphant with the bullet which had been lodged all night against her rib. Valuable forensic evidence – but would Caireen still have the gun?

They had all tried to persuade Rowena to receive proper treatment at Truro, but she was adamant that dealing with Caireen should come first. If evidence was to be sparse, then her reaction to Rowena's reappearance should be witnessed...

DI Lovatt spoke firmly to the security guard at the gate before they freewheeled down the rutted drive. Soon the northern façade of Uplands reared above them. There was no discernible movement inside the house.

As noiselessly as possible they climbed out of the car, and Rowena stood off the side of the stout front door with Keith while the officers approached to ring the bell. She held her breath; they rang three times before a vague scuffling sounded within, followed by the scrape of bolts being drawn.

'It's DI Lovatt, Mrs Malone. We're sorry to bother you so early in the morning.'

'What's the problem? Couldn't you have telephoned?' Caireen sounded querulous – and rusty. Perhaps she had been drinking.

'I'm afraid not. Someone with us would like a word with you...'

Smartly he stepped aside and Rowena took his place. She saw Caireen, dishevelled in an ash-pink dressing-gown, looking very middle-aged without her careful make-up. Only her eyes, still violet behind a thin bloodshot web, held any life: they started with horror at the sight of Rowena.

'Hello, Caireen,' she said. 'I left a few things behind.' Rowena was satisfied that the police had heard Caireen's involuntary gasp, seen her appalled expression.

'Er... yes. Come in.' Caireen made a vague gesture, a game attempt to rally herself, but it was far too late. DI Lovatt took his turn once more in front of her, his own eyes icy. 'Caireen Malone, I am arresting you on suspicion of murder...'

Rowena lodged in a room adjacent to Keith's at Chy-Growyn while Kevin, with the ill grace he knew was expected of him, allowed Keith extended leave.

Within days they heard that evidence against Caireen was building up: the pistol and blonde wig had been found, and suspicious stains in the Golf were expected to match Ginette's blood group. One afternoon Pendrea himself came to the guest house with another discovery.

'I thought I'd save your ankle,' he said to Rowena as he entered the sitting-room.

'Thank you.' She had been heartily relieved to find that the bones were not shattered, as she had feared at one point, nor even cracked. The lateral ligament, however, had been badly strained and she still limped around with the foot in strapping.

He sat heavily on the uneven sofa. 'These photographs were found among Mrs Malone's belongings,' he said. 'Were they yours or Ellie's?' He handed over a wallet-sized album and leaned back with a sigh as she examined the contents.

Rowena felt a catch in her throat as she realized that this was the little album June had described: Ellie's special photographs from childhood onwards. She saw Peppy the pony, various dogs, Alan, June, Jonathan... and herself – twice. One photograph was a copy of her own favourite, the two cousins laughing in the sun, a head and shoulders shot. (So Caireen *had* known her identity all along, just as she had claimed.)

The second picture was one she had never seen. Two girls in tennis whites – Ellie and herself – smiled widely at the camera as they were about to climb into a car. Rowena's father was just visible at the wheel, while on the right Oliver was rushing into shot, pulling a face and holding his blue helicopter high.

Her heart began to bang in heavy, sombre thumps. She remembered that game of tennis at her father's local club. It was during

Ellie's summer visit, only weeks before Oliver's death. Ellie must have handed her camera to Rowena's mother and asked her to take the picture...

Pendrea was watching her. 'They've all got writing on the back,' he said.

Numbly she flipped the plastic section to study the reverse of the print. 'Ro and me – with "OK" and that wretched helicopter we hid,' she read. The solecism was typical Ellie, but it was the other part which riveted her attention. Ellie had never been told the ultimate fate of the helicopter. She had clearly had her film developed and written her caption before Oliver's accident. And Caireen...?

Caireen knew that Oliver was dead. She had proffered a gambit and struck gold. A few key words, and Rowena's mind had filled in all the rest.

Rowena stared dry-eyed at the careless writing, her mind a maelstrom of emotion. *Why* had Caireen kept this incriminating album? Surely Brett had not been aware. He would have removed it from her grasp like the silver.

Information...Caireen was addicted to information. She couldn't bear to destroy something of potential value. Supposing June or Alan had come to consult her about Ellie...even tiny details could prove telling. Caireen may have planned eventually to acknowledge that Ellie had died somewhere else in the country, far from her family and friends. Precision, however, would elude her.

The thought sent a wave of pure rage through her body. She rounded on Pendrea. 'Do you intend to charge Caireen Malone with Ellie's death?' she asked. 'I've heard it's only Ginette so far.'

'We're assessing the evidence,' he said soothingly. 'A lot depends on Mr Saunders. He's hiding behind lawyers in London at present, but – let's just say he might soon see which side his bread's buttered.'

She nodded, not trusting herself to speak further. With Caireen irrevocably tainted, she felt that Brett could now be relied upon to put self-preservation before loyalty to his mother. Much, however, still needed to be done.

Two days later Rowena peered round Chy-Growyn's sitting-room door. 'You're sure you don't mind if I leave you this afternoon?' she asked Keith.

'Course not.' He was sitting with a cup of tea and a paperback thriller; the sky outside was grey and uninviting.

She gave him a lightning smile and returned to her room to brush yet more gleam into her hair. The previous evening she had telephoned Adrian, speaking frankly and at length about her hidden agenda and relationship with Ellie. He had accepted her heartfelt apology with surprising grace, and agreed to meet her this last time before she left for London.

As Adrian's vehicle drew up outside she hobbled down the stairs and opened the front door.

'Rowena...' He looked lean, handsome and pleased to see her.

'Adrian. Thank you for coming.'

'Where to, mademoiselle?'

She glanced at the gathering rainclouds. 'Somewhere with a view of the sea,' she said. As he helped her into the car she saw Keith behind the sitting-room curtains of Chy-Growyn.

Ten minutes later they were parked in a lay-by on the steep hill approaching Mousehole. Mount's Bay stretched wide and grey to the left, and the Mount itself was blurred by rain-mist.

'Adrian, I'm so sorry,' said Rowena as the engine coughed into silence. 'I should have trusted you.'

He shook his head firmly. 'No. You had no reason to trust me. You didn't know me.'

'Except in the biblical sense,' she murmured.

'Except in the biblical sense. I must admit, it would have helped if I'd been aware that you were Ellie's cousin on a mission. We'd have discussed everything openly and maybe even found some answers.'

'You were so mysterious about that bloodstain.'

'Yes. I'm sorry. That must have seemed very suspicious. Truth was, I didn't want to talk about it. I kept on a few dairy cows along with the beef herd, and they were all special and had their own names. One of them, Jenna, had a very bad time at the hands of an inept trainee vet in that barn. He was lancing an abscess and managed to hit an artery. She survived, but only just, and the stain soaked into the wood.'

'I see. There were two other things that worried me about you. One was a noisy quarrel Ginette claimed to have heard between you and Ellie just before Ellie vanished, and the second was a story about a missing shotgun.'

'Oh. Fancy you knowing about that.'

'It haunted me. That and the stain together seemed so sinister...'

'I can imagine. The gun had been my father's. I kept it locked in a cupboard on the top landing, but when the police asked to see it, there it wasn't.' He made a sound almost like a chuckle; Rowena felt offended that he could dismiss a serious matter so lightly. 'Sorry to laugh,' he went on. 'I couldn't help it. I was thinking of Madeleine. She confessed yesterday.'

'Confessed? To what?'

'To taking the shotgun. She very properly gave herself up to DS Pendrea, then they both came to visit me. It seems she was very anxious about my state of mind some months ago and persuaded herself that it was her duty to remove "temptation", as she called it, from my house, namely the gun. I felt quite humbled; she had to overcome all kinds of Christian inhibitions, but deemed thievery the lesser evil. So one day she took the key from my drawer, found the gun cupboard, removed the twelve-bore and locked the door again. I had no idea.'

He shook his head wonderingly. 'It's the next bit that creases me... She hadn't told Charles, and she couldn't think what to do with the gun, so after hiding it overnight in an outhouse she decided to drop it into Cober Pool. She took an old rowing boat and tried to row to the deepest water, but there was a hole in the bottom and she suddenly found herself sinking!'

Rowena felt tears of mirth springing to her eyes. 'Poor Madeleine,' she choked.

'Yes. And she was only trying to be a good friend.'

Rowena rapidly wiped her cheeks, unable to shake off the image of Madeleine going down with her ship. They had more in common than either of them had realized...

'Poor Charles, as well,' she said more soberly. 'All his plans have come to nothing.'

'I'd call it a narrow escape,' said Adrian.

'Perhaps you've had one of those.' Rowena's voice was soft.

He turned to look at her, resigned affection in his eyes. 'You were wrong to suggest I saw you as an Ellie-substitute,' he said. 'To me, you are different and just as special. But maybe you didn't really believe the claim yourself. Maybe you saw other reasons why we couldn't make a relationship work, and were using it as a more acceptable excuse. It's all right; I understand.'

That's more than I do, thought Rowena sadly. Deep down, though, she felt glad of his words of release. 'I think Ellie would have made you a good wife,' she said. 'She loved the countryside. I think she was searching for something elusive, and found it when she came to Anwith.'

He sighed. 'At the end I treated her badly. You asked about that quarrel... I'll tell you. I was upset about the heirlooms Patrick Sullivan had stolen: they were irreplaceable family things, yet I knew he'd taken them lightly, would sell them for just a few pounds and would forget all about it. When Ellie arrived that evening I met her in the yard and said I was surprised she'd shown her face. She asked why. When I told her she claimed she'd known nothing of Patrick's intentions. I refused to believe her. We ended up shouting at each other... eventually I said all right, she might not have known Patrick was planning to rob me, but she had twisted my arm to employ the man and was at the very least a rotten judge of character. Not very edifying, I'm afraid.

'She looked at me, those blue eyes brimming with hurt and agreed yes, she *was* a rotten judge of character... then she ran off. I never saw her again.' Adrian grimaced. 'So you see, I know all about guilt and lack of trust. I don't blame you for being unsure of me.'

'Good luck when you go back to London,' he went on. 'If you ever want a holiday you're welcome to use one of my super luxury cottages.'

She smiled in happy surprise. 'You're going to rent them out to tourists?'

'I never turn down good advice. Ann Trelowan will help me renovate them – with Madeleine chipping in – and do the necessary cleaning for a fair wage. I've offered her the use of my car: that should bring traffic to a halt all over the peninsula...'

The mood was amicable as Adrian turned the car round and drove carefully back to Chy-Growyn. Outside the door he gave her a brotherly kiss. 'Keep in touch, Rowena. A Christmas card?'

She returned his kiss and added a hug. 'At least. Maybe even a letter.'

'*So*,' said Kevin Bastable as Rowena stood in his office on her first day back at work, 'you've finally returned from your sabbatical.'

'Didn't you receive my last set of articles?'

'We got them. Not bad, some of that stuff. But where's the *big* one? The exposé of Caireen Malone? You were there, damn it. You were involved.'

'It's *sub judice*, Kevin. I'm a witness. I can't write about Caireen for our paper or any other.'

'Give the story to Keith, then.'

'No. We can't risk compromising the trial.'

'I see,' he said nastily. 'You're saving it all for your book of memoirs, are you? That should earn you a bob or two.'

'Of course.' She knew he understood sarcasm. There would be no books from her on this topic, no lucrative newspaper and magazine spin-offs. Not now, not ever. Let others bare their souls to the jaded gaze of the proletariat.

After some more sparring, which had doubtless set up Kevin for an enjoyable day, Rowena entered the open-plan room where her colleagues milled and chatted. At the back stood a lumpish girl with straggly brown hair and a notebook. 'Who's that?' she murmured to Ed Tranter, making a subtle jerk of her head towards the corner.

He glanced up. 'Chloe.'

Chloe? Hah! Rowena looked again. This girl was surely the most irredeemably ugly, or pulchritudinously challenged, or whatever one was supposed to say, individual she had seen in a decade. Rowena glowed with inner satisfaction.

'What about that blonde girl just behind?' She glimpsed a willowy figure and a face resembling that of Michelle Pfeiffer.

Ed sighed. 'I told you: Chloe.'

She swallowed and sat down hurriedly at her desk. Perhaps it was time to view Keith in a new light.

'Supper, Gordon!' Rowena strode across the garden to the rabbit hutch, shivering as the January frost bit into her limbs. She undid the hasp, placed the bowl of steaming bran on the wooden floor and stroked Gordon's glossy ears. His flanks were still very solid: her attempts to impose a slimming diet over the previous few months had yet to yield discernible results. 'I suppose you need the insulation in winter,' she conceded, changing his water and hanging a blanket over the mesh of the door.

Keith's flatmates had been desolate to lose their foster pet, and had demanded full visiting rights. She smiled in the darkness. It was Saturday, and tonight they were all going to a rock concert.

Back in the warmth of her flat Rowena turned on the bath taps and poured a generous aliquot of apricot essence into the swirling water. As she pottered around the bedroom waiting for the bath to fill, she picked up a letter she had received from June that morning. Her eyes alighted on the second page. 'I felt guilty at first, reading Ellie's most private thoughts, but then somehow I sensed her approval. It's a typical teenager's diary, every emotion magnified – all primary colours, peaks and troughs. It made her come alive again. I thought you might like to see this entry...'

Rowena moved on to the photocopied page of writing she had read several times that day. '...Ro and I played Scrabble then Oliver wanted Monopoly. They played for *hours* while I read my book. She's really good with him. Jonathan never plays anything with me. He's such a vinegar-face. When Ro went to fetch us all some ginger beer I asked Oliver if he liked having a sister and he said yes, she was the best...'

'Thanks, Ellie,' murmured Rowena into the air. 'Now the little wretch is in your hands.'

She turned off the taps, recalling for a moment Keith's relieved comment as they returned to the metropolis, 'No more psychics!' Caireen was at this very moment only weeks away from trial on two counts of murder and, bizarrely, one charge under the newly amended Fraudulent Mediums Act. Yes, Caireen had been a cold-blooded deceiver. But the others?

Downstairs in her telephone book Rowena had written a London number she had recently acquired – that of Dorothy Lambrook.

Just in case...